Vok brought forward another tall, thin alien and presented him to Captain Kathryn Janeway . . .

"This is Ban. He is able to travel more easily on these levels, and he knows the area well. It will be he who assists you, should you require anything."

"You are very gracious," Janeway told him. Vok did not change expression, nor did Ban. They merely turned and walked away, leaving their visitors in silence. The others, who'd not uttered a word during the entire confrontation, followed in silence. The Captain touched her commbadge thoughtfully. "Voyager, this is Janeway."

"Yes, Captain?" Chakotay's reply was nearly instantaneous.

"Did you notice an alien presence in our vicinity just now on your scanners?"

"Negative, Captain. Nothing since we lost those in the desert."

Turning to Tuvok with a quizzical expression on her face, Janeway quickly filled her first officer in while the Vulcan began a local scan with his tricorder.

"Nothing, Captain," Tuvok said at last. His expression was grim. "It is as if they had never been here at all."

STAR TREK VOYAGER™

CHRYSALIS

David Niall Wilson

POCKET BOOKS
New York   London   Toronto   Sydney   Tokyo   Singapore

An *Original* Publication of POCKET BOOKS

POCKET BOOKS, a division of Simon & Schuster Inc.
1230 Avenue of the Americas, New York, NY 10020

A VIACOM COMPANY

STAR TREK is a Registered Trademark of
Paramount Pictures.

This book is published by Pocket Books, a division of
Simon & Schuster Inc., under exclusive license from
Paramount Pictures.

ISBN: 0-671-00150-7

First Pocket Books printing March 1997

10 9 8 7 6 5 4 3 2 1

Printed in the U.S.A.

CHRYSALIS

CHAPTER
1

"ON SCREEN."

All eyes on the bridge spun to the viewscreen as the image of a large green-and-blue world snapped into focus. Captain Kathryn Janeway gazed at the planet in silence, tracing the lines of the continents, taking in the blue of large oceans. Her brow was furrowed in a frown of deep concentration.

Voyager needed supplies. They'd gone as long as they could, limping through several sectors without coming in contact with a world that could provide what they lacked, and she wanted very much to believe that this would be the one, if for no other reason that, seeing it there on the screen, she was reminded suddenly, and intensely, of Earth.

Voyager was light-years from home, so far that the distance hardly seemed real. They'd been dragged from their home quadrant suddenly, without warning, captured by the Caretaker, an extremely powerful being whose sole purpose had been the protection and sheltering of a race known as the Ocampa. *Voyager* had been pursuing a Maquis rebel ship that had disappeared. It, too, had been dragged to this quadrant, but that ship had not survived.

Now with the Maquis captain, Chakotay, as her first officer, and a mixed crew of Starfleet and Maquis personnel on board, they were trying to make their way home. With the lack of facilities and support from the Federation, certain limitations had been placed on the ship's systems, among these the replicator system. It was now necessary to outfit the ship for survival in ways to which Captain Janeway was not accustomed. It was becoming continually more difficult to provide for the needs of the crew.

It would take nearly seventy years to make their way home, even at top speed, and with the rationing they'd had to impose on their partially defective replicator system, scavenging and trading had become part and parcel of her duties as captain.

"I want a complete scan, Mr. Kim," she said at last, turning abruptly to make eye contact with her operations officer. "If there's anything we can use, I want to know about it. Get with Neelix to determine what is edible, and have The Doctor do a complete analysis of the air and the water.

"And, Mr. Kim, if there's anyone down there, we'll need to know that as well."

"Aye, Captain," Kim replied, turning at once to the panel before him and busying his hands at the controls. She watched him for a second, a smile playing at the corner of her lips, then turned away.

The others on the bridge were still staring at the viewscreen, and Janeway let her eyes travel back to the world they now faced, as well. The pang of recognition, of nostalgia, returned. So much like home. Considering the light-years that separated them from anything familiar, it was a bittersweet sight.

"There are some odd readings coming from the planet, Captain," Kim said. He seemed perplexed, and his fingers were flying over the control panel, adjusting bandwidths and frequencies. "I'm getting a life-sign reading, very low, nearly off the scale, but it spreads out across the surface—like it was covering it. I can't pinpoint a location. The reading seems to come from everywhere at once!"

"Is there any indication that it might be some sort of interference, or a system malfunction?" Janeway kept her face carefully neutral.

"None that I can detect. I've already run a system diagnostic, and we're fully operational. There's no sign of subspace interference. I've tried varying the bandwidth and frequency of the scan to both ends of the spectrum, but I get the same reading. It's as if this life-force permeates the air down there."

"Well, get a lock on it." Janeway turned from Mr. Kim's console and slapped the communications badge on her chest. "Mr. Neelix, to the bridge."

There was a moment's silence, then Neelix's cheerful voice floated out from the computer's speakers. "But Captain, I have this wonderful

N'llanthyan stew on the stove! The leaves are of a delicate nature; they must be stirred at precise intervals to insure there is no loss of flavor. The crew has been looking forward to it."

"Very well." Janeway stormed off the bridge and into the lift, her face a mask of stoic perseverance. Neelix was an invaluable asset to her crew under their present circumstances, but at times it was difficult to remind herself of this. Despite constant reminders, Starfleet protocol would never be listed among his strong suits. On the other hand, N'llanthyan stew was one of his more edible preparations.

She entered the mess hall quickly, moving directly to where Neelix stood behind a shiny metal counter, his chef's hat perched jauntily to one side and an apron dangling from his neck. The room had undergone a remarkable metamorphosis since the day he'd commandeered it for his galley. Somehow, anachronistic as it was to be cooking over live flames on a starship, he'd managed to make it comfortable and pleasant. He was a man of many talents, but one of his primary joys in life seemed to come from the time he spent cooking.

"Captain, Captain," he called out. "So good of you to come down. I assume we are near to Urrytha?"

"We are," she answered curtly. "We came within scanning range about fifteen minutes ago. That is what I wanted to talk to you about. I thought you told me there was no life on this planet?"

He turned to her with a quizzical expression on his dappled shiny face. "There is none that I am aware of, Captain," he answered. "Have you discovered someone?"

"Not exactly." Janeway quickly described the strange readings they'd taken from the planet's surface, and Neelix, listening intently as he continued to stir his stew, grew thoughtful.

"You know, Captain," he said at last, "there are rumors about this planet among my people, stories I was told as a child, but that I never paid any attention to. The stories were sort of magical, tales of huge stone temples and ruined cities. They spoke of a race who lived here once, quite an advanced civilization, from all accounts, but I was told that they died out many, many years ago. Frankly, I've always thought them nothing more than legend."

"What kind of stories, Mr. Neelix, and why didn't you tell me this when you mentioned this planet?"

"I've never encountered anything but plant life in this area, Captain," Neelix assured her. "The planet has a substantial supply of Blort roots, and I only thought to avail myself of them while we were nearby. They make a pot pie of marvelous texture, you know."

"I'm certain they do." Janeway smiled slightly. Neelix was infectious, and despite her ire at his lack of attention to detail, he was hard to remain angry with. "But that doesn't answer my question. The stories?"

"Well," Neelix said, "my grandfather used to tell a story about this planet. He told us he'd come here as a young man with a few of his friends . . . purely an exploratory visit, mind you . . . and they found the most *remarkable* ruins.

"They found them in the middle of a jungle, as he told it. Grand ruins with huge stone pillars and temples, lush gardens—but there was no evidence of a society that could have developed them. All signs of civilization had vanished, leaving the ruins to mark their passing. I've visited this planet myself on several occasions, and I've seen no ruins, nor any sign of habitation.

"I'm afraid that that is all I can recall, Captain. My grandfather told a great number of stories, but, really, no one took him seriously. He could really spin a tale, as they say. I remember once he was telling us about a female from the Edanis sector that . . ."

"That will be all, Mr. Neelix." Janeway spun toward the door, but before she exited the mess hall she added, "And thank you. That stew *does* smell delicious."

Neelix watched her go, his hand continuing its steady stirring motion, but his eyes were far away. It was a strange voyage fate had cast him into—a wanderer with no home guiding a crew who'd lost theirs.

He knew, better than most, in fact, how low they were getting on supplies. Part of his job in running the mess hall was to make certain that it was well stocked. He'd been making do with very little for quite some time, and the crew was getting a bit tired of the same old meals.

Neelix felt a sudden pang of loneliness, remembering his own planet, his people, who'd been destroyed in an apocalyptic battle, and found himself wondering where Kes had gotten herself to. No doubt she was locked in with The Doctor, studying. The medical knowledge seemed to come very easily to her, and the work kept her mind at ease—much as his cooking did for him.

The thought of his slight blond love brought the smile back to his face, and he brought the ladle to his lips, giving the stew a taste.

"Ah," he said to no one in particular, "perfect."

Janeway made her way back onto the bridge and called out, "Any luck, Mr. Kim?"

"We've scanned the entire surface, Captain," Kim answered, "but no matter how I configure this, I keep coming up with the same readings. It seems as if there's something alive down there, at least that's what the life-sign would indicate, but there's just no way to know where it is, or what. It's possible that the life-form we're seeking is very insubstantial physically, but very spread out, or even that there is some microscopic creature so rampant that it reads as a single entity. The only other thing I could think of is that someone might be jamming our signal in some way, causing a false reading."

"Mr. Chakotay," Janeway said, turning to her first officer, "any thoughts?"

"I'm not certain on this one, Captain," he admitted, "I've never encountered anything quite like this. Something is blocking our efforts, but there may be a few more ways to configure these scanners that we haven't tried. I know we need the supplies, but I'd like to get a better reading on the planet before we proceed."

"Agreed." Janeway nodded curtly. "Get Torres up here and see if there's anything she can do. Neelix tells me there may be a primitive agricultural society on this planet, which might be one way to explain these readings. If this is true, we need to stay clear of them. The last thing we need is to frighten off the inhabitants. Mr. Tuvok, will you assist?"

"Gladly," Tuvok replied.

As Kim and Tuvok continued to reconfigure the scanners, the captain headed for the door. "Commander Chakotay, you have the bridge. I'll be in my ready room if you find anything."

"Aye, Captain," Chakotay answered, nodding. He was already bending over the scanners beside Kim, lost in the problem at hand.

As the door slid shut behind her, Janeway relaxed her shoulders a bit and let out a heavy sigh. Moving to the comfortable chair behind her conference table, she fell back into it heavily. She took her responsibilities as captain very seriously, even more so now that she had to hold together the loyalty and respect not only of her own crew, but of a crew of former rebels as well.

She needed to keep a bold face on in the presence of the crew, even when her own heart and mind were down. To most of them, she represented the promise that they would find their way through this, that they would see home and their loved ones again. It was not an easy burden to bear.

Seeing the blue and green sphere of Urrytha had bothered her more than she'd let on. It was very much like Earth.

Most of the time she was able to shunt her feelings aside and concentrate on her job, on the work at hand, living from moment to moment, but it didn't always work. As the heaviness descended on her heart, she realized that this was developing into one of those times.

There was a sudden tone, indicating that someone was requesting to enter the space, and she sat up quickly, straightening her hair.

"Enter," she called out sternly.

Lieutenant B'Elanna Torres, the chief engineer, stepped quickly into the room, and the door slid silently closed behind her.

"Yes, B'Elanna, what is it?"

"I'm not sure, Captain. We haven't been able to isolate the source of that life-force reading, but a visual scan has picked up signs of a primitive civilization. We started with the forested area, but the scanners couldn't penetrate the foliage. That was where the life-force seemed strongest. When we expanded the range, that is when we found the settlements. There is every indication that there are natives down there, somewhere, a very basic agricultural society, no space travel, but we can't locate any beings of any sort."

"Are the settlements near to where we need to

harvest Mr. Neelix's roots? We have to get some food on board here, or we'll all be trying to fry bits and pieces of our boots."

"That's what is strange about this, Captain," Torres continued. "The settlement we located is in a desolate isolated region of the planet. All of the vegetation seems centered in one or two locations—almost like oases, but the natives have gone out of their way to avoid settling near those areas. There is water in the jungles and an abundance of plant life, even a few lower-level species of animals . . . just no clear sign of intelligent inhabitation. Certainly nothing that could explain the readings we are getting."

"Are you telling me, Lieutenant, that these . . . people—whoever or whatever they might be—have built their homes as far as possible from the most obvious sustenance on their planet?"

"That is how it appears, Captain."

"Tell Mr. Paris to bring us in a bit closer and get that area with the vegetation on screen. I want a look at these 'oases,' and I want some answers. We can't just go barging in on these people if it's a problem of our own that's keeping us from locating them."

"Yes, Captain," Torres replied. "But, Captain, those jungles are thick with overgrowth—we're not going to be able to get much more than the tops of the trees."

"Noted," Janeway acknowledged, already heading back into the world of her own jumbled thoughts.

B'Elanna exited the ready room purposefully, and Janeway stood, straightening her hair once more and smoothing the fabric of her uniform.

When Janeway made her way back onto the bridge, they already had the lush gardens of planet Urrytha on the viewscreen. Torres hadn't been kidding. From above, it looked somewhat like the rainforests on Earth. They could see the lush growth atop trees that soared hundreds of feet in the air, patches of huge ferns and flowering plants that reached several times the height of a large man. The colors were bright and vibrant.

"Computer," she said, "magnify the image by a factor of one hundred."

The image shifted. Suddenly blossoms that had been nothing more than a splash of color were clear. Large insects of several varieties were flitting about from flower to flower. A bird soared across the screen, then spiraled down into the trees below. Nowhere was there a break in the greenery large enough to make out the ground, although in a couple of places rivers were visible, blue ribbons cutting through oceans of green, overhung with branches and dangling vines.

"No sign of anyone in there, Captain," Tom Paris reported, "though there could be an army hiding under those branches, and without full use of the scanners, we'd never know it." He added, "One hell of a place for an ambush."

"You're certain there is nothing we're overlooking here?" she asked, knowing the answer, but unable to make it all fit together in her mind. Paris's comment about ambushes had left an uneasy feeling in the pit of her stomach.

"Quite," Tuvok cut in. "We have run every type of

scan we are capable of, and we have taken the visual through most of this vegetated area. If there are native inhabitants on this planet, they are even more adept at hiding themselves than they are at building dwellings and raising crops."

The door to the lift opened, and Neelix entered the bridge, a big smile pasted across his face. Taking in the landscape on the viewscreen, he turned to the captain and winked. "There they are, Captain, Blort plants . . . a garden full of them. Those roots will solve our problems for some time to come, and I can prepare a large variety of dishes from them . . . some quite exquisite."

"I'm more concerned with these inhabitants we can't seem to locate, Mr. Neelix. Your roots may have to wait. It is possible that they have some naturally shielded hideaway that we have been unable to scan. I don't want to beam down there and scare these people into a new religion, nor do I want to take an away team somewhere that I can't be certain is safe."

"I can understand your concern, Captain," Neelix rejoined obsequiously, "and yet I myself have visited this very jungle in the past and met no one. It would be embarrassing to find an entire race of beings who'd taken me for a god. . . ."

There was some general laughter, but Janeway did not share in it. Noticing the seriousness of her expression, Neelix changed tacks. "Captain, we have to have those supplies. With what we have available, we have a week, two at best, and that is on the paltriest and blandest of diets I can imagine. Our water supplies are also getting low."

"I'm aware of the status of our supplies, Mr. Neelix," Janeway assured him, though in truth she hadn't wanted the others to know just how bad things had gotten—not yet. The situation was not yet out of hand, but there were shortages that would not be ignored much longer; in that, Neelix was correct. "I guess that we'll just have to take our chances.

"Mr. Kim . . ."

Before she could finish her order, B'Elanna let out a small cry. "Captain, I've got something."

Her fingers danced across the control console, and the viewscreen shifted to a scene of rocky crags and cold stone. Vegetation was sparse, but in the background they could just make out some sort of village.

"What is it, Lieutenant?" Janeway asked, moving to Torres's side and glancing down at the monitors.

"This is the settlement I told you about, Captain. There were no inhabitants earlier, but a small group of humanoid beings has appeared," B'Elanna replied excitedly. "I don't know how we were missing them before, or where they might have come from, but there they are."

"It would appear that the inhabitants *are* living in that bleak place," Janeway mused. "Well, there's no accounting for taste. Mr. Tuvok, I want to form a landing party and get down there as soon as possible. We're going to need Neelix for his roots, and I'd like

Mr. Kim to accompany us, as well. I'll lead the team."

"Do you think that is wise, Captain?" Tuvok cautioned. "It is my duty to remind you that your safety is a paramount concern."

"I am aware of the importance of my safety, Mr. Tuvok." The Captain smiled. "But there doesn't seem to be much of a danger down there, and I've been cooped up for too long."

Tuvok didn't answer her, merely nodding, but his disapproval was floating just beneath the surface of his eyes. He entered the lift and made his way to the lower decks to choose the rest of his team, feeling uneasy, but unable to pinpoint the exact reasons why.

Janeway stood for a few moments, watching the screen in silence. Finally, turning quickly, she headed toward the lift. She had preparations of her own to make before beaming down to the planet's surface.

"Commander Chakotay," she called out behind her, "you have the bridge."

CHAPTER
2

THE LANDING PARTY MATERIALIZED IN A CLEARING THAT was surrounded on all sides by lush green ferns and towering trees. Birds flitted between the branches, their songs blending with the buzzing whir of insects and the soft sigh of a breeze that ruffled through the foliage above their heads. It was as if the entire fertility ration for the planet had been gathered and concentrated in that one area.

The air was heady with the perfume of exotic flowers, and the sudden burst of color from the myriad blossoms and multihued brush nearly blinded Janeway as she beheld it, up close, for the first time. She stood very still, taking it all in and savoring it, breathing deeply. It was, in a word, *breathtaking.*

Reflexively, she brought her tricorder up to chest level and began a routine scan of the area. Years in

Starfleet had burned the harsh lessons of alien landscapes into her psyche, and she wasn't about to endanger herself or her companions unnecessarily . . . not even to enjoy the beauty of such a remarkable place. There would be plenty of time to explore and to take in the scenery once they'd determined as well as possible the inherent threats.

Neelix was not so cautious. With a chortle of glee, he rushed to the side of the clearing, snatching at a green leafy palnt and yanking it upward. It came free of the moist earth easily, revealing a long slender root, pale and tubular. He raised it to his nose, sniffing deeply, then turned to the rest of the landing party, eyes sparkling. He called out to Janeway with his prize held high.

"I told you, Captain, Blort roots! There are enough here to keep us in rations for another two months!"

"Just gather what you need, Mr. Neelix. I hope that there are other plants here that will be suitable as well? I don't like the idea of taking a valuable food source from this planet if there are beings living here. We might be taking food out of their mouths."

"Oh, there's plenty for everyone, Captain," Neelix assured her, bustling off to the other side of the path to inspect another batch of shrubs. "One thing about Blort roots—you don't find them just anywhere, but when they grow, they are nearly impossible to get rid of. Only about thirty days from seedling to the stewpot. We have enough here to feed an army."

Let's hope we don't meet *that army,* Janeway mused, returning her attention to her tricorder.

Aloud, she added, "There's no sign of any of the inhabitants, but we don't know if it will stay that way. I want us out of here as soon as possible. That life-force reading we scanned makes me nervous, and I don't like the way those natives just *appeared* on our scanners."

"Perhaps," Tuvok commented, his eyes glued to his own tricorder, "we should begin another more intensive diagnostic on our scanning system. There appeared to be nothing odd about that village we scanned, and their level of technology does not indicate any viable method of cloaking, and yet they walked on screen as if materializing from thin air."

Janeway nodded absently, her mind slipping subconsciously between her concerns as captain and her enjoyment of their surroundings. They moved inward, following what appeared to be an overgrown trail leading into the interior of the lush garden.

She thought about that for a moment. It was more like a garden than a jungle, despite the untamed appearance of the place. There was too much symmetry to the layout, too much order in the divisions of trees and plants. If it could have been viewed from above, she was certain that there would be an immediately obvious plan to the area. Somewhere behind all this greenery, there was rational thought.

It occurred to her that if this were true, then perhaps that cloaking technology wasn't quite as far beyond the people of this planet as Tuvok assumed from the outward appearance of their village. There were different ways for a civilization to achieve greatness besides technological advancement, and it would do them all well to keep that fact in mind. Nature herself could provide adequate defenses in most situations, given enough time for the process of evolution.

In any case, the idea that it was all a big overgrown garden made her more cautious. They didn't need any surprises.

As they moved in deeper, Janeway lost herself in the beauty of the place. Neelix was busying the others with the gathering of the supplies he needed, and Tuvok, in his usual fashion, was scanning anything and everything in search of hidden dangers or clues to those who inhabited the place. He took his position as security officer seriously, and he was very good at it. His vigilance gave Janeway an opportunity to savor the abundant life that surrounded them, to take in the fresh air and the moist scents of plant life and rich earth.

All of these sensations had taken on the novelty of something alien after so many months in space, as if she were walking through the pathways of some half-forgotten dream. She'd last shared such a place with a lover she might never see again, and if she closed her eyes, concentrating very hard, she could still conjure up his image, the scent of him, holding her close. She found her mind drifting, her concentration slipping, and she was lost in a world of memories and places light-years distant when Tuvok's voice brought her suddenly back to her senses.

"Captain!"

She looked up, her eyes focusing ahead on the

path, and her jaw dropped in shock. The seemingly endless forest had given way just ahead to a large clearing, and from that clearing, crumbling walls of stone rose. They towered over the landing party in some places; in others they were falling down, returning to the earth.

The ruins were of obvious antiquity, neglected and overgrown with vines and small trees, but the foundations of the place were still basically intact. The sheer size of the stone blocks and columns, combined with the immensity and obvious complexity of the architectural design, was staggering.

She turned to Neelix quickly, questioningly. Her eyes held a bit of the anger she felt, but she kept herself under control.

"Mr. Neelix, I thought you'd visited this jungle before."

"I assure you, Captain," he said hastily, "I have never seen this place before." His stance, and the obvious surprise etched across his features, proved his sincerity. Staring up at the ancient ruins, he added, "There are Blort roots along the fringes of the jungle, and I never ventured much farther in than that."

Turning to the ruins again, he added, "Rather imposing, isn't it?"

Janeway didn't answer, but her mouth was set in a grim line. It might be true that the inhabitants of this planet did not live in these monstrous gardens, and then again they might just be well hidden. It was obvious that, whether anyone lived there at present or not, someone had lived there in the past. Another surprise. Something else to add to the worries that were already building in the back of her mind.

She chided herself for not ordering more intensive scanning before embarking the landing party, or for not sending scouts ahead to check the place out. There was no way to know what they might expect from such a place, no way to plan for the unexpected.

"I suggest that we give those walls a wide berth," Tuvok said, interrupting her thoughts, "and finish gathering our supplies. They afford suitable cover for an ambush."

"But Tuvok," Kim cut in, "aren't you curious to know who built this place?" The young officer's eyes were wide and staring, captivated by the decaying magnificence that faced them. It was a grand sight, whispering of days past and faded grandeur.

"Well," Neelix cut in, "they certainly must have been *large* creatures. Look at the cut of those stairs."

He was pointing at an area of the wall that bordered directly on the path. It was becoming easier to see the slightly overgrown trail as the remnant of a major thoroughfare, to picture the gardens—Janeway could now see that she'd been right to think of them as gardens—as a huge courtyard around a great keep. It was like a deserted city from some fantastic tale of fantasy.

Despite her misgivings, and the common sense—logic—behind Tuvok's warning, she felt compelled to know more. It wasn't in her nature to turn away from a mystery, or a problem, without at least taking a shot at the solution.

"I'm not ready to go back just yet," she told them. "Let's get a closer look and see if we can learn something. Maybe there's an answer here to those life-force readings, or to whatever it is that's blocking our scanners. Anything that we can learn about this place is bound to prove helpful." Turning to face Tuvok, she added, "And, Tuvok, if this quadrant has such a cloaking technology, don't you think that we need to know more about it?"

Tuvok's expression was disapproving, but he said nothing further as they proceeded. He walked with one hand on his tricorder and the other hovering near the phaser at his side.

Kim, who was unable to conceal his awe at the antiquity and majesty that the ruins implied, walked near the front of the party, near Captain Janeway. He took it all in, swinging his gaze from side to side and sweeping it over the ancient walls and crumbling stone. There was an aura of age about the place, of permanence that transcended the rot and decay eating away at the walls themselves. There was no feeling of abandonment, more a feeling of expectancy.

Two of the others that had been selected for the party walked at his side: Ensign Kayla, a young Bajoran woman who'd come aboard when the Maquis ship had been sacrificed, and Ensign Fowler, a junior engineer. As Kim stared in amazement at the ruins and the imposing walls of the jungle looming to either side, Kayla took the chance to stare at him. Her eyes were appraising and approving, and Fowler, walking just to the other side of her, grinned as he noticed.

"Nice view," he commented, tapping Kayla on the shoulder.

Kim turned at the exchange, just in time to catch Kayla's probing gaze before she turned to acknowledge Fowler. He blushed at the frank appraisal apparent in the depths of her eyes, and he turned quickly back to the ruins. Kayla moved a bit closer to him, sending a heated disapproving glance Fowler's way.

They had been in space for quite some time—away from interaction with anyone beyond their crew, with a few exceptions, and it was becoming clear that couples would form in *Voyager*'s crew. There had been one baby born to them already; the eventual pairing off of crew members seemed inevitable.

Kim made a great show of examining his tricorder and hurried his steps to come abreast of Janeway. He was embarrassed, but more than that. He'd felt some of the attraction that Kayla so obviously felt, and the guilt that washed through him was instantaneous. His fiancée waited for him, he knew, to return to his home. If he allowed someone to become part of his life in the Delta Quadrant, at least in that fashion, he knew it would be a sort of surrender, an admittance of defeat.

Kayla stayed back, for the moment, engaged in a

hushed conversation with Fowler. Kim blushed again, nearly certain that he was the subject of that discussion, yet not certain how to put an end to it. Kayla was a lovely young woman, and if circumstances had been different, he might have encouraged her. Instead, he found himself forced to deal with the issue of how he was going to communicate his feelings to her without seeming to reject her outright.

He would also have to deal with the emptiness, the void in his spirit that his fiancée had filled. Kayla's attentions had inadvertently reminded him of his loneliness. Turning back to the jungle, he tried to lose himself in his surroundings.

As they moved farther in, they found other structures, some of which were better preserved, more complete than the first building they'd passed. The stones that had once paved the street were still visible in places, and several structures stood untouched. It was almost possible to envision the builders of the city, their society intact, sitting inside at meals or lost in pleasant conversation.

As they neared the center of the ancient city, the buildings themselves grew larger and more imposing. They did not stretch upward in the manner of the skyscrapers of Earth, but instead they were wide and thick, adding to the feeling of solidity and permanence they exuded. They had been built to last.

Neelix scrambled up one of the sets of stairs, huffing and puffing with the effort. Each step reached nearly to the center of his chest, and he had to pull himself up, swinging one leg at a time. When he stood on the top step, he called out to them.

"You should see this, Captain. There is a garden inside this courtyard . . . a very impressive garden. I can see several plants that I recognize from here. It is overgrown and neglected, but I believe we can find a lot of what we need right here. I'd like to make this the starting point for our onload, and I think we should get samples of some of these for Kes's hydroponics bay."

Janeway found herself smiling openly at Neelix, despite his infuriating lack of respect. His enthusiasm was infectious, and she made a decision on the spot.

"I think we need to know more about this place. Mr. Tuvok, I'd like you to find a suitable spot for a base of operations. Mr. Kim, take Ensign Fowler and join Neelix in that garden up there. See what else you can find that might be of use. I'm going to have a look around over there."

She pointed to where the road bisected another trail up ahead. It appeared to be a plaza of some sort, perhaps the town square or central market. There was a raised platform in the center where several thick stone columns jutted up toward the blue sky above.

The area was surrounded by a series of low-slung buildings, mostly solid, and what appeared to be benches protruded from the walls, facing the square. In the center was a fountain, choked with weeds and buzzing with insects.

Tuvok looked as if he might press the issue, voicing yet another protest, but he apparently thought better of it. "Very well, Captain," he said. "I'll arrange to have the necessary equipment beamed down near the garden. It is a secluded well-protected spot, and since Neelix has chosen it for his gathering, it would be the logical location for a base."

"Agreed." Janeway nodded.

Neelix, Fowler, and Kim, who looked relieved to be moving farther away from Kayla, if only for the time being, were already entering the garden, disappearing between a pair of large columns at the top of the oversized stairs. Tuvok followed, still eyeing the structures about them suspiciously.

As they moved away from her, Janeway dismissed them from her mind. The opportunity to lose herself for a time in speculation over a race long gone loomed pleasantly, and she moved off toward the platform in the square. The sounds of the jungle swallowed her, and it was easy to feel time slipping away. The air was fresh, and her breathing seemed easier. The sounds of *life* surrounded her, even as the ghosts of the past beckoned.

As she neared the stone pillars, she noted with excitement a pattern of characters that formed a band about the width of her hand inscribed around the circumference of the nearest monolith. The characters were present on each of the pillars as she inspected them in turn, different patterns but similar in nature.

Janeway slapped the commbadge on her breast

and said, "Mr. Kim, could you join me over here for a minute?"

She continued to examine the ancient glyphs in fascination, running her fingers lightly over the impressions and trying to make sense of the pattern. The language was obviously based in mathematical symbology of some sort, but the symbols themselves meant nothing to her. It was their symmetry that caught her interest and piqued her curiosity. It reminded her of her years at the Academy, hours spent pouring over equations and theory. It had been one of the happiest periods of her life.

She heard someone approaching, and she turned. She saw that it was Kim, and she moved aside slightly so that he could see what she was looking at.

"Can you make any of it out, Captain?" Kim asked.

"No," she replied. "It isn't quite like anything I've ever seen. I want you to get a visual scan on these for later study. I'm pretty certain that the language is mathematical in nature, and the computer should be able to work it out fairly quickly."

Kim nodded, running his fingers over the ancient characters in fascination, much as she herself had done only a few moments before. They were fascinating.

Janeway knew that Kim would likely appreciate the challenge of deciphering the hieroglyphics, and she knew as well that he would be up to that challenge. She'd have liked to work on it herself, but she couldn't pull her thoughts away from the place itself, the freshness of the air, the mystery of the ancient forgotten city. There were not likely to be too many more opportunities such as this, in a place so like home and yet so different. She didn't want to miss a moment of it.

She'd also noticed, with some amusement, the exchange between Kim and Kayla, and she knew he'd be happy to get away from the others and get his mind on something besides the attentions of a certain ensign. She knew how he felt, if only in the shared pain of separation from her loved ones.

"*Voyager* to Janeway," Chakotay's voice crackled over her communicator.

"Janeway here," she replied briskly, her mind snapping to focus instantly. "What is it, Commander?"

"We've lost those beings again. They dropped right off our scanners as if they'd never been there at all. The life-force readings have increased slightly, as well, though there's still nothing specific that we can pin them to."

"Keep trying to get a lock on that signal," she instructed. "And keep trying to locate those Urrythans. I'll have the others wrap up what they're doing here as soon as I can, but there are some truly fascinating ruins down here, and I can't resist this chance to learn something about them."

"I'll keep you posted if anything changes," Chakotay assured her.

"Very well, Janeway out."

She continued her walk through the ancient city, but the knowledge that they were unable to detect the inhabitants of the planet kept itching at the back of her mind. Was it possible that their appearance in the odd little village had been a decoy? A trap? If they concentrated their efforts in scanning that desolate location, were they being set up for an attack here? Were these beings toying with them?

There were too many questions with far too few answers to suit her. They were in an alien, potentially hazardous environment, and she needed to keep that foremost in her mind. The last thing *Voyager* could afford was for four of her officers and the cook to walk blindly into a trap.

Her mood spoiled by the sudden pressing weight of responsibility, she turned and headed back toward the garden where she'd left the others. Tuvok had been right. The best thing for them to do was to gather what they could find and make their way out of this place as quickly as possible. At least she could help Kim with the translation of those odd hieroglyphics once they were on the ship.

She made her way into the garden where Neelix and Ensign Fowler were enthusiastically harvesting vegetables and roots. She stopped to watch. Heaving a sigh of resignation, she motioned Tuvok aside.

"They've lost contact with those beings," she told him. "We need to get what we came for and get out of here. I just don't trust this place—no reason I can put my finger on."

"Agreed." Tuvok nodded. "Though it is highly illogical to let one's emotional impressions dictate action."

"Captain!" Neelix was hurrying to their side, a long reddish root dangling from one hand. "I've made quite a discovery. These are a variety of Grondian tuber I've never seen in this sector. They will make a marvelous stew, and . . ."

He stopped short, staring, and Janeway spun to see what had caught his eye. She and Tuvok had drawn their weapons as they turned, and they found themselves face to face—or rather, face to torso—with a small assemblage of very tall and thin creatures in long white robes.

The beings stood nearly three meters in height, and suddenly the oversized steps leading to the garden made sense. Their limbs were extra-jointed, facilitating their excessive height. Their features were highlighted by long sad eyes staring down from beneath the snowy hoods of their robes. Their skin was an almost translucent blue, and it seemed to shimmer with captured light.

They held their hands clasped before them, and Janeway noted that the digits of those appendages were long and serpentine. They stood very still, watching her as she watched them. Janeway waited for them to break the silence, wondering how they would react to the "magic" of the Universal Translators.

Reaching across to Tuvok's arm, Janeway pressed it down toward his side, indicating that he should lower his weapon. Hers was already down at her side, showing no threat.

Stepping forward, she called out in firm but friendly tones, "I am Kathryn Janeway, Captain of the Federation *Starship Voyager*. We mean you no harm."

The creatures regarded them for a moment in silence, obviously digesting the fact that aliens were standing on their planet, talking to them as if it were a natural occurrence. At first they did not react at all, then finally the tallest of the aliens moved forward, sort of a sinuous multijointed shuffle, stopping a few yards from Janeway and looking her over carefully. He seemed merely curious, showing no sign of alarm.

"I am Vok," he said in a light musical singsong. "I am High Priest of the gardens, keeper of the ancients, one with the voice of the spirits and the lord of the *Ambiana.*"

Vok did not smile, not in any fashion discernible from his expression, and yet Janeway could detect no animosity in the tone of his voice.

"We are pleased to meet you, Vok," she replied. "My people and I are far from home, trying to make our way back. We require supplies, food and water, and we'd hoped to find those here. We did not detect your civilization."

"My people prefer to make their homes in the caverns of the ancients," Vok said. "The light is not a friendly place for us. We come to the gardens for ceremonies and worship, for meditation, but we spend most of our hours beneath the ground."

"This is your city, then?" Janeway asked curiously. The ruins did not strike her as the work of a people who spent most of their lives beneath the surface of the planet, and yet it was obvious from their size that the place fit them. They seemed *appropriate* to the garden.

"It was the home of our ancestors, the ancients," Vok explained patiently. "It is the city of that which has passed and that which will come again. It was destroyed in the last *Ascension,* and it is said that it is both our past and our future."

"I see," Janeway said, seeing nothing.

"You are welcome to the fruits of this garden, and to water from the streams farther in," Vok continued. "We have our own extensive gardens in the caverns—what is here is wild and free for the taking. You may have it with our blessing."

Janeway found Vok's speech patterns quaint and enjoyable. "We thank you," she replied politely. "We won't trouble you for long."

Turning, she asked, "Are you about finished, Neelix?"

"I would like to gather a few more samples, Captain, if it is possible."

She turned back to Vok, who was watching her expressionlessly. She wondered how welcome they actually were, and she was weighing that question in her mind when Vok broke the silence once more.

"You are welcome to stay as long as you like," he assured her. "Your presence is no intrusion upon us. If we had not happened through here on our way to visit the ancients, our paths might never have crossed."

Smiling, Janeway nodded toward Neelix. "Try and finish soon," she told him. Turning back to Vok, she gestured toward the ruined city that surrounded them.

"Your ancestors created a very impressive home

here," she said. "They must have been very advanced."

"It was a glorious civilization," Vok said, his voice betraying a bit of emotion that was still absent from the sad mournful lines of his face. "They built this city to honor their own ancestors. It has been nearly twenty thousand years since they laid down the first stones here, nearly half that since they themselves began the *Long Sleep*."

"The *Long Sleep?*" Tuvok asked.

"We believe that once we have been lain to the final rest of this body, we will rise again to a new life—a new birth," Vok intoned. "It is the goal we dedicate our lives to. It is the goal our ancestors sought, as well. They left this city behind when they began that journey. Now, while they sleep the *Long Sleep*, we tend them, waiting for our own chance to join them in the *One Voice*."

Janeway felt another tug of memory—of pain. The thought of death and rebirth was a familiar one—a belief her own people had fostered and that she felt very much separated from, lost as they were in a quadrant so far from home. She didn't know what to say, so she settled on silence.

"We will leave you to your gathering," Vok said. "We will be here if you need us, but I've been out in the light as long as is comfortable for me. The closer I get to the *Long Sleep*, the more difficult it is to move about on this level. There are others, younger than I, who will assist you if you have need."

Gesturing to one of the others who stood at his side, Vok brought forward another tall thin alien and presented him to Janeway. "This is Ban. He is able to travel more easily on these levels, and he knows the area well. It will be he who assists you, should you require anything."

"You are very gracious," Janeway told him. Vok did not change expressions, nor did Ban. They merely turned and walked away, leaving their visitors in silence. The others, who'd not uttered a word during the entire confrontation, followed in silence.

The captain touched her commbadge thoughtfully. *"Voyager,* this is Janeway."

"Yes, Captain?" Chakotay's reply was nearly instantaneous.

"Did you notice an alien presence in our vicinity just now on your scanners?"

"Negative, Captain. Nothing since we lost those in the desert."

Turning to Tuvok with a quizzical expression on her face, Janeway quickly filled her first officer in while the Vulcan began a local scan with his tricorder.

"Nothing, Captain," Tuvok said at last. His expression was grim. "It is as if they had never been here at all."

CHAPTER
3

THE CAMP TOOK SHAPE RAPIDLY IN THE SMALL GARDEN.
Captain Janeway still wasn't comfortable with the
idea of a world inhabited by beings that she could
not trace, but there seemed nothing to be done
about it. They'd been given permission to forage
for supplies, they seemed to be causing no great
stir among the aliens themselves, and *Voyager*'s
needs had to take precedence over her own nervous
worries.

She ordered a small work force down to the planet
to assist Neelix and to forage farther into the gardens. Since the opportunity was presenting itself,
she wanted to be certain that they came away from
this as prepared to face the next few weeks as
possible. There was the issue of water, too, which
she knew they'd find farther into the gardens.

Although Tuvok's security force had remained

vigilant, there had been no sign of the slim pale aliens since the initial contact. This surprised Janeway more than a little. The arrival of a strange starship on one's planet couldn't be that regular an occurrence, and yet they'd been left almost completely alone. The obviously private, secluded nature of the Urrythan civilization calmed her nerves a bit. It was refreshing to meet a race content enough with their own ways and level of advancement that they weren't constantly after that of others.

As her crew went about the business of replenishing *Voyager,* she found herself drawn more and more to the ruins that surrounded them. She spent her own time walking the twisting overgrown pathways and exploring half-crumbled buildings, trying to visualize the ancient civilization that had built them. She felt as if there were answers here for her, of some sort, if she could only find the right questions.

A small group of crewmen passed her on their way farther in. They carried the necessary equipment for gathering fresh water, but it was obvious that the magic of the place was affecting them in much the same way it had her. They were laughing, talking freely, relaxed. It was good to see smiles on their faces, considering the circumstances. There had not been enough smiles on Voyager in recent days. She noted that Ensign Kayla was among the crew and she couldn't help but smile. Kim would be relieved.

Urrytha was having the same effect on her. She hadn't felt as energized, or refreshed, in years. The air, the birds and small animals, even the ancient stone buildings—all of it combined to weave a tapestry of peace and harmony. It was as if the planet itself were singing to them. She laughed at the notion, hurrying to follow the group that had just passed her.

She followed them in, but at a slower, more leisurely pace, taking in all the sights and sounds the gardens had to offer. The trees and shrubbery were slowly giving way to a proliferation of a single large flowering plant with expansive golden-yellow blossoms. The stems of these flowers stood nearly the height of a tall man, and the blossoms resembled huge lilies, their surfaces dusted with a fine coating of pollen.

She saw many of the oversized insects she'd viewed from *Voyager* earlier, flitting from flower to flower, apparently gathering the pollen and distributing it like Earth's bees. She was fascinated, but she gave the creatures a wide berth. No way of knowing if they might bite, sting, or worse, and alien toxins could prove extremely dangerous, particularly when the only medical officer available was a hologram and confined to the ship. Just one more handicap the universe had dealt her when she was pulled from her own quadrant—another bit of responsibility to rest on her shoulders.

The insects went their way, and she hers, and if it hadn't been for the sudden cries of dismay from up ahead of her, she could have walked among them, watching them work, for hours.

Taking off at a run, she slapped her commbadge

and called Tuvok for backup. He was already on his way, and she turned back to the path, concentrating on catching up with the team ahead. The overgrowth of weeds hindered her stride somewhat, but she caught them in only a few short moments. As the path opened ahead of her into a small clearing, she stopped short, taking in the situation at a glance.

On the ground, Ensign Kayla was lying in a heap, her eyes glazed. The others were gathered about, leaning over her with concern etched deeply into their faces—faces Janeway had seen so recently smiling and laughing, without care. Ensign Fowler had his tricorder in hand and was attempting to administer first aid, but he looked bewildered. Janeway assessed the situation quickly.

"What's happened here?" she asked, kneeling to check Kayla's vital signs. Her pulse was weak but steady, and her breathing, though very slow, was also regular. She appeared, almost, to be sleeping.

"I'm not certain, Captain," Fowler replied, obviously perplexed. "We were searching for water, and I'd just spotted that stream over there"—he pointed to an opening in the foliage to their right—"when Ensign Kayla collapsed. We saw no sign of anyone besides our party in the area, and all my tricorder picked up is that odd life-force interference signal."

"She wasn't stung by an insect, one of those?" Janeway pointed at one of the large beelike creatures.

"I'm certain she wasn't," another crew member piped up. "I was standing right beside her when she collapsed. One moment she was staring at these flowers, the next she was falling, and I was trying to catch her. There were none of those creatures close by. We've been keeping our distance from them."

"*Voyager,* this is Captain Janeway. Get The Doctor on line."

"Yes, Captain?" The Doctor's slightly arrogant, constantly annoyed voice crackled over the line. It was amazing the depth of personality the programmed image had taken on in the time they'd been stranded. It was hard to think of him as anything but a member of the crew. "What is the nature of the medical emergency?"

"I'm not certain," Janeway answered, "but we've got a crew man down, collapsed for no obvious reason."

"If you will run your tricorder over her, Captain, I'll see if there is anything I can do from here."

Janeway complied quickly, keeping a constant watch on the display of the girl's vital signs. Kayla was breathing very slowly, but regularly. Her skin had always been a bit pale, but now it seemed drained of blood. Her pallor gave the impression of death, and Janeway could see from the tricorder reading that her circulation had weakened. The captain reported each change in the readings and varied the controls as directed by The Doctor, feeding the information directly to *Voyager*'s computer.

"Her vital signs are weak," The Doctor said. "Has she had anything to eat or drink, been exposed to anything unexpected that the others have not? It appears that some contaminant has been introduced to her system, but I can't pinpoint it without further tests."

"No," Fowler answered quickly. "None of us has had anything to eat or drink beyond the rations we carried with us. Your orders, Captain—only Neelix can okay these plants for consumption."

"I do not recommend beaming her to the ship yet, Captain," The Doctor said quickly. "I haven't got enough information to know what has infected her, or if there is a danger of contagion. I have no files on this planet, or its life-forms."

Kes spoke from the sickbay. "I can beam down and gather any samples The Doctor needs," she said. "We can set up a containment field in medical and beam the samples directly there. And you can use my help down there, in case any more of the crew become infected."

"Agreed." Janeway looked up just in time to see Tuvok burst into the clearing, followed closely by Kim, Neelix, and two members of his security team.

"Let's back out of this clearing," Janeway ordered sharply. "Tuvok, it looks as if we'll be spending a little bit more time on this planet than we'd planned on. I'm not sure what's happened to Kayla, but The Doctor wants us to wait before beaming up, just as a precaution.

"Let's get back to those ruins and see if we can't find our Urrythan friends. Maybe they'll be able to shed some light on this. Kes will be joining us to gather samples for The Doctor, and to tend to Kayla and any others who might need her in the meantime. We need to find out anything we can that might prove helpful, and we need to finish taking in the supplies. That is still our purpose here."

Tuvok took charge of the situation quickly, directing several of his men to raise Kayla's limp form and carry her between them.

Kim moved in and took Kayla by one arm, a grim pained expression painting his normally cheerful features. Somehow, he felt guilty. He'd suggested to Tuvok that Kayla be selected for the foraging party, thinking it best to keep some distance between them. Now this.

With an unknown threat surrounding them, Tuvok's instincts had taken over, and his normally intense vigilance had doubled. Despite his increased caution, the group made good time on the return trip, and it seemed only a few moments before they reached the outskirts of the ruined city and made their way into the small garden where their base camp waited.

Kes was waiting for them when they reached the town square, and Tuvok directed them up the stairs and into the partial security of the garden as quickly as possible. More equipment had been beamed down as well—medical supplies and sleeping enclosures. If possible, they didn't want to be on the planet long enough to put it all to use, but it was best to be prepared.

Neelix had already started a small mess, with a stove and an odd assortment of pots, pans, and implements. Using an odd assortment of the roots and herbs he'd been gathering, he had whipped up a stew that sent a pleasant odor wafting through the encampment.

Tuvok directed that Kayla be placed on one of the expandable cots that had been beamed down, and he, Janeway, and Kim gathered around behind Kes as she conducted a more thorough scan.

"She has traces of an organic compound that the computer is unable to identify," Kes relayed to The Doctor, who was monitoring her results from Medical. "It appears to have slowed her metabolism. . . . It's as if she's gone into some sort of . . . hibernation."

"The largest concentration of the compound is in the area of her nasal passages," The Doctor observed. "It would appear that some type of airborne contaminant—a pollen or a bacterial agent, or a bacterial agent *contained* in a pollen—is the cause, though I can't be certain until I have the samples in hand."

"Can you reverse the effects?" Janeway asked quickly.

"I will have to research the toxin, Captain, before I can make a definitive answer to that question," The Doctor replied calmly. "I estimate that it will take me twenty hours to complete my analysis, once the samples are in hand. Of course, that is taking into account the worst possible scenario."

"You have twelve hours, Doctor. After that we're beaming aboard and taking our chances," Janeway replied, cutting off the communicator before he could reply. Turning to Kes, she said, "Get him those samples on the double, then see what you can do to make Kayla more comfortable. We'll have to keep a constant monitor on her condition. Keep The Doctor informed of any changes, and I want to know the minute we have anything definite."

"Yes, Captain," Kes replied.

Kim stepped forward, blushing, and pulled Kes aside momentarily. "I'd appreciate it if you'd let me know if there are any changes," he said softly. "I . . . I'm just a bit worried, that's all."

Kes smiled at him quizzically, waiting for an explanation, but Kim turned and walked after Janeway, leaving her to her own conclusions.

Now that she was on the planet, Kes was all business. She set quickly about making a comfortable place for Kayla to rest, listening to Neelix prattle on about the food they'd found and his fears that she should not have been exposed to whatever had caused Kayla's illness, nodding her head every now and then to show she was listening, but not really concentrating on what he was saying. Something was itching at the back of her mind, a sort of hum of energy, and it was distracting her.

Neelix was saying something about a root, but the

words suddenly began to fade away. His face distorted oddly, slipping in and out of focus, and the humming in the back of her mind grew stronger, insinuating itself into her thoughts.

She turned from Neelix, who was moving toward her with a look of concern on his face, and staggered a few steps toward the entrance of the garden. The tricorder she'd held in her hand dropped to the ground with a clatter, forgotten. She could hear voices calling to her, several voices, very loud, but slow, or were they too fast? She couldn't make out the words.

They were being overpowered, brushed aside. Something else was calling out to her as well, something deep, powerful, and insistent, but not malevolent. It wanted her to join—something—someone. Understanding dangled just beyond her mental grasp, and she reached out, as if to embrace some entity that none of the others in the clearing could see, then she dropped softly to her knees in the lush grass.

She felt herself struggling upward through a sluggish stream of—mental energy—struggling up toward what she dimly recognized as reality—her own consciousness. She could feel hands shaking her by her shoulders, and the voices were growing more insistent—more constant.

She fought against the heavy dreamlike pull on her mind, fought her way back toward the concerned faces of her friends, which were beginning to come back into focus, to take on color and form. She reached out with her mind to Neelix. His image, the worried frown that had invaded his ever-cheerful face, was all it took. With a sudden snap, her mind parted itself from the invading vision, and she found herself in control again. She shook her head to clear her muddled thoughts.

"Kes! What is it? Can you hear me?"

It was Captain Janeway speaking, and Kes found herself staring into her clear gray eyes as her own vision focused once more. The captain was leaning over her, and it was her hands that held her shoulders.

"I'm okay," she said, trying to rise, then sinking back down slowly. "It was . . . amazing. I felt harmony, and power, more power than I've ever felt in one place. And it was growing. Whatever it was, it was growing stronger. There was such . . . joy, in that sensation, Captain, a great expansion of joy. I can't explain it, but whatever it was, whatever it meant, it was wonderful."

"Do you think that what you just felt might in some way be responsible for what's happening to Ensign Kayla?"

Before she could answer, Neelix piped in: "Do you think it will affect you again? Perhaps you should return to the ship. . . . Perhaps we all should."

"We aren't going to risk infecting my ship," Janeway snapped, "until I find out just what's going on here. Can you tell us any more, Kes?"

"No, Captain," Kes replied, "but I'm certain that whatever, or whoever, that was, they mean us no harm. I don't think it has anything to do with Kayla, but there was a trace of Kayla in what I felt, Captain. Again, I don't know how to explain that. I just know that there was nothing malevolent in what I felt—that it involved joy and harmony, not harm of any sort."

"I agree," Tuvok cut in. He had a serious concentrated expression on his face, as if he were listening to something. "I cannot make anything in particular out, but there is an energy in the air. It does not feel dangerous, but it is powerful, and since we do not understand it, it is a potential threat."

"Our phantom life-force reading?" Janeway asked thoughtfully.

"Perhaps," Tuvok replied. "It is not concentrated in one spot, but seems to permeate the air. Also, it is not like the mental energy of any single mind I've encountered."

"Mr. Tuvok," the captain said, "I want you to take a couple of the others and return to the spot where Kayla collapsed. I've been thinking about what The Doctor said about pollen. I want you to bring some samples from those large yellow flowers. Get in and out of that area as quickly as possible."

Tuvok nodded, gesturing to Ensign Fowler and one other crewman, who began immediately to gather the equipment they would need. Moments later the small team was moving away briskly.

Janeway turned back to the others. "I don't know what kind of communications devices they may have, Mr. Kim, but I want you to see if you can't raise our friends somehow and get them back here.

We need some explanations, and I don't intend to lose any crew members waiting on them."

"Yes, Captain," Kim replied eagerly. Among the equipment that had been beamed down was a small communications console, and he went immediately to work, hailing the Urrythans on different wavelengths and frequencies.

Satisfied that they were doing all that it was in their power to do for the moment, Janeway sat down against the stone wall surrounding the garden to wait. The savory scent of Neelix's stew reminded her that it had been a while since she'd thought about eating. There was something about this place that stole her concentration.

"Captain?" It was Kes, walking up quickly with a tricorder in her hand. "I believe we've got something. It appears that the compound that has affected Ensign Kayla has a chemical makeup particularly reactive with the Bajoran nervous system. That would explain why none of the rest of us passed out immediately, but it is likely that we have all been affected to some degree. Until we've isolated the various components of the compound, we can't guess its exact effect on different races."

The captain remained silent for a moment, lost in thought. Now she had a new concern. She herself might be in danger of infection by this compound . . . might, in fact, already be under its influence. If it was true, it could explain her inability to concentrate—and it brought up new problems.

If they had all been infected, then it might be only

a matter of time before herself and the others reached the state that Kayla was now in.

"Now that you've isolated the compound, does The Doctor have any ideas on how we might reverse these effects?" she asked.

"Not yet," Kes replied, "but he's confident, now that he has more of an idea what he's working with, that it will not take him long to solve it."

"Keep me informed. We'll have some more samples to beam up in a little while. I've sent Tuvok back to those flowers. What we got from Kayla will not have the same concentration as the plant itself can provide. Maybe there will be something in the cellular structure that will be helpful."

"I'll tell him to be expecting them, Captain," Kes said, turning back toward Kayla briskly.

In her mind, Janeway was chiding herself. Tuvok and the others would be getting a second dose of that pollen, and she had sent them to it. She wondered, just for a moment, if whatever that compound was had already had a negative effect on her ability to think rationally. She only hoped that whatever amount of the compound Tuvok's party took in would not be enough to incapacitate them.

The beauty and greenery surrounding her had begun to take on a more ominous nature—more threatening. For the first time since reaching the planet, she wished she were on *Voyager*, in her ready room or her stateroom, sipping a cup of warm tea.

She was snapped out of her melancholy by Kim's voice. "I've got them, Captain," he said. "They have a very primitive transmission setup. Vok says he will come personally."

She nodded, fighting to keep her thoughts centered. She hoped the Urrythans weren't far away. She didn't know for sure that Vok and his people could help them, but she didn't know where else to turn. They might be running out of time.

CHAPTER
4

JANEWAY HAD NO WAY TO KNOW HOW FAR AWAY THE Urrythans had actually been, or by what method they would return. She kept a constant watch on the jungle surrounding them, monitoring her tricorder, and *Voyager* scanned the area carefully, but there was no sign of anyone—nothing.

Vok was as good as his word, however. It was less than an hour before the solemn group returned to the garden, and he walked at their head, emotionless as before. It was difficult to read emotions on their stoic faces, but his movements were jerky, less graceful than she remembered. Something was different, and warning bells were going off in Janeway's mind as she watched his approach. He seemed agitated.

She hoped it was not nerves brought on by guilt. Things had seemed perfectly amicable at their first meeting, and she'd thought she could trust him, and one of the things she hated most in life was to be proven wrong. It was possible that it was nothing more than the necessity for his continued exposure to sunlight that was bothering him.

"Your message informs me that you and your party have encountered some difficulty?" Vok asked without delay. He appeared concerned, but his movements were furtive, as if his concern was not directly with the problems of his visitors.

"One of my crew members has fallen ill," Janeway answered briskly. "She was with a party foraging deeper into the gardens in search of water. In a clearing surrounded by large yellow flowers, she passed out, though there was no one near her at the time. My medical officer, who is unable to leave the ship at this time, has informed me that the condition has been brought about by some sort of biological contaminant—a contaminant we have all been subjected to."

"The *Ambiana*," Vok breathed. "The *Ambiana* is always present, but it does not have this effect on us—not so quickly. I hadn't thought to mention it to you, because I believed your visit would be too short for any to feel its effects."

"Not so quickly?" Kes cut in, her eyes bright with interest. "Then you know of this condition?"

"Oh, yes," Vok replied. "We seek it. She has reached the *Long Sleep,* the dream from which there is but one awakening. I have personally been seeking such a state of harmony for over two hundred years.

Even now, the *One Voice* calls to me . . . it will not be much longer before I reach the *Long Sleep* myself."

Janeway could only stand and stare. Two centuries? She wouldn't have placed the being's age at more than forty or fifty years from his appearance. There were a lot of things about these beings she needed to know, it seemed, and she needed to know them fast.

"If you are familiar with the condition," she said slowly, "then perhaps you know how we might reverse the effect?"

At that moment Vok showed the first actual emotion they'd seen. He backed up a pace, as though he'd been physically slapped, and he turned his head quickly to trade glances with those who stood behind him. Clearly, Janeway's question had been the last thing he'd expected to hear, though she couldn't understand why that would be.

"Reverse the *Ascension?*" he said at last. "Why would one wish to reverse the natural order of the soul's travel to rebirth? If the harmony has called one into its song, why would they wish to be separated from it? Why would one return to a lower plane?"

"Ensign Kayla is not suffering from the natural order of her soul's travel," Janeway replied grimly. "This state may be normal for your people, Vok, but you yourself have stated that to reach such a condition has taken you a very, very long time. It cannot be natural to drop into such a state in only a few hours' time. What she is suffering is an adverse reaction to a biological contaminant, and any information you might have on that substance may well save her life."

"It *is* remarkable," Vok agreed, nodding his head slowly. He seemed to be considering the implications of her words, but his next statement belied this.

"Your follower is truly blessed. We have not had one go to the *Long Sleep* so quickly in nearly five hundred years. It is a great honor."

Communications were obviously breaking down, and Janeway's patience was nearing its end. "Your beliefs are not ours, Vok. My 'follower' is not going to go into any *Long Sleep* or *Ascension* here without her consent, no matter what you think. Kayla must be awakened. Can you help us?"

"It would be wrong to return a gift from the ancients," Vok noted sagely, his tone that of an instructor explaining something to a stubborn child. "It is just that you do not understand, do not feel the underlying harmony that calls her home. We cannot allow you to interfere in this, not so near to the sacred resting grounds of our ancestors.

"Already her voice is joining with those of the elders. She is weak, but she will strengthen soon, and she will be welcomed. She will come to a new life, a new birth. It is her destiny. We must begin preparations for her *Ascension.*"

Janeway didn't know what to say. It was obvious that these beings were not only bent on *not* helping with Kayla's condition, but that they were actually rejoicing over it. They appeared to be taking it as some sort of sign from their own ancestors. A religious miracle.

"There will be no preparations for my crew members unless they are made, and sanctioned, by myself," she said at last, fighting to keep the tone of her voice even and reasonable. "We came here peacefully, hoping only to gather supplies and to continue our journey home. You indicated that this was not a problem for you. If this has changed, then we will take what we have and be on our way . . . just as soon as our Doctor has found a way to reverse the effects of this *Ambiana.*"

Vok did not answer, but again he turned to his followers, ignoring the captain and the rest of the away team as if they were nonexistent. Then he turned back to the garden and began to move forward at a measured, practiced cadence. His followers moved behind him in silence, and their features were taking on a glazed, entranced expression.

When they neared Kayla's prone form, they began to circle her reverently. Tuvok reached for his phaser, but Janeway restrained him by placing one hand lightly on his arm once more. What was happening was unacceptable, but thus far there had been no act of violence from either side, and she wanted to keep things that way if at all possible while she worked out a solution to their problem.

The Urrythans had begun a slow monotone chant that seemed to emanate from deep inside them. It rose and fell in pitch and shifted with eerie precision between subtle backbeats, filling the air with a sort of calming energy. Their voices were so closely entwined that the harmony they produced formed chords that melded to sound like a single voice.

Kes felt the familiarity of it, and nearly cried out. It was the same as the sensation that had overwhelmed her before, only subtly changed. The depth was not there, the pureness of the emotion was flawed. What she'd experienced the first time was utter peace, a harmony with existence that transcended anything she could have described. This was different, and yet somehow the same. A lesser shadow of the harmony.

As she sank into the sound, she felt that other voice, that other, brighter song, filtering through and around her, blending with the voices of the circled aliens. She could sense, faintly, Ensign Kayla's mind as it was joined, thread by thread, note by note, into the *One Voice* of the planet. The chant was helping her to mesh, clearing the way and synchronizing her mind to the great chord.

In the background of the chant, she could detect a hunger, a yearning. It was as though a great void was calling out to be filled, as though some entity full of loneliness and pain yearned for its home, for . . .

"Enough!" Janeway's voice cut through the sound, breaking its spell like a stone through a thin pane of glass. The Urrythans appeared startled, as though what she'd done was beyond their comprehension. Their chant fell away, and they backed off from Kayla's body slowly and uncertainly. For a long moment they stood watching, confused, then Vok moved forward once more.

"You have broken the ritual," the tall stolid alien chided her softly. "She needs guidance to the next level, a bridge between her own song and that of the ancients."

"You will guide yourself and your followers out of this garden," Janeway said, her voice betraying the barely controlled fury that Vok's actions had brought upon her. "We have done nothing more than you agreed that we might, and I will not have you interfering with the health of any member of my crew. We will find a way to reverse Kayla's condition ourselves, and the moment that I'm certain this virus, blessing, curse, or whatever it is will not infect my entire ship, we will leave you and your planet behind. I am sorry if we have troubled you, but I'm afraid I must ask you to leave. Now."

Vok did not answer, but he did turn away from Ensign Kayla and moved toward the gates. The others seemed more reluctant, clinging to their space in the proximity of Kayla's form. It was obvious that they did not want to leave her, that they were attributing some sort of significance to her condition that was beyond Janeway's comprehension.

In the end, Vok's presence proved the stronger, and they pulled themselves away. The group left the garden behind in silence, but there was none of the friendly harmony that their first visit had instilled. Rather, there was a feeling of menace to the air. Although they'd left peacefully, Janeway thought that it might prove to be a bit *too* easily. It might be only a regrouping, a preparation for a different attack.

Janeway was startled, looking down. Her hand had brushed her commbadge, and she realized that, despite the danger involved, she'd been about to request that they all be beamed back to *Voyager*.

"*Voyager*, Janeway," she said, hitting the activator absently. "I don't suppose you found a way to keep our friends on the scanners this time?"

"No, Captain," Torres's perplexed voice crackled over the circuit. "They just come and go from the screen, fading into that life-force emanation as if they'd been a part of it all along. Even when they were standing right there in front of you, it was difficult to keep a lock on them. And that life-force reading is still growing in intensity. If it gets much worse, we won't be able to detect them at all."

"Any progress on the contaminant?"

"None, Captain," The Doctor's voice snapped on line. "I have isolated the compound to its various components, but I have not found a way to reverse the effects. It is a powerful, yet subtle blend of anesthetics and depressants. It slowly relaxes the central nervous system. It causes no *fatal* damage to the body's systems, but it *does* cause an eventual cellular reorganization. It takes over the system and . . . modifies it."

"Well, I suggest you work faster, then, Doctor," Janeway said, staring off into the distance through the garden's entrance. "I don't want Kayla's cells rearranged, and I want us out of here at the first possible moment. The welcome mat has been pulled out from under us, and I don't want to wait and see what that might mean to our new acquaintances."

Just then, Tuvok and the others returned. Ensign Fowler had a large pile of the yellow-blossomed flowers over one shoulder, but there was something odd in the way he was walking. He seemed disoriented, and there was a serene smile pasted across his face. If he'd merely walked into a room where Janeway had been watching, she'd have said that he was either drunk or under the influence of some chemical.

Tuvok seemed oblivious, but he was staring straight ahead as he walked, acknowledging nothing, obviously light-years away and lost in thought. Pursing her lips, the captain stepped forward and grabbed her security chief by the arm, dragging his attention back to the moment.

"Mr. Tuvok," she said quickly, "isolate those flowers, quickly. Their pollen may well be what caused Kayla's condition. I can't afford to lose any more people to this."

"Aye, Captain," Tuvok answered. He raised one eyebrow quizzically, almost smiling. On his severe Vulcan features, the smile did not sit well. It came across as a leer, though Janeway chalked that up to her own sudden fears. She was losing control of the situation rapidly. She wondered if he'd been walking to the beat of an alien song—a song that involved a chord and yet only one voice.

Darkness was fast approaching, and the away team spent the next couple of hours readying their camp for whatever the night might bring. The sleeping structures were erected and supplies secured against scavenging animals.

Tuvok, who seemed to regain his awareness slowly once the flowers had been safely beamed to *Voyager*, concentrated on security, as usual. He set a watch on the perimeter of the camp, giving each of his men strict instructions to call him if anything out of the ordinary occurred. Everyone was given a watch, but he tried to keep his own people spread as evenly as possible so that there would always be a few of them well rested.

Neelix, who'd never stopped cooking since they'd lit a fire, served up a stew of the Blort roots he'd dragged them to Urrytha to find. The concoction was tasty, if a bit exotic, considering their surroundings. He served the meal with a worried grin, and he kept glancing over to where Kes was ministering to Kayla. It was obvious that he was on the verge of making a scene and insisting that she be sent back to the ship.

Kes had had no further visions, but it was clear that whatever it was that their scanners on the ship were picking up from the planet was having its effect on her. She had a serene blissful manner about her, and her movements were more slow and graceful than usual. She seemed very at home in the small clearing, as did several of the others, notably those who'd been with Tuvok to gather the flowers.

Janeway managed to have Tuvok tactfully exclude each of these from guard duty for one reason or another, without explaining exactly why. She didn't want any of them panicking, but she knew that there was no way to know how the alien pollen would affect each different race represented in her crew.

She was thankful that Kayla was the only Bajoran who'd beamed down.

The humans seemed to be holding up well, and despite her mental link with the planet, Kes showed no signs of the druglike effect. While she was able to make a connection with the musical interference, she seemed able to break that link just as easily. This might prove a strength, in the end, and Janeway made a mental note to try and come up with a method of putting that strength to use.

Tuvok was even more calm and focused than was his norm, but at the same time he was more relaxed than Janeway had ever seen him. His usual attentive scrutiny of the garden was cut short when he decided, on the spur of the moment, to sit down with Neelix and have a bowl of stew.

"Doctor," Janeway said, taking a seat and preparing herself to stand the first watch, "if I've ever needed you to come through for me, this is the time."

As two alien moons rose to lend the gardens and ruins an eerie luminescence, she settled back against a stone pillar and waited. There was nothing else to do. She scanned the landscape around her wearily, feeling a sort of numbing vibration working its way up through the ground and into her bones.

When it came time to awaken Kes for the second watch, the captain never even rose from her seat. Her eyes had grown unaccountably heavy, and dreams of home had stolen in to replace her concentration on her duty. When the Urrythans returned near the midpoint of the night, they passed her in silence, and she did not move. There were no others awake to greet them, none to challenge them.

They melted from the shadows, slipped through the camp past Kes's resting form, and lifted Kayla's inert body gently. With the Bajoran woman draped easily across two sets of slender shoulders, they returned to the shadows, disappearing from sight and baffling *Voyager*'s scanners. Their escape was swift and unhindered.

CHAPTER
5

THEY MOVED SOFTLY AND SILENTLY ACROSS THE LANDS of their ancestors, their feet in tandem, their minds in harmony. There was no hesitation, no discord. It was a special moment of balance, and they could feel the voice of their ancestors vibrating through the ground, reaching out to them, binding them one to another and to the song. There was a deep soothing sensation of approval accompanying the song—of belonging, as if their actions were causing great joy.

Vok pushed ahead, the only one with the slightest twinge of doubt over what they'd done, over what they were about to do. His were deeper memories, longer years. Things had changed a great deal over the span of his lifetime, and this was not something he believed would have happened in the days of his own youth.

The female was a miracle, that much was certain.

To react in such a way to the *Ambiana* was an indication of a great soul—a destiny. In his heart, he knew this—believed in it implicitly. His mind, though, was another matter. Vok would have given anything to be in her position—to know the communion with the *One Voice* that she was experiencing, but the years had also given him perspective. What the starship captain, Janeway, had said also made sense.

Two hundred plus years he'd struggled through the hardships of life, watching his brothers and sisters and friends make the *Ascension,* watching generations of young ones grow and join those who sought the great harmony. His own journey was not a long one, by the standards of his ancestors, and yet the younger ones did not linger as he had. Things were changing, and he did not fully understand those changes.

Now these aliens had come along, their captain so polite, so direct, and her words had instilled the seeds of doubt that two centuries of life had been unable to teach. If the *Ascension* was not a part of these people's beliefs, were they merely ignorant of the *Long Sleep*—the harmony—or were they different? Did they have their own paths to follow, or was it in Vok's destiny to be their prophet, to lead them to understand what their own backgrounds had not prepared them for? Too many questions, and he was too near his own *Long Sleep*.

This female they carried, she was not of their own. Special as her *Ascension* might be, it was not the way—not the *proper* way to follow the ancestors to the final rest. And they were not her ancestors. At the moment his followers were in a state of ecstasy over this, but in time they might come to resent this Kayla, with her immediate *Ascension* and accelerated initiation into the harmony.

Part of it, he knew, was the increase in the strength of the ancestor's voice. He could hear it singing through his psyche, even as he walked, and he knew that, at their own levels, they could sense it, too. It was building toward the *Awakening,* and there had not been one in the lifetime of any who walked the planet.

Still he pushed on. For good or ill, his people had demanded this. There was a great fear that the star travelers would awaken the woman, that the gift of the ancestors would be rejected, and that this rejection would reflect on their own afterlives, or, worse yet, that the aliens might in some way prematurely end the *Long Sleep* of the ancients and in some way harm them.

When they'd confronted him outright, demanding that something be done, Vok had assented. He was but one individual, and he was an individual with doubts—unworthy of the role bestowed upon him. He was eldest among the walking, last of his generation to ascend—wisest. The wisdom was no special quality of his person, but only the weight of years, piling one upon the other, driving him toward his destiny. He was eldest, he would serve. It was the way of Urrytha.

The doubt faded slowly as they neared the caverns, as he'd known that it would. The voice of the old ones called out to him, embraced him, and there was no room in such an embrace for doubt. He moved as if in a dream, the harmony gripping him and rushing through his system like a drug. He led the way to the central square of their settlement, within sight of the entrance to the halls of the ancients, and they placed the woman's body gently on a large stone altar.

Without a word, they dispersed, leaving only a single guardian to watch over the woman's prone form. There were things to be done, things to be gathered. Preparations would need to be swift and exacting, given the nature of her condition. There was little time, and the voices of the ancients were already weaving their spell about her. It was time for her ritual. It was time to encase her in the vehicle that would carry her through to the afterlife.

Vok stared about him at the massive pillars, ascending themselves until their uppermost reaches were not visible, as though they were reaching for the sky. One day, he would reach as they did. This day, it would be the one called Kayla. He stood rigid for a long moment, imagining the walls of his own vessel rising about him, imagining the womblike security, the constant connection with the *One Voice*, the majesty of *Ascension*.

With a heavy sigh, he turned and disappeared after the others. There was not much time, and it had been some time since he'd performed the rite of passing. It wouldn't do to make a mistake with another's soul hanging in the balance, not when his own people considered her some sort of saint.

In the solitude of the small square, Kayla stared blankly at the clouded skies stretching above her. If she was in any way aware of her surroundings, she gave no indication of it. The smile on her lips was unshakable, and her breathing, though a bit softer and slower even than it had been before her abduction, was steady.

Janeway was awakened by the crisp tinny call of her commbadge.

"Voyager to Janeway."

Awakening in a matter of seconds, she responded, "Janeway here, what is it?" As she listened, she scanned the camp quickly. Had she been relieved on watch? How could she have fallen asleep?

"I'm not certain, Captain," came Torres's voice, in a tone of uncertainty. "I've been realigning the scanners, trying different combinations to break through whatever type of screen is hiding the Urrythans from us. A little while ago I noticed a strange variance in the life-force reading.

"It seemed to grow stronger in the area where your camp is located, then it steadied out again. What it appears to be is a slight fluctuation, as if there were some signal that was a part of the whole, and yet not entirely in synch with it. I wouldn't even have noticed it, but I was recording the signal over a period of time for more intensive study."

"Can you tell anything from the variance?"

"Nothing certain, Captain, but I checked back over the computer logs of our earlier readings. We didn't notice it at the time, since we were concentrating on scanning for the Urrythans, but when your friends visited you yesterday, a similar variance occurred."

"Janeway out."

Levering herself to a sitting position, she continued to scan the camp for anything suspicious. Silently she berated herself for her lack of vigilance. Nothing seemed to have changed. The others lay undisturbed—sleeping soundly. Ensign Fowler had also been on watch, and she could just make him out, leaning against a tree near the gateway to the garden. She breathed a sigh of relief. She'd been disoriented when she awakened, but it seemed as if someone had been watching, if she had failed.

Wide awake now, she decided to get up and have a look around. Something in the way Vok and his followers had acted during their last encounter had lessened her trust of the tall quiet aliens. Possibly it was her own imagination getting the best of her, or the stress of the situation, but there had not seemed to be any note of finality on the issue of Ensign Kayla.

The history of the Federation was littered with situations where religious fanatics had been out of control. Wars had been fought, coups enacted. Entire races had been wiped out for less than the circumstances of their meeting with the Urrythans, and there was no way to gauge the reactions on their emotionless faces to know how fanatic their own beliefs might be.

She made her way quietly through the camp

toward Ensign Fowler's post. He made no move to challenge her, and as she drew near to him, she noticed that his head was lolling oddly to one side. Hurrying her steps, she heard the soft regular sound of snoring. He was asleep!

Boiling with sudden anger, at herself as much as her crewman, she crossed the remaining couple of yards to the man's side and grabbed his shoulder, shaking him roughly.

"Ensign Fowler!" she said sharply. "Ensign Fowler, wake up."

He didn't move. In fact, as she continued to shake him, he slumped further to the side, dropping to a heap on the ground beside the stone column he'd been leaning against. His head struck the ground rather sharply, yet he didn't even moan from the pain. His breathing was shallow but regular, and his eyes remained closed.

Suddenly she sensed a presence at her back and spun. It was Tuvok.

"What is it, Captain?"

"Take the watch, Mr. Tuvok. It would appear that Ensign Fowler is falling under the same influence as Kayla. I'm going to check on her."

When she reached the low-slung cot, Janeway stopped and stared in shock. Kayla was not there. Kes was still curled up on the ground nearby, and all of the supplies and instruments they'd laid out remained untouched, but the Bajoran woman was simply not there.

It took only a few moments to rouse the rest of the

party, but it was obvious from the way certain crew members were carrying themselves that their problems were only beginning. Tuvok and herself seemed relatively untouched by the effects of the *Ambiana,* and the few hours of sleep they'd been afforded had cleared her head somewhat. Not all the others were so fortunate. Kes was wide awake and coherent, but there was a faraway distracted look in her eyes that made Janeway nervous. She felt the reins of control slowly slipping through her fingers.

"Voyager, Janeway."

"Yes, Captain?" It was Chakotay's voice that crackled across her commbadge.

"We've lost Kayla." She quickly informed him of what had transpired, including an explanation for Tuvok and the others of what Torres had found that had roused her from her own deep sleep.

"Excuse me, Captain," Kes cut in, after hearing this last bit of information, "but I have a thought on those readings."

"Yes?" Janeway asked hurriedly. "I'm ready to listen to just about anything that will clear this up."

"Well," Kes continued, "you remember when I went into the trance yesterday. There was a feeling of extreme calm—an almost hypnotic musical rhythm in the air. I believe that what I felt may have been the same life-force your scanners are registering. If the scanners picked up the Urrythans at their remote encampment, but not here, it seems logical that the readings are generated from here."

"But how would this explain our inability to

detect them when they are right here in front of us?" Janeway asked, intrigued but skeptical.

"I believe that, as they fall more and more deeply under the influence of this *One Voice,* they fall into synch with one another on some primal level. The closer they come to this place, to the source of that signal, the closer they bond one to the other, and the more difficult it would be to distinguish them individually. What you are reading *is* the aliens, you are just reading them all at once."

"A group mind of that sort would be formidable," Tuvok commented.

"Formidable," Kes agreed, "but not necessarily dangerous. What I felt was not in any way violent or aggressive. It was a feeling of unity and harmony. It is that which they seek—I'm certain of it—and they believe that Kayla has already found it. Also, I doubt that any of those we've met is powerful enough to bend the power of that group mind to his own purpose. It is more as if they are being swallowed within it.

"There is also the fact that, though they are one with this life force, they are not *completely* one with it. All of them still have auras of their own, a bit of individuality that keeps them from becoming one with the whole. This must be what Torres was able to detect—the ripple of their own discord with their planet."

"If this is true," Tuvok mused, "then it would be illogical for them to harm Kayla in any way. They would be preparing her for a sleep of thousands of years. This should allow us enough time to find out where they've taken her and attempt to free her."

"Chakotay," Janeway said finally, "I want you to configure all the scanners around the variances in this life-force reading. If we can't spot these aliens individually, maybe we can read the overall picture and use it as a sort of map. We have to find Kayla, and we have to do it quickly. I don't want to lose any more people to this, and we've already got Mr. Fowler down hard. Some of the others are showing signs of lethargy, as well.

"Doctor, have you made any progress?"

"Yes, Captain, some, though preparing an anti-dote is proving a bit more problematic than I'd anticipated. The effects of this pollen are caused by a very subtle mixture of a great number of toxins and—"

"Just find it, Doctor. I want us off this planet as soon as we find Kayla. Is that clear?"

"Quite."

"Chakotay, keep me informed of *any* variance in that reading."

"Yes, Captain."

Janeway signed off, then turned to scan the expectant faces around her. It was a bad position, and it was time to make some decisions about how they were going to deal with it. Their present sit-back-and-wait policy was failing, and she felt the need for action, for positive results, to keep both her own sanity and her control of the situation intact.

She noted the expression of disbelief and shock on Kim's face, and she frowned. It was obvious that he had not been able to rid himself of the feelings of guilt he'd had earlier, and she needed him to be as sharp as possible in the hours to come.

Ensign Fowler had come around finally. He was groggy, but Kes had given him a stimulant, and he seemed aware enough of his surroundings. It seemed that the reaction in his system, despite the fact that he was human—as Janeway was—was progressing pretty rapidly. At least he wasn't gone completely, as she'd feared. How could they maintain any type of security if there was no way to know when one of them would just drop off into dreamland?

"It is obvious that Vok and his people are going to do nothing to help us learn more about this *Ambiana*," she began, "so we're going to have to work on that ourselves. If their ancestors built this place, then they must have had the answers to our questions.

"Mr. Kim, Tuvok, we're going to start into the ruins and see if we can't locate something that will be of help to us. The rest of you will remain here, in case Vok should return. Tuvok, Kim, and myself seem the least affected by the pollen, and Kes, you will be needed here to care for those who fall too deeply under the influence. I want you to remain doubled up on the security watches, and the moment you feel the influence of this *Ambiana* becoming too much for you, get someone up to relieve you."

"I'm not certain," Tuvok cut in, "that it is wise to venture in farther. We have no idea what kind of safeguards the Urrythans, or their ancestors, might have put in place to stop us. We have no idea of their weapons capabilities, nor do we have any evidence that the answers we seek will be available to us."

"I am not certain, either, Tuvok," Janeway answered firmly, "but I *am* certain that we are going to accomplish exactly nothing if we remain here in this clearing waiting for the inevitable. I want to know more about this place, and I want to find Kayla. Our only course would seem to be straight ahead, and I mean to take it."

"They mentioned caverns, Captain," Kim cut in eagerly. "Maybe we can find an entrance to them near here?"

"Good thinking, Mr. Kim. We'll start at once. And while we're at it, maybe you'd better get started on trying to decipher that writing we found earlier. It won't do us much good to find answers we can't understand."

"Right, Captain." The young man's face was more animated than she'd seen it in a long time, and Janeway nearly smiled. It was a shame, she thought as they readied themselves to depart, that it had taken such a disastrous turn of events to bring that expression to the surface. She just hoped he would be able to concentrate on the task at hand and not worry too much about Kayla.

"Kim," she said softly, pulling him aside.

"Yes, Captain?"

"She'll be fine. Quit blaming yourself."

"I'll try, Captain," he replied earnestly. Janeway nodded, turning to Tuvok and tilting her head in the direction she intended them to take.

As they started off, with Janeway and Tuvok

carrying the bulk of the supplies, Kim busied himself with his tricorder. He walked with his head bent, eyes glued to the small device, and Janeway moved protectively closer. The least she could do, she thought, was to keep him from running into a tree.

"Captain?" Kim said uncertainly, stopping short for a moment.

"What is it, Mr. Kim?"

"My tricorder. I can't seem to access the ship's computer. It's as if my signal were being blanked out somehow. . . ."

Janeway quickly checked her own tricorder, and she noticed that Tuvok was doing the same. Nothing. She switched her controls a bit, and saw that the life-force readings were still growing in intensity.

"It would appear that we are on our own on this one, Kim," Janeway mused, putting her tricorder away and heading back up the path. "It seems that this *One Voice* is beginning to grow a bit loud."

Back in the small garden, the others were making final preparations to hold their position against invasion. There was no way of knowing if Vok and his followers would be satisfied with just Kayla, or if they would insist on the *Ascension* of every crew member who fell under the influence of the *Ambiana*. Fowler was already showing signs of weakening, and Kes still had the faraway dreamy look that made Janeway wonder how much their Ocampa companion might be beginning to sympathize with the aliens' point of view. She certainly seemed to enjoy the sensation that the *One Voice* of the planet brought her.

Janeway caught herself drifting off, getting lost in the colors, sounds, and scents of the giant gardens, and she shook her head violently. She was not immune to the *Ambiana* any more than the others, and yet, so much more than they, it was imperative that she keep her wits about her. Kim and Tuvok showed no signs of the pollen's effects, and for that she was grateful. Somehow she knew that, whatever was to come, they were going to need to be alert.

"Captain," Tuvok cut into her reverie. "There is a slight fluctuation in the life-force readings ahead. I'm not certain if it indicates one of the Urrythans, but there is something different . . . there."

He pointed ahead where a growth of the surrounding foliage was particularly thick.

"And, Captain?" he added.

"Yes?"

"It is stronger. All of it. It has been growing slowly but steadily in strength since we arrived."

Janeway said nothing, but she hurried her steps. When she reached the point in the brush that Tuvok had pointed out, she thrust the leaves aside quickly. Behind the foliage, rising up through the ground where the years and the weather had buried it, was the tip of another of the strange pillars they'd encountered farther out.

Janeway reached out to touch the surface of the thing, running her fingers lightly across it. She cried out suddenly as a small spark of energy seemed to jump from the thing to the tip of her finger. It was vibrating. The ground was vibrating. There was an energy surrounding them that was undeniable in its growing intensity. It was a calming peaceful vibration.

She had a sudden vision of color and joy. The vibration worked its way through her, the sound permeated her being, reaching deep within her to pluck at bits and pieces of her mind that she'd not been previously aware of, molding them, bringing them into syncopation with the whole. She felt drawn in, and that drawing in was a wondrous thing, a blissful sensation.

"Captain," Tuvok called out. When she failed to respond, he grabbed her roughly by the shoulder and pulled her away from the pillar. "Captain!"

"Wha . . . I . . ." She shook her head violently from side to side and stood, staring down at the stone. She'd felt . . . just for an instant . . . a joining with that energy. Sudden understanding of what Kes had been talking about flooded her senses. There was also a quick flash of respect. Kes had felt that, felt it constantly, on some level, and yet she'd pulled herself free.

"Keep moving in," she said, her voice slightly shaky. "Something tells me these pillars are getting older as we move toward the center of the garden. If I'm right, we may find more of their history carved in the bases of those farther in. Maybe we can find something we can use. They seem to be buried more deeply here, and that would indicate more years of existence."

Tuvok's gaze intimated that he thought the likelihood of finding anything but trouble farther in very slim, but he kept his silence. Kim barely noticed their exchange. His eyes were glued to his tricorder as he worked feverishly to decode the alien script. Janeway turned and began making her way down the ancient trail, leading them into the ever-deepening shadows of the Urrythan jungle.

CHAPTER
6

"VOYAGER TO KES, DO YOU READ ME?"

Kes had been meditating, exploring the sensations of the planet's powerful yet soothing mind, and she shook her head, trying to clear the cobwebs that the experience had brought. She felt momentarily guilty, as though she'd been shirking some responsibility, but it passed. Coming back to the surface of her mind was like swimming up through thick warm water. Groggily, she answered, "This is Kes, what is it?"

"We can't seem to contact the Captain, Tuvok, or Kim," Chakotay's worried voice crackled over the communicator. "We've lost them on the scanners, all three of them. We had them as they left the camp, then suddenly they were just not there. They were swallowed up in that . . . whatever it is. That life-force reading. The communicators are as useless as the scanners."

"It is getting stronger," Kes replied.

"*What* is getting stronger?" Chakotay asked quickly.

"The harmony," Kes replied. "The feeling that I get from this place, the joining. It is one big life-force reading, Commander, that is why you can't single them out. The Urrythans are one entity most of the time—and the oldest of them are that way *all* of the time. Now that they have moved toward the source, the central location of the signal, the captain and the others may well be shielded as well."

"You're saying that their minds are joined?"

"Not joined, really," she replied thoughtfully. "That would imply that they were separate in some way. They are not separate minds joined, Commander, they are *one mind.*"

Chakotay's mind raced. He had a great responsibility on his shoulders, and it had just doubled. The captain was in danger, that much he was certain of. If he could have gotten a lock on them all, he'd have beamed them aboard, damn The Doctor's complaints, but it wasn't possible. With no fix on their position, or on their condition, his hands were tied.

He'd been trying to reach the captain to tell her that he couldn't locate a signal for Ensign Kayla. They had been searching for the young Bajoran woman since she'd been abducted, looking for the variances in the life-force reading that would indicate where she'd been taken. He'd assumed that she would be the easiest variation to track, but instead she seemed nonexistent. She didn't show up as a variance at all. She had been there, then after the aliens had whisked her away, she'd begun to fade.

He'd already noted that the life-force reading from the planet was growing stronger, but he'd not been aware, until Kes pointed it out, that it was more than one entity he read. They were linked so closely, so intimately, that it was impossible to tell which signal came from where. There were points where it was stronger, though, and it seemed that the captain and her party had marched straight into the middle of the most powerful node.

The worst of it was that the longer the away team remained on the planet, the further under the influence of this *Ambiana* they fell, the less likely he could be of any help to them, even those in the areas where the life-force was less concentrated. If the signal continued to increase in strength at the rate it was presently growing, he would soon lose them entirely, nor would he be able to track their movements on the planet by any means he now had available. Already it was unlikely that he could beam anyone out—there was too much chance of losing them in the interference.

He considered his options. He could go down himself, taking a small team armed for confrontation and shielded against the biological hazards, but there was no way to be certain that he could find, or even catch up to, the captain and her group. That didn't seem a viable option. It was frustrating, infuriating.

"Commander Chakotay?" It was The Doctor's voice, and the viewscreen on Chakotay's desk came to life, showing the hologram's stern visage.

"Yes, Doctor, what is it?"

"I believe I have isolated the toxins. I should have an antidote ready within the hour."

"That would be better news if I knew where your patients were located," Chakotay snapped.

"Excuse me?" The tone of The Doctor's voice was both shocked and a bit pained.

"Sorry," Chakotay said, forcing himself to speak evenly and slowly. "It's just that this life-force on the planet is swallowing them up. The longer they stay there, the more impossible it is for us to trace them. I can't get a lock on any of them to beam them up, and even if I send in an away team to get them, I'm not certain where to send it."

"Oh." The Doctor paused, considering. "I take it that this compound I'm working on is what draws them into the planet's life-force?"

"I assume so, yes," Chakotay answered.

"Then it is possible that if we get this antidote to the surface, they might be able to release themselves from the planet's hold, allowing you to get a transporter lock. If I understand Lieutenant Torres's assessment of the problem, they would show up as discordant 'glitches' in the life-force reading."

"Get me that antidote, Doctor," Chakotay ordered. He hesitated, then added, "And thanks. I don't know if we can pull them in through that interference, but if your antidote can help us locate them, then there is hope that we can get them out."

The Doctor nodded, then the screen went blank. It wasn't much, but it was something.

"Hold on, Captain," Chakotay said softly. "Just hold on."

CHAPTER
7

Vok stood alone in the shadows, watching as the others moved about Kayla's silent form. She lay on a bed of stone, softened by the blossoms of the *Ambiana*. Though she was not of his own people, her features were soft and gentle—at peace. The voice of the ancients was calling her home, lending her its beauty and its harmony. With such an expression on her face, she could have had the appearance of a large insect, and still the beauty would have shone through to one as closely attuned to the *One Voice* as he.

The preparations had begun for her *Ascension*. There was a great deal to do, and it was not such a commonplace event as to be simple in its enactment. Though the rituals were well preserved, they were not without a touch of danger, in and of themselves.

Everyone would have to understand fully, and there would be no room for casual errors. There would be danger for the young female, but there would be equal, and possibly greater, danger for Vok and his followers.

The *Ascension* depended on an intricate string of chants and songs that would lead the soul of the one ascending into the *Long Sleep* in perfect harmony with the *One Voice*. The danger was that, if the ritual somehow failed, or if it were not completed for some reason, those involved in the chant might not be able to withdraw from the union. It would draw them into the *One Voice*, giving them a taste of what was to come in their own future, but it would take the snap of energy that the new voice entering into the harmony would cause to break them free. They were taking a great chance with the alien girl. What if she didn't meld?

One thing was certain; he'd not seen such energy in this place since the long-lost days of his own youth. He did not feel the energy himself—or, more precisely, he felt it as it joined with the elders—with the *Long Sleep*, with that which was to come. He felt it from within, but the others, they could feel it surrounding them. He felt it as a part of the great whole, but he could no longer feel it as his followers did. They chatted excitedly among themselves, rushing about to finish their preparations, throwing themselves into the daily meditations and rituals with new vigor.

Vok had a vague memory of such individual temporal emotion, and for some reason, the attention they were paying this stranger, the emphasis they were putting on her condition, was troubling. He'd have been happier were it just a bit closer to his own time for *Ascension* and their efforts concentrated on himself.

One of the others broke away from the crowd and moved his way—it was the young one, Ban. Ban considered himself a leader among Vok's followers, but he had known but ninety summers. Though he knew the legends, the teachings, for him that was all they were, thus far. He had not joined with the ancients in full communion.

There was a love of singularity, a love of *self* floating in the depths of the young Urrythan's eyes. Ban could feel the elders, but he was not yet ready to give himself over to them. He still considered himself important *as* himself, and that was the greatest lesson one needed to learn before *Ascension,* that the *One Voice* was everything, and the self nothing without the harmony.

Vok nodded as the younger man neared him, turning an attentive ear politely toward him. As elder, it was always his lot in life to listen.

"They are moving inward, Elder," Ban informed him. "The one who calls herself *Captain,* the tall one whose ears point to the skies, and one other. They are approaching the resting place of the most ancient.

"I have been talking with the others." Ban gestured toward a large group who stood to one side, watching their exchange curiously. "And among them it is thought that these star travelers may be after the secrets of our ancestors, that they must be stopped before they steal, or profane, that which they do not understand."

If he had not been in complete control of his own mind, Vok would have smiled then. This youngling, this "new soul," was worried over the comprehension of their elders by a race of beings from the stars of which he knew absolutely nothing. He himself had no real grasp of what concepts were at stake—not really.

It was interesting, intriguing, even, that this Captain Janeway would make her way inward toward the resting place of the ancients, but it was of no consequence. There was nothing she could do to disrupt the inevitable. More likely, the closer she and her followers came to the truth, the less they would be able to resist the correctness of it all. He wondered briefly if Janeway had chosen to move deeper into the gardens, or if they'd been drawn there.

"It is well," Vok assured the younger man. "Continue as you are; complete the ritual. There is nothing they can do, nothing that they can learn that could in any way change things, except for their own betterment. Do not concern yourself with our visitors, for I fear that they are distracting you, and this is a time in which distraction may prove deadly.

"Instead, look inward—delve more deeply into the *Ambiana,* into the harmony. Seek that which is promised, draw it into your mind and hold it—

rejoice in it. You know the ways—the teachings and the legends, and you know the ritual. Complete it. All other pursuits are trivial and secondary."

"But their presence will desecrate that which is holy, Elder. Surely you cannot forgive this? The halls of the ancients are not for casual visitation, nor should they be ransacked by those who do not even believe."

"It is not mine, nor yours," the old Urrythan added calmly, "to forgive or to not. There is nothing that they can learn, nothing that they can do, that will in any way disrupt the *Ascension.* You give proper reverence to the ancients, and this is good, but you forget that they are not without power of their own. Their voice alone will protect them."

The younger man nodded, but it was clear from the flicker of emotion that transited his eyes and the quick toss of his head that, though he respected Vok, he did not believe what he'd been told. There was a fire within him, a singularity, that only time—and temperance—might burn away.

"I do not want you to follow them in," Vok added softly. "It would be an affront to the forefathers to invade their resting place for such a reason—for violence. It would be wrong. Conduct your ceremony, but leave this Janeway and her other followers alone. There is nothing to be gained from further strife."

Ban turned away slowly, not acknowledging Vok's words one way or the other. It was clear from the set of his shoulders that he did not feel he'd been advised correctly, but there was no way to read from his stance, or his manner, what he would do with this information. He was young, and he was fiery, but to this point, he'd been obedient to his elders, and to the harmony. Vok knew he could only wait and watch. Such was his responsibility.

Ban, and others like him, had developed a great following among the younger generations. In these later times, the *Ambiana* blossoms grew freely, and the *Long Sleep* came in a matter of two or three hundred years—nothing compared to the thousand summers Vok's own father had seen.

Vok had followed those wild ways himself in his earlier years. Without the kind of energy that Ban and his fellows exuded, there would be no progress, no survival, and without that survival, there would be none to make it to the *Ascension*. It pained Vok that it was so, now that his own years had taught him both temperance and wisdom, but he had neither the energy nor the inclination to change the order of things at such a late point in his own journey. He was nearly ready for the ceremony of *Ascension* himself—nearly ready to join the elders in their sleep.

He saw that Ban had returned to the others, and he saw as well that he had drawn several of them aside, where they conferred softly as the preparations for the outsider's ritual of *Ascension* continued, but he could not hear their words, and in any case, he had nothing more to add to the situation.

If he were to go to them, to reiterate what he'd told Ban, it would be seen as a sign of weakness, and that was not an option. He was eldest. Unless they were willing to throw away all that had come before them, the wisdom of generations, they would heed his words. He wouldn't be around that much longer to advise them, but he had to have faith in what he'd learned, belief in his followers—assurance that they would listen while he was.

With a heavy sigh, he settled back into a small alcove and rested himself against the cool stone of the mountains' roots. He could feel the voices of the elders, joined as one, resonating and growing in strength. The others could feel it as well, but none so completely as he, none so perfectly. Vok knew that a part of what the others felt was himself. He was their closest link, and when he led them in the ritual meditations, they grew closer to the ancients.

He wondered, though, at the strength of the *One Voice*. It had been growing, expanding—filling his mind and stealing his thoughts. He hadn't been able to concentrate for days, spending longer and longer periods in full communion.

Awakening.

The time was near. He knew it, prayed for it. He wanted, just once, before his own time came, to see the wonder of it for himself, to know the truth of the ancients as a vision, not conjured by his own mind and imagination, or from the influence of the harmony. He believed in it, he lived for it—he preached it and taught it, begged for it and dreamed of it, but he'd never seen it. None alive had ever seen it. It was a matter of thousands of years of faith, generations following the words of their forefathers. Faith alone was their guide into an unknown future.

The resting places of the generations of elders littered the gardens now. They rose toward the skies, stark and stony, only the vibration of their contents belying the image of death and desolation. Farther in, even the ground itself was reaching slowly up to swallow them. When it was possible, Vok slipped away to those inner places, laying his cheek against the cool exterior of the pillars one by one and feeling the soft undulating thread of life that bound them all—bound him—in one perfect weave of fate.

It was enough, and yet he still wished for that vision—a memory to carry into his great sleep. He wanted very much to witness an *Awakening*. The voices of those who'd gone before spoke softly to him, and he knew they spoke truly. If he held on, if he could but put off his immersion in the harmony a bit longer, that vision would be his.

Vok closed his eyes, letting himself drift into the *One Voice* of the elders, letting the planet itself drag his senses away as he contemplated all that was to come. He didn't see the others sneaking hasty looks his way, checking to see if he'd faded from their reality, or if he remained in control of his senses. None of them looked comfortable with the deception, though Ban and a few of those closest to him were flushed with the excitement of the moment.

When it was certain that Vok would not be rising soon, the others gathered around Ban, and he led them from the small settlement and off through the surrounding countryside. They left behind just enough to complete the ceremony, just enough to keep the volume of the chant at a level where Vok would not notice the fluctuation in the *One Voice* that would indicate to him that they had left.

Ban watched the elder furtively as they passed, but Vok never flinched. He sat against the foot of the mountain, his cheek resting against the cool stone. He never felt the small ripple they sent through the *One Voice*. His visions, and the song of the ancients, were far more powerful, and they were calling him home.

The small party, Ban at its head, made its way toward the gardens, moving across the surface of the planet, through the light they normally shunned, through the world that had been their ancestors' home. They would protect that home, would drive the intruders away and keep the gardens pure. That was the plan, nebulous and half-formed as it was.

They really had no idea what they would find when they arrived in the gardens. The dangers that the invaders and their star craft might present were vague uncertainties in their minds, but they felt that the act of defense itself was enough. Surely it was not right that their most holy places be visited by those who did not belong. Just as surely, they must prevent it.

The voice of the *One Life* swallowed their essence as they neared the gardens, and they felt it wrapping about them, welcoming them home.

"There!" Torres's voice cut through the thick brooding silence on the bridge sharply. "The reading just fluctuated again—near the outskirts of the gardens."

"Get on it," Chakotay ordered, galvanized to action. "Doctor, how much longer on that antidote?"

"It is ready now," came The Doctor's voice.

"Let's get it down to the surface, then," Chakotay ordered. "See if you can contact Kes."

The young Maquis that had taken the operations console nodded, sweat beading on his brow. He wasn't an officer, not on *Voyager,* but he'd worked such consoles often enough on the Maquis vessel, and he had plenty of experience behind him.

"Eg'gyrs," Chakotay muttered.

"Yes, sir," the boy replied, thinking the comment had been meant to get his attention. His eyes were locked on to his console. "I'm getting nothing, sir. I've hailed them all on every frequency we've got . . . something is jamming the signal."

Chakotay didn't say a word, but his frown deepened. He hadn't really expected that they could get a signal through, but he'd tried because he wanted to avoid the decision that came next.

Someone else was going to have to go down there. Another risk. Another life, the loss of which might possibly be on his own head. He wanted desperately to be the one, but with the captain gone, he couldn't leave them alone. There were no others on board strong enough to carry them through. Command wasn't something one could just step into, and there were uncounted dangers waiting out there for them.

It had to be someone else, someone he could trust. He had to make that decision, and make it fast.

"I'm not chancing the transporters, not with that

life-force drowning out everything we've got. I'd be afraid of losing someone in the transit. There's no way to tell how strong a lock we can get on someone, because they're all being swallowed up by the influence of the *Ambiana.*" He was speaking aloud to no one in particular.

"Mr. Paris, take Chief Eg'gyrs with you, and get a shuttle down there. Get that antidote to Kes, and get those people ready to beam back up here. We'll lock on to your patterns as soon as you hit the planet, and the moment the drug takes effect on the others enough that we can pick them out of that haze, we'll start lifting them out as well. Assuming, of course, that we can use the transporters at all."

Paris nodded, but he hesitated.

"Kim and the captain are down there, and Tuvok. If we get the others out, I'm not leaving until I find them."

"I'm ordering you to the planet, and back," Chakotay said evenly, his eyes conveying what protocol would never allow him to speak. "You are to find those left in the camp, administer the antidote, and get them out of there." He hesitated for a moment, searching the younger man's eyes. "Am I understood, Mr. Paris?"

The pilot stood staring at him for a long time, taking it in and gathering his own courage. In the end, he merely nodded. No further words were exchanged, but both men knew the truth of what was to come. If they were to get home—to transit all the way to Federation space—they were going to need every asset available to them. Leaving the captain, the security officer, and the operations officer on the surface of an unknown planet was just not an option.

Eg'gyrs looked at his former Commander, an odd glint in his eyes. The young man was part Romulan, part human—an odd mix, to say the least. Chakotay couldn't tell if he were honored to be chosen for the mission or questioning the wisdom behind it.

The door slid shut behind the two, and Chakotay turned to face the viewscreen again. He searched the terrain below, watching the steadily increasing levels of the life-force carefully. The glitch that B'Elanna had pointed out was moving slowly and steadily toward the point where their base had been situated. He hoped that Paris and Eg'gyrs would get there before the Urrythans did.

There was something different, something ominous, in the way the ripple moved across the screen. Somehow he knew the time for friendly visits was long past. That was fine. Chakotay was not feeling all that friendly himself.

Let them come, he thought. *Let them come, and let's get it over with.*

CHAPTER
8

"KES?" NEELIX'S CONCERNED VOICE WOVE ITS WAY through the ever-strengthening spell of the planet's song to tug her back to reality. It was growing more difficult to pull herself free, more difficult to *want* to be free. She concentrated, and the small camp began to come back into focus.

Shaking her head, she answered him, "Yes, Neelix?"

He was standing there, hands clasped before him in concern. Part of this, she knew, was for her, but she could not deny the pull of the harmony to ease his burden. She did not feel as though she were losing control, but she needed to understand, to draw forth what she could from the sensations. It made her feel more useful, and in the face of medical training that was serving her poorly at the moment, it was good to have another skill to fall back on, uncertain as it might be.

"I'm not certain," Neelix said, "but I believe that Ensign Fowler may have lost consciousness. He's been asleep when I checked on him before, but I was always able to get him to shake his head, or mumble something back at me . . . now he just lays there. I was attempting to get him to take some of this broth I've made—I'd hoped it would soothe him—but I can't get a response."

Moving slowly, Kes rose, her movements graceful and sleepy, like a cat stretching after a long nap in the sun. As Neelix watched her, she saw tears forming slowly in the corners of his eyes, and she smiled at him. Her sometimes excitable lover was concerned for her, and with the enhanced energy that the planet's *One Voice,* as Vok had called it, had lent her, she could feel the depth of his caring in a way she'd never been able to, even with her own psychic abilities. She wondered for a moment what it would be like if she could draw Neelix into the song, into the chord that surrounded them, to share in what she was experiencing. More than any other, she wished she could experience it with him. If nothing else, it would help to ease his worry.

"I'll come and see what I can do for him," she said, laying her hand softly on Neelix's shoulder. She knew that there was little to be done, actually, beyond monitoring life-signs and looking out for the physical comfort of their patients. It was horribly frustrating, and, in truth, it was the reason she continued to immerse herself in the experience that the *Ambiana* was forcing upon the rest of them. It helped to calm her, and it helped her to understand what they were going through. If they could not be awakened, at least they were not in pain—were not suffering.

The only two still on their feet with any regularity were she and Neelix, and it had been quite a while since they'd heard anything from the captain, or from *Voyager.* She'd tried on several occasions to check in with The Doctor, to find out how he was progressing with the antidote, but her communicator had proven worthless. She knew that when the antidote was ready, they'd find a way to get it down to her, but it would have been nice to know for sure what the status of things was.

Still she could not truly worry. The energy that surrounded her, growing in strength with each passing moment, was in no way negative. It was beautiful, filled with rich harmony and devoid of pain. She could sense the auras of the others around her, Ensign Fowler, even Kayla, though that signal was more vague—less sharply defined—among the vibrations. They were not suffering, and yet they were being absorbed into the *One Voice* slowly, their individuality sloughing from them like melted snow. She suspected that at some point, not too far in the future, their bodies would begin to change as well. She didn't know in what way they might change, and she certainly didn't know how she knew that they *would* change. It just seemed that their mundane humanoid form was too crude to contain the beauty.

And there was something more, a feeling of impending *change* that seemed to make it all appear to be a natural progression.

She made her way to Fowler's side, bending low to run her tricorder over the length of his body. Nothing new, really. All that had changed was the level of the life-force that surrounded them. It was increasing steadily—a fact she was all-too aware of without the aid of the instrument in her hand.

Although he was resting calmly, Fowler did not seem any further affected than before. He was just in a very deep sleep, a sleep enhanced by the pleasurable sensations of the dreams that accompanied it. Anyone in such a situation would be difficult to awaken.

As she worked, Neelix remained like a statue at her side, watching carefully, only letting his gaze wander now and then to her face. He was watching her when Fowler's eyes fluttered, then opened. The man let out a small cry of dismay, half-rising to a sitting position, then falling back. His eyes focused on her, coherence flooding his features. He made no further attempts to rise, but he could see her, and he managed a weak smile.

Kes turned quickly to Neelix, her eyes questioning. She hadn't done anything in particular to get this response from Fowler. He'd only been resting. Neelix met her gaze, then dropped his own suddenly, looking quickly toward the ground, as though ashamed.

"I only told you he wouldn't respond because I was worried about *you*, Kes. I stood there in front of you for nearly ten minutes, just watching you, and you didn't even know that I was there. You were lost—somewhere—somewhere I couldn't follow, and I was afraid. I was afraid that this place had taken you from me, that I was losing you. I couldn't stand that."

"I'm *fine,* Neelix." Kes smiled at him in mild exasperation. "I'm in tune with the voice of this planet, true, but the *Ambiana* does not seem to have any effect on my system. You yourself are immune to it so far. Perhaps it is something to do with our being from this quadrant.

"Because I'm aware of what is happening, I can share in their emotions, their feelings—but I'm not falling under the influence of the drugs, as Kayla did. I only want to understand. I've learned so much from The Doctor, from you, from Captain Janeway—none of it seems to be helping. This is something I can do, a way that I might find out something that could help. You have to understand."

Neelix didn't look convinced, but he smiled at her tentatively. It was obvious that he believed she was just covering up, making things sound better for his sake. It was his nature to worry over things, and this, it seemed, would be no exception.

Finally, after the silence had become almost unbearable, he spoke.

"Now that you're awake, would you like some of my stew?"

Kes's smile broadened. "I'd like that very much."

Before the two of them could turn from Fowler's side, however, a rush of air and the sound of engines announced the approach of one of *Voyager*'s shuttle craft. The stew forgotten, the two of them made their way to the garden's entrance and watched as the small ship touched down in the clearing that had once been the city square.

They hurriedly clambered down the oversized stone steps and across the trail as Lieutenant Paris and Chief Eg'gyrs clambered down to meet them.

"We've been unable to get you on the communicators," Paris explained quickly, clasping Neelix's arm tightly. "We weren't certain if the transporters would work under these conditions, so we've brought The Doc's antidote here in person. Chakotay didn't want to beam us down and strand us here like the rest of you, or worse yet, spread us out through the atmosphere."

The group took the medical kit Eg'gyrs had carried down from the shuttle and returned to the clearing. Kes spent a few moments clearing her thoughts. She pushed aside the planet's "voice" with an effort, giving her total concentration to the task at hand.

While Neelix brought the landing party up to date on the Captain and her party, she went over the instructions The Doctor had provided and began to prepare to dispense the drug. She was glad, finally, to have something to occupy her mind. It was exciting to be the one with the cure in hand, as well, and she was eager to see if the serum would work. It had to—they were out of other options.

"So, there have been no signs of the Urrythans since Kayla's disappearance?" Paris asked at last.

"None," Neelix said.

"B'Elanna reported, just before I left, that there was a ripple in the life-force reading moving in this direction. If she's correct, those ripples indicate the movements of the Urrythans when they leave the direct vicinity of their settlement."

"You think they are returning?" Neelix asked. "Perhaps they have seen the error of their ways and intend to return Ensign Kayla to us?"

"I wouldn't count on that," Paris answered, giving the grounds a quick once-over to familiarize himself with the layout. "I'd say it's more likely that they are coming back for the rest of you. You reported that they consider the influence of their drug to be sacred . . . maybe they're coming back to see if the sacred stuff has taken over."

Just then Fowler, who'd been the first to receive the antidote, sat bolt upright on his cot, staring about himself wildly. Kes was at his side, and she quickly moved to put her arm around his neck, supporting him and speaking soothingly into his ear.

The man's eyes were vacant, as if there were no coherent thought behind them, and he looked frightened—perhaps lost. He had the appearance of a man whose world had been yanked from beneath him, and it was obvious that his system was having difficulties dealing with the shock.

Then his eyes cleared, slowly, and he lay back with a sigh.

"Ensign Fowler," Mr. Paris called out to him. The man turned his head to return the pilot's concerned gaze, and he smiled weakly. He looked pale and haggard, but relatively normal for all that. Paris breathed a quick sigh of relief.

"Where am I, sir? What happened?"

"It's a long story," Paris answered, "and when we're all back, safely on the ship, I'll tell you about it. Chief Eg'gyrs, get back to the shuttle and see if we can establish communications with *Voyager*. I know the commbadges aren't functioning, but we have a better range from the comm panel. Tell them Mr. Fowler has returned to us, and see if they can get a clear-enough signal to get a transporter lock on him now."

The others were waking up around them, and Paris and Neelix worked side by side with Kes to ease them back to reality. There seemed no long-term damage, and for that they were thankful. Gathering the small company into a tight knot near the center of the garden, Paris explained what was happening as best he could while Eg'gyrs contacted the ship.

Kes stood off to one side, the faraway look of concentration returning to her eyes. She'd felt something, a motion in the *One Voice*, a slight sequence of discord in the harmony. It had jolted her back into the stream of the planet's energy and she went with it, searching and probing as it drew her in. She did not recognize what the disturbance was, but it was moving rapidly toward them, and she turned, staring blankly off toward the garden walls that bordered on the direction of the disturbance's approach.

"Kes?" It was Neelix again. "Kes!"

She dragged her mind free again. "Tom is right. They are coming—someone is coming. It is not natural, the sensations are changing—shifting. There is something going on that is not a part of the normal pattern. Whoever, or whatever, it is that is coming here is creating an imbalance in the *One Voice*. I can trace them by it."

"How far?" Paris asked, already moving toward the entrance to the garden to check on Eg'gyrs. None of the tall natives were in sight, and the chief was waving frantically to him from the shuttle.

"Not far," Kes answered. "I can't be certain—it's a sensation, not exact, like a scanner presentation."

With a quick curse, Paris sprinted out of the garden, taking the steep steps in leaps and bounds, covering the ground as quickly as possible. He didn't know who or what might be watching from the cover of the gardens, and he didn't plan on making himself an easy target and finding out the hard way.

As he approached the shuttle, Eg'gyrs called out to him, "I have them, sir. They say that they have a firm lock on all of us. It must have been the influence of that drug that was blocking them."

"Get over there and gather them together, then," Paris called out, swinging up and into the shuttle's pilot seat. "I'm not leaving this ship here for them. I'll tell the transporter room to get you out the moment they have a lock."

Eg'gyrs hesitated, as though he didn't want to be the one to go, or didn't want to leave Paris alone, but after a few moments he nodded reluctantly and took off across the overgrown trail toward the camp, as ordered. Paris watched him go, his own heart beating more rapidly and loudly than he'd have believed possible. Just because he was staying behind didn't mean he wasn't afraid.

"Bridge, Paris."

"Go ahead, Mr. Paris." Chakotay's voice was thin, competing with a hum of static, but readable.

"Beam them out when you're ready," he said, almost too softly.

"You aren't with the group," Chakotay barked.

"I'm bringing the shuttle back," he explained, knowing that his lie was unnecessary, knowing that it would be spotted for what it was the moment he uttered it. "You're the one who's always telling me we can't afford to lose another one."

"Are you sure you can get it out of there?"

"I'm not certain of anything, but we can't just leave it here for them. Besides, I'm going to hang on for a bit in case the captain and the others come back. We'd never know it, if they did."

"Very well. Chakotay out."

Paris could feel the unspoken words behind the first officer's sign-off. He could feel the weight descending on him like a dark cloud, the responsibility he'd fought so long and hard to ignore in his youth settling directly onto his shoulders with no relief in sight. The greenery that surrounded him, familiar and comfortable only a few days prior, when he'd first seen it on the viewscreens, now loomed dark and ominous. All his life he'd dreamed of being a hero; now he could see that it might not be all it was cracked up to be.

"Paris, *Voyager.*"

"Go ahead *Voyager.*"

"We've got them . . . but . . ." The transmission died out with a hiss and crackle of static, but he'd gotten the information he most needed. He watched the entrance to the garden for a moment longer, and just as he was about to gather together the gear he'd stowed in the back of the shuttle and take off into the gardens after the captain, he saw a familiar figure striding through the gates of the garden.

It was Kes, and she stood there, framed by the huge stone pillars, gazing out across the trail at him. A moment later she was clambering quickly down the steps and trotting across the clearing toward the shuttle. She climbed aboard, a dreamy smile gracing her lips.

"What are you doing here?" he asked her, trying to be cross.

"I'm not certain," she answered. "I was there with the others, then they were gone. I felt nothing at all—not from *Voyager,* anyway."

"The Urrythans?"

"I think they were here. I think they were watching when the others beamed up, but I felt them moving away. I don't know why, but I'm certain they were not coming for those of us here in the camp."

"I bet you were trying to track them when *Voyager* went for the transporter lock," Paris said thoughtfully. "If being immersed in this *One Voice* is what kept them from being able to beam up Fowler and the others, you may have unconsciously blocked them."

"You may be right," Kes replied, but the look in her eye belied the accidental nature of that blockage.

"If those beings were here, watching us, but went on without stopping, then they might be following the captain and the others," Paris went on, his eyes growing wider.

Just then the comm panel crackled again, and another broken communication made its way through.

"Mr. Paris. I don't know if you can hear me, or for how long. We are losing communications. The life-force is growing in intensity again. That disturbance that was nearing your position has passed you by, heading inward in the same direction that the captain took." There was a burst of static, then Chakotay's voice continued. "We were unable to locate Kes . . . locate . . . aliens . . ."

The transmission died, and the empty hum of static that replaced it had a ring of finality to it. Whatever came next, whatever decisions they made, they were on their own. Barring the sending in of another shuttle, which Paris knew that Chakotay was not going to risk, they could expect no more assistance from *Voyager*.

"I'm going after the captain," Paris told Kes quickly. "I don't know how I'm going to find them, or what I can accomplish if I do, but if I can get them back to this shuttle, maybe there's a chance we can all get off this planet alive.

"I want you to wait here for me. You should be fine with the shuttle's defenses. We have a limited weapons capability, but it should prove superior to anything these aliens can come up with, and I'm certain that the shields will hold if they attack."

"I'm going with you," Kes said, laying her hand on his arm and staring intently into his eyes. "You can't find the captain or the others without me, and you can't tell where Vok or his followers are, either. I can sense them. I can feel the voice of this planet."

"It's too dangerous. Neelix would kill me if I let anything happen to you."

"I'm not asking you, Tom. I'm telling you—I'm going."

He hesitated a moment longer, considering how he might change her mind, but there was no time to argue. Also, there was the small point that she was right. He had no way to follow Janeway, Kim, and Tuvok without her, nor could he even follow the Urrythans themselves. He nodded, and the two of them began to gather all the equipment they could carry that might be of use.

Dropping to the ground, Paris looked at Kes questioningly, and she hesitated for only a moment, then started off down the trail. He followed, sweeping his gaze and his tricorder from side to side carefully. A few moments later he put the tricorder away. Too much interference for that, as well. They were truly going to have to rough it this time.

He became even more cautious, not relaxing his guard for even a moment. He might not be able to detect danger in the same manner that Kes could, but that was no reason not to be prepared for it if it came.

* * *

The moment Neelix stepped from the transporter pad, he was talking. He'd known, even as they were being beamed from the planet's surface, that Kes was not with them. He'd tried to move from the spot where he'd been standing, to reach out for her and drag her to him, but he'd failed. One moment they were standing on Urrytha, side by side, and the next he was whisked away, leaving her to whatever fate awaited her on the planet's surface.

"Where is she?" he cried out, leaping to the deck and heading for the control panel. Mr. Carey, second in command of Engineering, stood behind the console, and he looked as perplexed as Neelix was upset.

"I'm not sure, Neelix," he answered. "We locked on to every clear signal we could find, but it was as if she wasn't there at all. She was there when we spoke with Paris, but when we beamed you all up, she was gone. It wasn't a bad lock, or a weak signal—she just didn't appear to be there at all."

"Well, she was there, all right. I don't know what happened, but I know what has to be done about it," Neelix replied, stomping back toward the transporter pad. "Beam me back down there immediately."

"I'm afraid I can't do that," Carey replied. "I've got strict orders to get as many of you aboard as possible, which is what I've done, and, besides, we've lost what clear signals we had from below—there's no way to tell if you'd ever make it there alive. I couldn't beam anyone in or out of there the way the interference from that life-force is intensifying. You're lucky to be standing here alive."

"I don't care," Neelix replied stubbornly. "I'm

not leaving this space until you activate that transporter and put me back on that planet."

Carey shrugged, but made no move toward the controls.

"Transporter room, Bridge," Chakotay's voice cut through. "Do you have them?"

"All but Kes, sir," Carey replied. "There was no signal for her, nothing to lock on to. One moment we had her, and the next she'd disappeared from my screen. She seemed to be swallowed up in that overriding life-force signal."

"Sir," Neelix piped up, "I was just demanding that I be sent back down there. I can't allow you to leave Kes on that planet alone. If I have to be stranded with her, that is fine, but I must insist that you set me back down."

"She isn't alone, Neelix," Chakotay said calmly. "She is in the shuttle with Paris, or she was a moment ago. I'm certain that he can handle whatever is going on down there."

"Then he'll be flying her up immediately?" Neelix asked, his expression hopeful.

"Not immediately, no," Chakotay hedged. "Mr. Paris wants to take a shot at finding the Captain, Kim, and Tuvok."

"Then I insist you send me back down to help them." Neelix crossed his arms and returned to his spot on the teleporter pad. "If need be, I can pilot another shuttle."

"I wish you'd reconsider," Chakotay said softly. "With you on that planet, the crew has had to suffer from the lack of both good food, and your services as morale officer. With Captain Janeway gone, it's been quite a burden on the other officers. We have a lot of scared people here, Neelix, and a good meal would go a long way toward relieving that stress."

Neelix cocked his head to one side, obviously weighing his responsibilities to the crew, and to Kes. He really did like to fit in, and he took his job as morale officer very seriously—it helped to give his life on *Voyager* purpose.

"You say she's with Paris?" he asked at last.

"Yes, she was with Paris when we lost communication."

Neelix didn't say another word, but he left the room and headed straight for his galley. He and Tom Paris had not always been on good terms, but they shared one thing in common that steadied the small man's nerves for the moment. Both of them were more than a bit fond of Kes. If she was with Paris, he would see to her safety. He knew he would just have to settle for that.

Mr. Carey heaved a sigh of relief as the small man departed the space. He wasn't certain he could have beamed the man down to the planet, even if he'd been forced to try, and he hadn't wanted the responsibility of trying to control him, either. It was hard enough on the Talaxian to be stranded in space with no people and no planet to return to—he hoped to God, or whatever entity ruled this sphere, that Kes would return to them in one piece.

On the bridge, Torres was shaking her head angrily. "It's no use, Commander. I've lost Paris, and there's no way to track Kes. She seems to have blended somehow with the rest of the planet. I have no idea where they are. I can't even locate the shuttle."

Chakotay nodded. "Track the aliens, then," he ordered, "as best you can, and we'll all have to pray that Paris and Kes have a better way of following than we do."

"Pray, sir?" Torres asked.

"It isn't the worst thing we could do," he replied, turning to watch the planet below on the viewscreen. "It would seem that, in many ways, this is becoming a matter of faith for us all. It's certainly that for the Urrythans."

For a long moment, as his words faded, the bridge was bathed in complete silence.

CHAPTER 9

As THEY MOVED FURTHER INWARD, THE PILLARS THEY passed had grown steadily older, many of them either sunken into the earth from centuries of natural settling action, or with huge piles of dirt washed up against their sides by wind and weather, all but burying them. As Janeway led them into deeper, more impenetrable gardens, the ruins appeared to sink deeper within the earth, their secrets more closely guarded than their more accessible descendants.

The ruins of the outer city had fallen away, and though they'd passed through smaller groupings of broken walls and squat buildings, there was no further evidence of the grand civilization that had erected the temples and palaces of the first set of ruins they'd encountered. These were more like simple settlements than they were like cities—resembling more the few surface dwellings they'd seen of Vok's people than they did the grandeur of the ancient city. Only the gardens remained relatively the same.

On the base of each of the monuments, if that was indeed what they were, they found more of the inscriptions they'd first scanned. Many of the symbols were repetitive of what Janeway and Kim had recorded near the central square of the city, and yet more were completely different. It was as if each separate pillar had its own tale to tell, but there was a formula within which that tale must be rendered. Also, there were subtle changes in the lettering and formations of words that seemed to indicate dialectic shifts, or perhaps merely a more ancient form of the same language.

Kim, who had been working furiously since they'd lost contact with *Voyager,* was beginning to look haggard, but the light had not left his eyes, and his enthusiasm had not waned. He'd been given a responsibility, and a challenge, and he was thriving on it. The weight of responsibility that Kayla's abduction had placed on his heart was easier to bear as long as he was contributing something positive.

If he could have had access to the full computer system of the ship, it would have been a simple matter, if not instantaneous, to translate the rudiments of the language. The mathematical basis of the symbols alone would have made it so. *Voyager* was equipped with records of the structures and nuances of every known language, and all language, in the end, has certain characteristics.

Without the ship's computer, he was forced to do a lot of the actual intuitive translation in his mind, then input it into the more limited capabilities of his Universal Translator and the computer in his tricorder. It was tedious, mind-wracking work, but he kept at it, exercising every iota of his powers of concentration and bending his will to the manipulation of the simple controls.

"Got it, Captain," he cried out suddenly. As the three of them stopped their forward progress and Janeway and Tuvok huddled around him, he keyed in a sequence of symbols, causing a printed message to begin scrolling slowly across the tiny screen. He let it pass for a few seconds, then he explained.

"It appears to be a sequence of dates," he said excitedly. "Each of the pillars we've scanned has had this pattern of symbols in one form or another, some more archaic than others, but always the same. The only difference from one to the next is the addition of these final sequences." He pointed to a series of numbers on one of the lines of data.

"I believe that the last symbol on each line is the date of a particular alien's death . . . but that's the odd thing."

"What is odd?" Janeway asked, raising her eyes to meet his puzzled gaze.

"The rest of the symbols seem to be histories, or legends—myths—religious parables. There are repeated references to something called the *Long*

Sleep, and the *Ambiana* is covered at length. There are stories of the city and the gardens, even mention of visitors from other planets, but nowhere on any of these pillars has any word that appears associated with the notion of death come into play.

"It appears that these pillars hold the remains of the ancestors of Vok and his people, stored against a time when they believe they will be lifted up—a time in which they will ascend to another level of existence. The *Ambiana* is some part of the preservation rituals."

"Like the pyramids of the ancient Egyptians on Earth," Janeway said. She turned, letting her gaze sweep up the nearest of the pillars, wondering what might be resting inside.

"It is illogical to assume that they do not believe in death because you see no evidence of it on these monuments," Tuvok cut in. "It is more likely that they are merely saying that *these* particular ancestors are not believed to be dead. That is not a completely illogical thought, in that we've been detecting this odd, all-encompassing life-force since we first scanned this planet."

Janeway's brow furrowed in concentration. Somewhere in the cryptic messages of these ancient beings, she had to find the answer to free her crew. If these ancients had known about the *Ambiana,* then it was likely that they knew more about it than Vok and his follower had been willing to share. There would appear to be more to the tales of *Ascension,* as well. One of the lessons of Earth's past was that legends and religious beliefs quite often grew from some factual background. There was no way to ascertain how much of what Vok's people believed was fact, and how much fiction. The notion of *Ascension* to a better life brought back memories of her own childhood—her own family's beliefs. Were they so different?

"But where are the remnants of these other earlier cities?" she said out loud. "Why are there ruins farther out, along with these same pillars, and yet here there are only the pillars? Is this some sort of graveyard, or are we missing something obvious?"

"It could be that the ruins are buried, Captain," Kim speculated. "These pillars are not all as tall as those farther out, near where we were camped. When they were erected, they would have been tall enough to have towered over any buildings that were nearby—perhaps time and decay have hidden the ruins from us here completely. If Vok can be believed, the beings buried in some of these tombs would be nearly ten thousand years old."

"Well," Janeway replied, turning back to the path and continuing toward the center of the garden that surrounded them, "let's hope everything isn't buried. If we don't find some answers here, we may very well end up like Kayla."

As the three continued on, they did not notice the sound that followed after them—the whispering voices, the soft tread of feet slipping softly through lush grass. They didn't feel the eyes upon them, stalking them. Tuvok kept his own gaze locked on his tricorder, but the planet's overriding signal was becoming so strong that it was nearly beyond the small device's ability to distinguish fluctuations.

Ban watched the star travelers, monitoring their progress from the depths of the shadows, his long sad eyes narrowed in concentration. They were a young race, compared to his own, but that did not make them weak or inferior, especially in matters of violence. Their starship and the devices they carried with them at all times were testament to this.

There had been such technology in the history of his own people, during the times of great cities and internal darkness. They had seen and built wonders, toppled cities and rebuilt them from nothing but the dust of what they'd destroyed. In those times, only the few were initiated—only a select group had aspired to *Ascension*. The others had lived for the material world, and for the gains it could bring them.

Since then, the enlightenment had come. Those who did not see the truth of what the *Ambiana* offered had long since departed, in one manner or another. Some had been picked up by passing starships, such as these aliens had arrived in. Others had merely fought among themselves until they were wiped away to extinction. The priests and the true followers had lingered, moving deeper into the caverns, drinking in the elixir of the *Ambiana* and waiting. For them, time was an ally, not an enemy. As their brothers and sisters were eaten away and crumbled, the *Ambiana* had preserved them.

There were legends Ban could recall, tales he'd been told as a child of war and strife, but none who now lived, not even Vok, blind old Vok who could not see the danger that presented itself to them, had lived long enough to actually remember the planet's last act of violence. Now, here he was, not even a hundred summers into his own life, contemplating being the one to return such a thing to his planet. It was a great responsibility, a difficult choice.

It was not an easy thing, the decision he'd made, and yet he felt the need in his heart to be the one to offer the protection the elders surely needed, to prevent these intruders from visiting places he himself would go only once, and that at his holiest of moments. He would make that pilgrimage, as was his right, just prior to his own *Ascension,* but no sooner. He would commune more closely with the elders then than he'd ever done before—he would prepare himself for the *Long Sleep.*

He motioned to those behind him to follow, signaling that they should remain as quiet as possible. They had no weapons to match those of these intruders, their only hope of victory would be in their superior knowledge of the terrain, and in surprise. Common sense told Ban that the superior numbers of his followers would eventually turn the tide if they could just get into the right position for an attack.

He began to move more swiftly, letting his long sinuous legs propel him forward. His multijointed limbs gave him an odd posture, the appearance of ungainly size and a lack of coordination. It was a *false* impression. He soon outdistanced Janeway's party, working his way around through the shadows and thick underbrush until he was in front of them, always careful not to make a sound.

There was a place that he knew, just ahead, where one of the most ancient temples protruded through the earth that had risen and blown up in the wind to all but swallow it whole across the span of centuries. He would be able to conceal his entire group within those walls, and there they would wait. Ban's senses were peculiarly alive—intense. Something in his system was reacting to the excitement of the moment. It seemed very fitting that it would be within walls built by his ancestors, those he was prepared to defend, that he would meet the enemy and repel them. It would be glorious, and when the youngest gathered to be taught their history, his name would become central—a hero.

Paris was moving at a trot, and he was surprised to find that Kes was having no trouble keeping up with him, despite her shorter legs and the weight of the pack she carried. They'd followed the emanations she sensed, making their way onto a trail leading into the junglelike overgrowth of the gardens, but moments after they started down it, she told him that the Urrythans had not taken the trail.

"This is the way the captain went," Kes said

thoughtfully. "Let's follow it in for a while. The variation in the harmony is off to one side. Perhaps they were just trying to remain out of sight."

After they'd traveled inward a few hundred yards, she turned with a fierce smile. "They followed," she said simply. "They are paralleling the path—there." She pointed to the left of the trail. "Whoever it is wants to know where the captain is going, but they don't want her to know that they are there."

"That can't be good," Paris answered grimly. "In all of our other encounters with these beings, they've come right up out of nowhere and met us head on. This must mean that their intentions have changed, whatever they were in the beginning. I've never seen a reason why a peace-minded race would hide their intentions."

"They appear to have changed their attitude when they kidnapped Kayla," Kes replied. "Prior to that, they didn't seem to mind our presence at all."

"Let's catch up with the captain," Paris said, concentrating on his breathing. There was no way to know how far in they'd have to follow to catch up with the others. "They may not know that they're being followed, and if that's the case, we need to try and get there before the aliens get around to doing more than following."

The two raced along the trail, trying as best they could to be silent. There was little they could do. If they wanted to remain discreet, they'd have to sacrifice time, and it didn't appear that time was something they had much of. They'd just have to count on the idea that the Urrythans believed they had beamed up to the ship with the others. They would not be looking out for pursuit.

As they went, Paris couldn't help wondering about the huge yellow flowers they passed beneath. Under any other circumstances, they would be beautiful—regal, even. They were so tall and lush, so full of quiet purpose. Now that purpose seemed darker and more sinister, and despite The Doctor's antidote, which he'd been injected with before leaving *Voyager,* he felt in the blossoms a silent menace.

I'll never look at flowers the same way again, he thought.

Then there was no room for thought, only pacing himself, running and dodging through the brush and the vines that had overgrown the ancient trail. It was like a dream, or some malfunctioning holodeck program. He and Kes were as isolated from their own worlds and their own people as he could ever imagine being. Even after his time in prison, he'd found the commbadge and the electronic lifelines of Starfleet comforting. Now they meant nothing, and only his own wits, nerve, and abilities would see him through. He could almost see his father, the admiral, wince, had he known how much now rode on the shoulders of his renegade son.

That made for an interesting image. There were a lot of questions he'd like to have asked the old man. The notion of the *Ambiana* and the *Ascension* made him wonder about his own spiritual roots. He'd never discussed that kind of thing with his father . . .

he'd never discussed much of *anything* with his father. He pushed it all aside for the moment, pressing his body for more speed.

Kes ran easily at his side, eyes bright and mind far away, tracking some spirit voice he could only imagine. She moved with such confidence that it was nearly impossible to imagine that she was less than two years old. What an amazing race hers was. Not for the first time, he regretted that he had not had the opportunity to meet her under other circumstances. She loved Neelix, and he himself had long since set his deeper feelings for her aside out of respect for him. They were an odd match, but they had that magic that many couples never achieved.

"Tom," she cried out, and he stopped for a second, breathing hard and staring down at the ground where she was pointing. In the soft ground they could clearly make out three sets of prints. They had stopped, shuffled about the stone pillar that rose through the ground in front of them, then continued on.

"These are pretty fresh," he said. "We must not be that far behind. Can you keep up this pace?"

Kes looked at him, nodding. He thought, just for a second, that she was surprised by his question, and he made a note to look further into the physiology of the Ocampa. If he had been guessing, he'd have said that her expression read something like *Of course, why would I not be able to?* His own lungs were starting to protest, and he could already feel the cramps that would assault his legs come the morning. Assuming that the morning was still in his future.

He turned and led the way on down the trail, keeping his eyes peeled for more signs of their own party, and watching the shadows for the Urrythans. He held one hand as near his phaser as he could without interrupting the motions of his stride; he just hoped that when the time came, he was quick enough and attentive enough to use it.

Vok awakened from his slumber and looked around. At first he noticed nothing odd—nothing strange. In truth, it was difficult to process the images of his waking world when drawing himself free from the *One Voice*. Then, as he shook himself reluctantly free of the influence of his ancestors, he began to comprehend just how much his meditation might have cost him this once.

They were still preparing the woman for *Ascension,* but there were no more than three or four of his followers in attendance. Barely enough to keep the chants going. There were others, gathering and bringing the blossoms to keep the *Ambiana* fresh, but not enough—not nearly enough. None were joining him in the meditation—none bustled about the domestic chores of the settlement. Ban was nowhere to be seen.

Vok rose, making his way slowly toward those involved in the ritual. He stood for a moment, watching them, aware that they were studiously ignoring him. They knew what he wanted to know, and they would tell him—he thought—but only if he asked.

He moved closer, tapping one of the young ones on the shoulder. The man turned to face him reluctantly.

"Where have they gone?" Vok asked softly.

"They will protect the elders," the young one answered. Vok searched his memory for a name, found it. Tel. The young one's name was Tel.

"The elders need no protection," Vok said softly, "as well you know. They have withstood wars, centuries—time itself. Our purpose is not to fight. Our purpose is not to protect. Our purpose is to join with them, to find our place in the *One Voice.*"

Tel nodded, but it was obvious that he was only partially convinced. Vok was the eldest, but Ban was full of fire, of energy, and they were all still too full of themselves. It would take long years, time and meditation, learning and the wisdom that came with life, to bring them to the knowledge he sought for them.

"The star travelers mean us no harm," Vok finished, turning away. "They came in peace. Now I must go to their aid before my own people make mistakes they cannot right. Though my hour to ascend is upon me, I must make this one last journey. I will go the place of the elders, and I will set things right, if I can. Finish preparing the girl—I can feel her falling into place with the elders. At least her spirit can find the freedom that should be our goal."

He turned then, knowing that he'd spoken the truth, and knowing with a deep sadness in his heart that it would be decades before that truth became obvious to any of the young ones. Some of them would not make it at all. If Ban and his followers had their way, things might change. The *Ambiana* might not bring them all to the light. It brought him great pain to feel that he might be one of the last of his kind to ascend.

And these others—his had been the decision that had set all that was happening in motion. He had been the one to authorize the taking of the woman, Kayla—the initiation of her ceremonies. He could be wrong. As long as he'd lived, he knew this to be true.

There were no others near him in age. A sickness had taken a great many of his peers, the others had all gone on before him. Now there would be none to teach, none to counsel. He wondered briefly if any would have listened. He could feel his ancestors calling to him, could feel the tug at his soul that would drown him in the *One Voice* forever, sending him into the long sleep that would bring him to his *Ascension*.

As the *Ambiana* proliferated, becoming more and more common—easier to attain—his people were spending less and less time between birth and the *Long Sleep*. With this, a lot of the wisdom, a lot of the personal balance, was lost.

He left the settlement quickly, heading deeper into the caverns. There were other ways to reach the eldest—ways that even Ban did not know. If that was where they were all headed, then there was still a chance that he could get there first—a chance that he could stop the ugliness he felt descending on them. He only prayed that he had the strength, and that he would not be too late.

CHAPTER

10

"CAPTAIN?" TUVOK CALLED OUT.

"Yes, Mr. Tuvok, what is it?" Janeway answered, distracted by the trail ahead of her and the seeming hopelessness of their situation. She turned to find him standing still in the path, staring down at his tricorder with the closest expression to frustration she'd ever seen grace his features.

"I am not certain what it means," he answered, "but the life-force readings are now growing in intensity at a greatly increased rate. I am unable to get a reading off anything because of it. I am afraid that whatever this force is, it has rendered our equipment virtually useless."

"So," Janeway mused, "we have no way at all of knowing if our friends are coming around to pay us a visit."

"We had no clear method before," Tuvok retorted.

"We will merely be required to exercise the abilities of our minds and our senses. It may prove an interesting exercise."

Janeway smiled. One day Tuvok was going to crack a smile, she just knew it. "You are correct, of course." She nodded. "We'll have to watch ahead and behind. There's too much overgrowth on the sides of the trail for anyone to sneak up on us that way. We'll have to assume that they will use the trail, just as we are. We've all been trained for situations like this—I just never expected to be *in* one."

"Maybe they're just pilgrims of some sort," Kim cut in eagerly. "We *are* heading straight into the graveyard of their ancestors."

"I hate to rain on your parade, Mr. Kim," Janeway replied, continuing on down the trail, "but if someone was threatening to invade the graves of your ancestors, someone who'd already shown an inclination to disobey the tenets of your religious beliefs, what would you do? Besides, I've never been one to bet on coincidence, and this would be a big one."

Kim didn't answer, but Janeway knew her point had been pounded home. Janeway didn't know if it was Vok himself that followed, or a contingent of his followers, but whoever it was meant them no good will. If they had, they'd have helped in the first place. That was one of the things about the entire mess that bothered her the most. She'd been utterly and completely convinced that Vok had meant his welcome as he'd voiced it. It bothered her more than she was letting on that she'd made an inaccurate judgment of such an important issue.

They rounded a bend in the trail where the narrow walkway widened into a rounded clearing. Here they saw the first signs of civilization beyond that which they'd left behind. These buildings were partially buried in the ground, and yet the same clear austere lines were present as in the later ruins. There was also a greater concentration of the odd pillar-shaped tombs here than there had been in the outer gardens. Some of the pillars were buried, others appeared newer and stood above the ground.

Had the aliens been more plentiful in the older times, or had they just felt the need to go to their *Long Sleep* in closer physical proximity to one another? There was no way to tell unless they could decipher it from the pillars themselves. More and more it was the cryptic carved messages that seemed their only link to a solution.

"Captain," Kim said suddenly, "I believe that if we can get down into the ruins of that building over there"—he pointed to the roof of a crumbling edifice across the clearing—"we might be able to access the lower extremities of those two pillars."

Straddling the ruined building were the very tops of two of the older pillars. They were a bit more chipped and worn, but otherwise as sturdy and enduring as the others. The earth had built up around them, leaving them more beneath the surface than above it. The building had apparently circled them, with the two pillars reaching to the stars like twin towers. An odd configuration, among many odd formations.

"If they have the same sequence of symbols as the others," Kim went on, "maybe we'll be a bit closer to what we seek."

"It would not be advisable to enter any sheltered spot that we cannot scan," Tuvok countered. "It could be a trap. We should not abandon the very training you were just mentioning, Captain."

"We may have to take that chance, Mr. Tuvok," Janeway said softly. "We are all trained in combat protocol. I suggest we stop worrying over the assets we no longer possess and begin to try and use the ones that we do."

Tuvok didn't answer, but he slipped his tricorder into place on his belt and pulled forth his phaser. Without a word, he began to make his way slowly toward the old building, sweeping his gaze over the jungle to either side with stern determined concentration. He moved with confidence and precision— as if it had been his idea to explore the ruined building all along.

Kim and Janeway slid into step behind him, Kim with his back to Janeway's and scanning the trail behind them, Janeway shifting her eyes from left to right and back again, watching for anything suspicious, any movement, or sign of life besides their own. It was an unfamiliar sensation, the lack of sensors and scanning devices, and yet, somehow, it felt good to depend, if only for a little while, on the assets she'd grown with . . . her mind, her body— her wits.

They made their way to the ruins without incident, but there was something in the air, something hanging just out of reach and tickling at her senses, that made Janeway hesitate before entering the building. She wondered briefly if the *Ambiana* might be influencing her thoughts, finally, if she might be becoming more sensitive to the odd life-force that permeated the place and picked up on the voice of Vok's ancestors.

"Mr. Tuvok, I . . ." She never got the rest of the sentence out of her mouth. The Urrythans seemed to erupt from the crumbling windows and the broken doors, pouring out and upward, swarming toward her startled little group before they had a chance to react. As they came, they chanted—an odd hypnotic sort of hum that seemed to give their movements cohesion.

There was nothing to indicate rage or hatred in their features, but the long sad faces suddenly swarming around them were uniformly determined. They meant to overrun the intruders at whatever cost, and something in their odd chant, and the strange way their multiple-jointed legs propelled them forward, communicated this without question.

"They are not armed, Captain," Tuvok grated, swinging his arm up quickly and spearing the first of the aliens with the beam of his phaser. It was set on stun, and the alien, crying out—his voice a high despairing keening sound—dropped like a sack of flour as the beam struck him full in the chest.

The others hesitated for an instant, seemingly shocked into the reality of the moment when their companion fell, as though only just realizing this as a possibility. Then they rushed forward with renewed speed, taking little or no further note of their fallen companion.

Kim, who had dropped a second alien, cried out in alarm. "There are too many, Captain. We can't take them all out before they reach us. Not in such an open area."

"Then we will fight," she grated, dropping a second assailant and swinging her aim quickly to the left. Kim was right. There were far too many of them, and they were attacking without regard to their personal well-being. This was a difficult strategy to counter, if it could be called a strategy at all. It was more like suicide, or would have been if the phasers were set differently.

Spinning so that her back rested against the wall of the old building, she called out, "Duck inside! It's our only chance to evade them, and in tighter quarters we'll be at less of a disadvantage."

They followed her lead as she dove through one of the window-like openings that the aliens had just exited. She hoped that their lack of apparent strategy would stretch back to a failure to include guards at their rear. Kim slid in last, and as he cleared the opening, Tuvok spun and let loose a burst of phaser fire over the younger man's shoulder, just in time to keep one of their attackers from wrapping his long slender fingers around Kim's ankle.

The interior of the old ruin was much darker, lit only by the sunlight that managed to filter both through the trees surrounding them and the few windows that were still free of vines and debris. It was a few moments before their eyes became accustomed to the sudden lack of light. They clustered as closely together as possible, back to back, and attempted to get their bearings as the enraged Urrythans, deprived of their element of surprise and with several fallen companions, paused to regroup.

"There are stairs leading down, Captain," Tuvok pointed out. "We may be able to buy ourselves some time by heading in there."

"Or we might run into more of them," she countered, thinking hard. "They're letting up for the moment, let's wait as long as we can before we commit ourselves to the lower levels. That might be exactly what they *want* us to do, and I'd like to keep sight of the outside world as long as possible."

There was a quiet babble of voices from beyond the wall. The Urrythans' obvious confusion lent Janeway confidence. In a real battle, she and her comrades could have been at the windows, picking them off as they milled about and discussed the situation. She was tempted to give that order, but she didn't want to become the aggressor in the situation if it was possible to avoid it. Were they to be overrun, such an act would be more difficult to explain away as self-defense.

The Urrythans did not seem at all comfortable

with the concept of strategy, and it appeared that whatever leadership had gotten them as far as they'd come was not holding up so well under closer scrutiny.

"I wonder if we could talk to them?" Kim said softly. "They don't seem in any big hurry to attack us now . . ."

As if they'd heard his comment, the Urrythans hit the openings to the underground ruin all at once. They did not hesitate at the darkness of the interior—if anything, their senses seemed suddenly heightened. It was the same attack plan they'd used when coming *out* of the windows, a mass swarm.

They live underground, Janeway reminded herself. *We're in their territory now.*

"Keep the wall at your backs," she barked. "Maintain steady fire and keep those weapons on stun. They can only come at us so many at a time in here; if we're careful, we can hold them off for quite a while. If we get enough of them, maybe we can run the others off."

Tuvok, who was spraying steady bursts from his phaser into the attacking throngs, was the first to notice that something was wrong. There were a lot of them—just as before—but not as many as there should be. They were attacking with the same unruly mob tactic as they'd used when pouring *out* of the building, and yet there seemed more to it this time.

Tuvok took precious moments to twist his eyes to

one side, then the other, trying to place the source of his uneasiness. To the left. There was someone there, though they were remaining out of sight. Then he felt the same thing on the right. A flanking movement. Very simple, hardly a strategic breakthrough, and yet it had used his own confidence, and that of the captain, against them.

"Captain," he called out, dropping yet another of the aliens. The huge ancient pillars stretched through the floor, then the roof of the room in which they stood. Their attackers were gathering behind the relative safety of the columns, then charging randomly from different directions. It was a crude tactic, but more effective when coupled with those hidden in the shadows off to the sides.

"Yes?" Janeway answered. She couldn't turn to face Tuvok, not with so many Urrythans bearing down on them. She didn't want to alarm the other two, but her own phaser's charge was getting low, and she suspected that theirs were, as well. If the Urrythans had brought any sort of weapons with them at all, it would have been over long before. Thus far it hadn't even occurred to them to throw rocks.

"I think there are more of them to the right and left," Tuvok continued. "I can sense their presence, but I cannot make them out in the shadows. There must have been side entrances to this ruin that we did not know about."

Momentarily, it was a standoff, but the feeling of tension in the air told Janeway it was only a second regrouping before the final rush. She knew that, as things were going, it was only a matter of time until their attackers broke through their defenses—only a matter of time until they were completely overrun. She'd believed at first that the aliens were cold-hearted, turning from their fallen comrades without thought, but a second thought occurred to her. They were mentally linked—they knew the phasers were only stunning them—and they might believe it was the strongest blast possible. Her charity might have given them confidence.

"Suggestions, Mr. Tuvok?" she said at last, sweeping her arm in a slow arc that kept the phaser at chest level and ready.

"It might be a prudent time to investigate those lower levels, Captain."

Janeway smiled grimly. "I believe you are right, Mr. Tuvok. Mr. Kim, lead us in; Tuvok, bring up the rear. Let's get moving before they have a chance to regroup."

Kim didn't hesitate. He slipped along the wall toward the ruined stairs and launched himself downward. With a wistful glance at the windows leading to the air, the jungles, and *Voyager,* Janeway followed.

The Urrythans, catching on a bit late that their quarry was heading underground, began to follow, but Tuvok laid down a pattern of fire that sent them scurrying for cover, and he backed carefully down after his companions. Seeing that they were not followed immediately, he hurried his steps, keeping his eyes on the shadows.

* * *

Ban didn't know what to do next. It was obvious that, as long as the intruders possessed the superior weaponry, without the element of surprise he could not take them. A quick check had shown him that his own followers were not dead, and yet he did not want to rush in and subject more of them to the stunning force of the star travelers' rays. Neither did he wish to allow them to continue as they now were, directly into the vaults of the most sacred areas of his ancestors. Ban himself had never been there, would not go there officially in many decades. He was shocked that what had seemed a simple action, a plan thought out in detail, had actually driven the aliens into the very place he'd wished to drive them *away* from.

That was the difficulty now. Neither Ban nor his followers were in any hurry to rush into a place that they had no right to be, even to protect it. It violated everything they'd ever been taught, every bit of training Vok had pounded into him. Was it acceptable, even in such an instance, to desecrate that which was holy? It was a painful thing—a thing that was causing many who now followed him to question the wisdom of their mission and, even more strenuously, the continuation of that mission. Still it had to be done.

Vok was old. His time of waking was nearly complete, and his thoughts and eyes were already turned beyond—to the *Long Sleep*. His years had stretched beyond any of his own generation, and even some of the younger ones—with the *Ambiana* more accessible—had gone on ahead of him. He did not see the danger these star travelers might present because he was not able to view the situation clearly. His perspective was at least a hundred years out of date.

If Ban and his people were not to go to the sacred places, why was it allowable for invaders with no belief whatsoever to do so? It could not be right, and in their capacity as guardians, it was their duty to see that it did not happen. Of course, he could remember no teachings that designated himself, or any of his people, as "guardians" of anything, but that was obviously an oversight caused by different times—different situations. In Ban's time, it was a necessity.

That is what Ban felt. His immediate problem would be to convince his followers. He had a few stalwart disciples that would follow him in, but he would need all of them, full support, to be effective in what was to come. Without the token advantage of numbers, their mission was doomed to failure.

His closest followers could be counted on to do as he asked, but the rest of them had come along more out of the novelty of the expedition than any true belief in Ban himself. It was something different—a change in their routine. Such an occasion was truly rare on the path to *Ascension*. Their allegiance, these thrill-seekers, would in the end be to the elder—to Vok—and Vok had already made his own opinions known. Ban had to act before this course of action presented itself to their minds.

There was the failure of their initial assault to consider. Some of the others, with good cause, were questioning the wisdom of continuing against an obviously superior show of strength. While none of his people had been killed—the star travelers' rays had proved very effective in incapacitating them. Many feared that if truly angered, the aliens might begin to end lives. Such a thing had not happened in millennia. It was unheard of. How could one die before even making it to the *Long Sleep?* Never to arise again? To be denied *Ascension?*

To ask them to risk this was a great responsibility, but Ban still felt in his heart that it was the only thing that they could do. It would be horrible to die in defense of the ancestors, true, but would it be less horrible if these intruders, roaming freely through their holy grounds, caused the death of one of the elders before he reached the *Awakening?* How much more horrible, after so many thousands of years of waiting and preparing, would that be. Besides, something in the nature of the battle they'd just endured led Ban to believe that, in at least one thing, the Federation captain, Janeway, had spoken truly—they meant no harm. It was their actions, in ignorance, that could not be tolerated.

He gathered his followers tightly about him, keeping a wary eye on the stairway that the intruders had descended, and he outlined the plan that was just beginning to form in his mind. There was still hope, he realized suddenly—they had advantages they had yet to press. He had forgotten basic concepts— or never considered them in the first place. They would be underground—they were on their own home planet. It was not yet time to give in to despair.

"The voice of the planet is so loud now," Kes murmured as she turned slowly, trying to get a bearing on the traces left by Ban and his party. "I think . . . yes, they went this way."

"How can you be certain?" Paris asked, frowning slightly. "If they are all small parts of one big life-force, how can you distinguish between them? What is it that's different from one note in a chord to the next?"

"There is a slight disharmony to those we are following," Kes explained, jogging easily at his side. She seemed buoyed by her short melding with the planet, her eyes a bit dreamy and far away. It was as if she were drawing energy from the air around them, while Paris's own faded into labored breathing and concentration.

"They are not following the accepted pattern," she continued. "What they are doing is actually *disrupting* the natural order of things."

They were nearing a clearing, and Paris noted that there were more and more of the strange monolithic pillars protruding through the soil around them. He would have sworn that he could feel something himself now, something crackling through the air about them. Everything seemed charged with energy, alive in some odd way that his senses were not equipped to understand. It seemed that it was growing strong enough for his senses to detect, but not for his brain to translate into any usable data.

"Wait," Kes cautioned him, coming to an abrupt halt and grabbing his arm. "They are very near."

Paris slipped into the brush to one side of the trail and pulled Kes in beside him. Moving more slowly, he made his way forward to where the clearing was visible. More ruins filled the small opening in the gardens—older, more deeply buried than any of the others they'd encountered. He was about to step forward into the clearing when he made out the shape of one of the aliens, just inside a crumbling window of the most complete of the ruins. A guard.

He pointed the alien out to Kes, who nodded. Closing her eyes, she concentrated, trying to weave her way through the harmony of the planet's voice, searching. It was a realm of patterns, a web of intricate sensations, but it was not beyond her ability to unravel. She tried not to cause any ripples with her own mental actions. There was no way to know how sensitive the Urrythans might be to such a thing.

"They are in there," she said at last. "These Urrythans here are slightly in variance with the voice, but the captain, Tuvok, and Kim are more glaring. I was able to locate them because they do *not* fit into the harmony."

"Then they're okay," Paris said softly. "What do we do now?"

Kes hesitated, then pointed to where the alien had

been standing just a moment before. "They are moving to a deeper level, where the captain has gone—they are following."

"I wonder if they'll leave a guard."

"I don't think so," Kes answered. "They are moving as a unit, though these are younger ones. I sense that they are only partially in harmony with the *One Voice*, not like the sensation I got from their leader, Vok, at all. They are, however, in harmony with one another—they are acting as a single mind with a single purpose."

"Vok isn't with them?" Paris asked, perplexed.

"No. I sense that he is approaching, but he is not responsible. He is very faint against the backdrop of the elders' voice—he is nearly one of them himself."

Paris didn't question how Kes knew all of this; for the moment the time for questions was past. If she said she knew, he had no choice but to believe it— he had nothing else to go on.

"They've gone," Kes said at last.

"Come on, then," Paris said, moving toward the ruined building stealthily. "Let's get inside and see if we can catch up and help."

Kes nodded, and together they moved to the nearest window and clambered inside, dropping to the floor beneath.

"There was a fight here," Paris observed. The dust on the floor was disturbed in several places, as though large objects had been dragged across them, and there were footprints everywhere, some from Starfleet boots, but most of them longer and more narrow.

"Apparently they haven't figured out our weapons yet," Paris observed.

"They have no weapons themselves," Kes said thoughtfully, running her hand over one of the odd pillars, caressing it. "This is not a violent society. The young ones are merely trying to preserve their ancestors until the *Awakening*."

"Whatever," Paris replied. "They went this way."

Without a further word, he plunged down the stone stairs and into the darkness beyond, and Kes followed. The shadows swallowed them quickly and completely.

CHAPTER

11

"COMMANDER." TORRES'S VOICE WAS TREMBLING WITH barely concealed frustration. "I can't make out anything. I've reconfigured for every frequency band, every type of available modulation. I can't penetrate this thing. It's as if the life-force of the planet was bubbling up and running over. Every system we have is picking it up now—it's causing fluctuations in the computer I can't even trace, let alone filter out."

"Then Paris and Kes are on their own down there, too," he said softly. Under his breath, he added, "I hope he knows what the hell he's doing."

"Sir?" Torres asked, looking up quickly.

"Nothing, B'Elanna, just thinking out loud." Chakotay didn't want to burden her with his own concerns. She had enough to worry over with the mounting problems in Engineering. He knew he should pull back, away from the interference, but he was holding off. It felt too much like giving up, and he wasn't in that mind-set yet. So far it hadn't affected any primary systems.

Those that had been beamed back aboard were recuperating. Ensign Fowler had assumed Kim's console and was aiding Torres in her efforts. As Chakotay stood pondering the situation, Neelix stormed onto the bridge. He was more agitated than the first officer had ever seen him, and it was obvious that The Doctor's order to get some rest had been ignored. In all fairness, relaxing while your lover was stranded on an alien planet and completely lost to all contact was hardly a popular suggestion.

"Commander Chakotay," Neelix called out, "have you located Kes and the others?"

"We can't locate anything on that planet, Neelix." Chakotay sighed. "That life-force is building up to something, something big, and we can't penetrate it with any methods or equipment we have available. It's grown so powerful that we're feeling the effects of it all the way out here. We're still trying."

"Then I demand to be beamed back to the planet." Neelix was standing, legs spread wide and a stubborn expression masking his features. "I'm not leaving her down there alone to face these Urrythan bandits."

"She isn't alone, Neelix," Chakotay reminded him. "Paris is with her. He's trained to adapt to difficult situations and conditions. They'll be fine."

"I still don't understand why she didn't beam up

with the rest of us," Neelix fumed. "She was standing right next to me!"

"She is too much in tune with the planet itself," Chakotay explained for probably the tenth time. "She was there one moment, then suddenly the computer didn't even register that there was a person next to you—not even after the administering of The Doctor's antidote. My guess is that she was trying to sense the location of the approaching Urrythans, and she dipped back into the life-force of her own volition. She's a brave girl."

"Send me down there, Captain," Neelix insisted. "I'll find her and bring her back, and if not . . ." His voice choked up, but he continued with an effort. "If not, then I'll die defending her."

"I'm not sending anyone anywhere, Neelix," Chakotay said softly. "I appreciate your desire to help, but there is really nothing you could do, and they are too spread out down there as it is. We may not be able to find them all and get them back, and I'm not going to be responsible for any further losses. It would make things that much more difficult for her if something happened and we had to spend time looking for you."

I see," Neelix said, barely controlling his voice. He was trembling, on the verge of giving in to his emotions and collapsing in tears. "Then I would like to do something, something that will help. I am not leaving this bridge until we have some answers." With a great effort, he drew back his shoulders and took a deep breath.

"Fine," Chakotay agreed, realizing that Neelix

just didn't want to be alone. "Go over and see if you can give Torres and Fowler a hand with those scans. Maybe you can think of something we've overlooked. We've run out of things to try, and we're fast running out of time, as well."

Neelix nodded and made his way quickly to the operations console, a new sense of purpose evident in his step. *Maybe he will think of something*, Chakotay thought, watching him. *It wouldn't be the first time he's surprised us.*

"How about sending out probes?" Neelix asked.

"We can't maintain contact with the surface," Torres answered, shaking her head. "We could get the probes down there, I think, but we'd be as unable to contact them as we are the commbadges or the shuttle craft, unless . . ."

Turning to Ensign Fowler, she went on quickly. "Kes said that this *One Voice* is a kind of harmony. That means it's made up of synchronized complementary signals. If we can determine what that harmony is, exactly, its frequency spectrum and components, then we might be able to configure a probe that would operate in *conjunction* with the signal. There is no theoretical limit to the amount of notes in a chord, what would one more hurt? We've spent all our time trying to penetrate this thing, why not try and use it to our advantage?"

"It might work," Fowler agreed. "If we added a single note to their 'voice' but didn't disrupt it, we might be able to configure the scanners to communicate with a primitive modulated signal, using the note as a carrier."

Chakotay hurried over to them. "How long will that take?" he asked quickly.

"I need to analyze the signal, then reconfigure the probes and the scanners—at least a couple of hours," Torres said, her fingers already flying over the console.

"You have one hour," Chakotay told her. He could see the lights flashing in her eyes and could almost hear the gears turning with sudden energy. "I want those probes ready and launched, spread out in a pattern that will give us the widest possible range. Concentrate efforts on the center of that garden, where we lost the captain's signal, and on that settlement in the desert. Somewhere down there, something will move, and I plan to be ready when it does."

Torres didn't answer. She was already intent on the work before her. Neelix hovered nearby, moving here and there to push a keypad or take a reading as directed.

"I'll go and get started on those probes," Fowler said, standing. "I can get them set up so that as soon as you have the frequency we can begin the programming."

Torres nodded, but she didn't speak. Her concentration had taken her to another level, lost in her own world of energy, microprocessors, and numbers. Fowler left the bridge, and Chakotay took his own leave shortly thereafter, moving into the captain's ready room where he could be alone to think.

The whole problem on this planet was arising over a conflict of belief systems. Chakotay knew from the experiences of his own heritage just how strongly such a system could affect one's psyche. He wasn't certain that he could blame these Urrythans for their reactions. They had taken Kayla because they truly believed that she was about to receive the highest privilege their own religion offered, *Ascension.* The problem was in the pushing off of one belief on to those who followed another.

He wasn't certain just how he felt about the ascension of a person's spirit, but he knew that there had to be something beyond the physical life he now lived. He'd been aware of his own spirit, in his own way, for many years, and he believed that he would continue his journey, through that spirit, beyond physical death. That belief—that *knowledge*—was one of the cornerstones of his being.

The Urrythans believed that they would come to harmony with their ancestors, go to sleep for thousands of years, and rise to a new and greater life. It was easy to scoff, to pass it all off as just another primitive explanation for the mysteries of life, but it was less easy in the face of the odd life-force readings from their planet. *Something* down there was alive, something beyond the confines of the Urrythans they had encountered, and whatever it was, it was growing in strength. Were they nearing some sort of spiritual climax? Could these strange beings be right, acting out of a duty to the souls of *Voyager*'s crew, rather than any malice?

In the end, he knew, it didn't matter. *Ascension,* or no *Ascension,* a fundamental truth among humans was that free choice was vital. The many races that formed the Federation shared that belief, for the most part. Freedom of belief and religion was as sacred as any right a sentient being might possess, and it needed to be defended.

They might be right, they might be wrong, but the Urrythans had no right to make life decisions for others, no more than *Voyager* and her crew had the right to disrupt the ways of this planet. There had to be some solution, some way to draw back and leave them to their world without losing any of their own crew. It was not an easy problem, and the solution would not come without thought. He only hoped he had enough time left before disaster pushed things beyond reasonable limits.

Placing his hands carefully on the desk before him, Chakotay let his mind relax. He might not be able to help, but it would be best to face whatever was to come with a calm balanced mind. He let himself slip inward, blanking out the feel, sounds, and sights of *Voyager,* seeking his personal place— his spirit guide. He didn't know what good it would do him, but he knew he needed all the help he could get.

Vok moved as quickly as he could manage, picking his way through the ancient tunnels, doubling back when the way was blocked, following the voice that filled his soul. The ways through the ancient tunnels had not been used as much in the later years. There were newer tunnels, and his followers did not feel comfortable coming in close contact with the elders until they neared their *Long Sleep.*

Vok hurried because he wasn't sure how far Ban would go on his misguided "mission," and because he felt the tug on his mind so strongly that he feared his time was limited. If he fell to the *Long Sleep* now, alone in the tunnels, there would be none to tend to him, none to administer the rituals or to erect the shell. He would merely lay there until he decayed and, eventually, died. That thought, the thought of his own death, frightened him more than any single other thing. Beyond that, even, he felt the needs of his people—the heritage of which he was the eldest living member.

Ban didn't understand that heritage, not fully, and he wouldn't understand until he was more firmly initiated into the patterns of the *One Voice*. He still thought too much on his own, cared too much about the physical world surrounding him and the worries of day-to-day life. He still worried more about the affairs of others, and their opinions, than he did about the state of his own spirit.

Traditionally, this had been the lot of the young ones. It was their responsibility to tend to the gardens, to gather the *Ambiana,* and to care for the needs of everyday life as the elders made their way to the *Long Sleep*. Conversely, it was the duty and purpose of the elders to train the young ones, to guide them on their journey into the future. It had always been thus, and until now, it had been an admirable system.

Ban saw Vok's leadership as the will of one being imposed over the will of many others, and thus he believed that his own decisions could be as viable, perhaps more so under certain circumstances, than those of an elder. What he didn't see was that it was not Vok who spoke, when matters were decided, but *all* of those who'd gone before. It was not one body telling another what to do as much as it was a huge mind sending signals to its various organs, moving limbs according to a single balanced plan.

Vok knew this was his own fault. When the others had demanded that the female intruder be taken, he should have stood firm, held them in check. He had not listened as strongly to the voices in his heart as he might have, and his lack of confidence in his own leadership had caused things to get out of hand. There were a few rebels among them, but the majority of them would have abided by his decision, and with only a handful of followers, Ban would have sulked for a while, then grown beyond it.

What had happened instead was a toppling line of events, one leading to the next, and all of them discordant to harmony. He only hoped that he could find a way to put it all right, to set the star travelers free so they could continue their journey home, and get his own children on the right path once more before his time was up and it was lost forever. He'd put off his own ceremony for too long, and he realized that the decision would soon be wrested from his control and thrust upon him.

As much as Vok wanted to become fully one with his ancestors, as often and fondly as he dreamed of the *Long Sleep* and the peace it would bring him, he did not want to be the last to take that path. He did not want to be the link in the chain that would end things, parting old and new irrevocably.

Each pathway he took deeper beneath the sun-drenched surface of his world led him closer to the center, closer to the almost overwhelming presence of his ancestors. It became more and more difficult to concentrate on continuing, but he forced himself to go on. Those who would follow him in his journey, those who would become elders, would be a part of the *One Voice*, and it was vital to continuity that they not bring discord into that joining. Only his guidance, and his ability to reverse the events he'd set into motion, could assure that this would happen.

He felt the gardens above him as he moved, knew when he passed beneath the clearing where he'd first met the strange woman, Janeway, and her followers. They had not sought the harmony, and yet there was a strength of spirit to these outsiders. They seemed to have a different sort of harmony, all their own, and they did everything with a purpose, albeit a purpose totally alien to Vok's mind or experience.

Perhaps he had been blinded by his own self-importance, elder to the tribe, next in line to lie down and rise again. It was a lesson he'd been eager to teach Ban, now he understood that he was not completely free of such sensations himself—such individual emotion. None of what filled his mind mattered to these visitors from the stars, and in retrospect he realized that there was no logical reason why it should.

He reflected on the arrogance of his own belief. Because another came before him who did not believe as he believed, he had considered them to be somehow less than he. What he should have realized, what all of them should have learned, was that different did not mean wrong. Each of them started out very different in life. Ban was distinctly different from Vok himself and from each of the others, but that difference was superficial—a difference of the physical material world. What mattered was the unity, the point where they became not different, one from another, but different parts of one whole. In a single note, there is no harmony.

He became slowly aware of a variance in the *One Voice*. It had been steadily growing in strength for him, drawing him in, but this was different. Now it was expanding at a greater rate, overwhelming everything about it. He felt a slight vibration beneath his feet—a tremor in the ground. What could it mean? He'd noticed the growing strength of the harmony, but he'd attributed that stronger sensation to his own growth. Now he saw that it was a reality for all. He'd never experienced anything like it.

He could also sense the others now. He was growing near to the center, and that was where Captain Janeway and her followers had come to. Had he been wrong? Had they, too, felt the power of the ancestors calling to them? The stronger the *One Voice*, the tighter the harmony, the more easily he was able to pick out those sounds, those sensations that did not fit.

Suddenly the life-force that was Ban came into

focus in his mind's eye, and his heart chilled for an instant. Just for one long moment, the harmony and balance that swelled within him hesitated and nearly stopped. Something was wrong. Ban had never been fully in tune with the *One Voice,* but Vok had assumed he would fall in line eventually. Now the young one stood out like a tumor against the beauty that was rising.

Something had gone terribly wrong, and Vok sensed that if he did not move very quickly, perhaps more quickly than was possible, it would be too late. Too late for Ban, too late for Captain Janeway—perhaps too late for Urrytha itself. For the elders. Something wonderful was on the verge of happening around them, and yet it bordered on disaster—a catastrophe beyond thought—because of his own negligence.

He doubled his speed, though it cost a great deal of his remaining strength, zeroing in on the sensations that would lead him to Janeway and praying to those who had gone on before that he would reach her in time.

"Got it!" Torres, grinning fiercely, looked up from her console at last. Not seeing Chakotay on the bridge, she slapped her commbadge and called out, "Chakotay, Torres. I've got the frequency, and I'm on my way to Engineering to help Ensign Fowler with the probes. We should be ready to launch in about fifteen minutes."

Chakotay's voice returned to her after only a slight

hesitation. "Do it. I'll be on the bridge, waiting to begin the scan."

Rising and taking a deep breath to reorient himself, Chakotay made his way back onto the bridge. On screen the planet below hung like a huge multicolored ball in the void of space. Somehow, his perceptions of the place had changed since they'd first arrived. It had seemed so much like home, so accessible, that he'd somehow forgotten that alien is alien.

There is little common ground between races, and when it appears that there is more, it is often deceptive. Their perspective and that of the Urrythans would never fully mesh, and somehow this lent an air of menace to the place. The most that could be expected was a mutual respect, one belief system for another, one lifestyle for another.

"Chakotay, this is Torres. We're ready to launch."

"Get those probes out there," he answered without taking his eyes from the screen above him. "It's time to bring them home."

CHAPTER
12

BAN SOON REALIZED THAT THERE WAS NO WAY HE WAS
going to defeat these aliens by any sort of direct
confrontational strategy, or by might of arms. In
both instances, they were superior to his force.
Surprise, as he'd initially surmised, was the only
hope they had, and though it would be more difficult
to achieve that surprise again, it had to be his
objective. He might chase them for a long time
through the tunnels, but unless he found a way to
trap them, they would reach their goal before he
could prevent them, and it would all be pointless.
Surprise was the only course that made any sense.

There were factors that worked in his favor. He
and his followers lived a great deal of their lives
beneath the ground. Their vision did not require the
same amount of light to function as the star travel-

ers'. In fact, they could operate for limited amounts of time with no visual stimulus whatsoever, relying on touch and smell to guide them. He'd never before thought of this as an advantage, had only taken it as natural.

There was also the fact that this was his own world. He did not know the particular passageways they would be traveling, but he knew many others much like them. He knew the way his ancestors, who'd built these passages and walls, had thought, and he could intuitively understand the tunnels in ways the intruders would never be able to fathom. His knowledge was instinctive, and he was certain that he would be able to find a way to slip up quickly, boxing his enemy in.

Once that was accomplished, it was only a matter of time before his superior numbers began to tell on them, and they fell beneath the attack. If his surprise were swift and decisive enough, he would be able to get them out of action without making another great battle of it. He found that his taste for direct confrontation had waned since leaving the settlement behind. All he wanted was to keep them away from his ancestors.

He directed groups of his followers into the passages to the left, and others to the right, instructing them to keep parallel to the central passage if possible. The idea was that one or both groups would find their way around to the other side of the fleeing star travelers. He knew that many of the paths they might try would dead-end, and there was no way to know which, or how many, of his followers would make it through. Hopefully it would be enough to accomplish his goal—surprise.

He himself led a smaller group straight ahead, in the wake of the intruders' passing. Their quarry were far from silent, and they left a clear trail in the accumulated dust on the floor. Without a solid source of light, their movements were more ungainly, less controlled.

Ban came after them very slowly, not wanting to give himself away before his people could move up on the far side and complete the trap. If he was too obvious, or came too close, they might bolt, and there was no way to predict what direction they would take, or how many would be injured in the process. If they chose the worst case, they would be among the resting places of the most ancient in a very short amount of time, and that he could not allow.

Janeway followed closely on Kim's heels. They had limited light, and they were wasting as little of it as possible. Ahead were more tunnels, all of them dark. The dust was rising as they passed, choking them, as they gulped down the already thinner air of the cavern. The billowing clouds blurred their vision further, confusing the already unfamiliar images that surrounded them. It was obvious that this was not a place that the Urrythans themselves came often, if ever. She guessed that no feet had trod the stones beneath hers for centuries. Perhaps millennia. It would have been an awe-inspiring journey, had it not been for the horde of fanatic Urrythans shadowing them from somewhere in the darkness behind.

The passageway itself was amazingly well preserved. There were niches in the walls that had presumably once held torches or some other source of light. The stonework was immaculate—smoothly chiseled and intricately worked. They passed a cistern, hollowed from the stone wall to their right, which was somehow fed from an underground stream. The water was cool and inviting, and each of them took the opportunity to rub some of the dust from their eyes and to clear parched throats as the others kept a watch on the passage behind them. They heard nothing, but that did not mean there was no one out there.

"Do you think they followed us, Captain?" Kim asked.

"I'm certain of it," Janeway replied. "They didn't chase us all the way to those gardens and ruins just to let us go when they finally have us cornered. Mr. Tuvok, are those readings any better in here?"

"That is negative, Captain. If anything, the life-force readings appear to be even more concentrated here in this cavern than they did above ground. There is absolutely no usable reading on any channel—for scanning, the tricorders are worthless. And the emanations are still growing in strength."

Janeway leaned toward the wall and placed her hand against it experimentally. It was vibrating slightly, and she believed she could even hear a muted hum. Just what was going on here, and what would it mean to the three of them, trapped as they were beneath the ground? If the strength of the vibration was growing in conjunction with the life-force readings, the whole place could come down around their heads.

Kim had moved to the far side of the passage where the base of one of the pillars protruded from the wall. He was kneeling in front of it, tricorder in hand, when he suddenly rose and turned.

"Captain!"

"Yes, what is it?" Janeway asked, moving quickly to his side. Tuvok did not join her, but turned in a slow circle, maintaining his vigil, sweeping his eyes up and down the length of the passage.

"Take a look at this," Kim said, holding his tricorder up so she could see what he'd been working on. "This message is more complete—different from the others. And look at that date. If this translation is correct, this pillar was constructed over ten thousand years ago."

Janeway listened to him on the periphery of her consciousness, but she was concentrating on the message on the tricorder's small screen. It was difficult to pay attention to what she was looking at *and* worry about the Urrythans on their heels.

"Here lies Lin, son of Les, brother to Mat," she read aloud. "He approaches the *Great Awakening* through the tunnel of the *Long Sleep* with open arms. He dreams and prepares for the coming wonder of *Ascension*. As his father before him, and in the hope that his brother will pass in his footsteps, Lin becomes one with the soil, reaching for the stars in repose as he will reach to them at the *Great Awakening*."

"This is much like the others," she commented, looking up. "Why do you find it so interesting?"

"Read on, Captain," Kim said eagerly. "What you just read came from the pillar. I found more, something completely different. The rest came from the stone *beside* the pillar——it would appear that Vok was either hiding something from us all along, or didn't know. I'm certain that no one has been here in years. Maybe he's never read these records——I wouldn't expect this sort of thing to be the favorite among the storytellers."

Janeway leaned back over the screen and scrolled down.

"This is to mark the passing of Mat, son of Les, brother to Lin, who was laid down for the final rest this day. He was denied the *Long Sleep* and stripped of the blessings of the *Ambiana*. He will never ascend, nor will he follow in the footsteps of Lin. May his soul rest in peace."

"Stripped of the *Ambiana* . . ." Janeway looked up quickly. "Then there is, or was, a way to reverse the effects. Possibly it's been lost over the years—— maybe they did away with the process. It certainly seems to be their most feared punishment."

"It would appear," Tuvok surmised, "that to a race who believed they would ascend to a greater level of existence, death on this level would be equivalent to eternal damnation."

Before they could continue their discussion, they became aware of the sounds of muted voices, of shuffling feet, both ahead and behind them. Their attackers were pouring down the passageway three abreast, and somehow they'd managed not only to catch up, but also to flank Janeway's small party and hem them in with no avenue of escape apparent.

Janeway put her back quickly against Tuvok's, and Kim stood with his back toward the wall between them. They began firing without hesitation, dropping the Urrythans as rapidly as they could fire, but falling behind almost as soon as they began. Janeway glanced down at her phaser. She was down to about a twenty-five-percent charge—not much left. She had to assume that the others' weapons were in similar condition.

There was no time for talk or discussion. Their attackers were closing in on them, using fallen comrades as cover, pouring from the shadows in a seemingly unending flood of slender sorrowful faces and long groping limbs. The situation was fast growing hopeless.

The vibration Janeway had felt earlier began to grow more violent, and dust and bits of crumbling stone began to filter down from the ceiling of the passage. The three could feel it against their backs, and they pulled away from the wall slightly.

"Captain!" Tuvok cried out. "I'm beginning to sense something, as Kes did earlier. The life-force is becoming so powerful that it is leaking into my mind."

Before they could discuss this new circumstance, a voice cut through the sounds of battle and the thrum of whatever force it was that now threatened to rip the place apart. That voice, though not extremely loud, was powerful—commanding.

"Stop!" At first the sound was too soft to make out, too weak, but somehow it blended itself with the vibration around them, echoing powerfully through the tunnel and causing a pause in the battle. "Stop at once!"

Janeway turned, looking back over the heads and shoulders of those attacking from her side—from deeper within the caverns and tunnels. A single figure stood, tall and proud, ignoring both the threat of phaser fire and the seemingly imminent collapse of the tunnels about them. An odd light leaped in the depths of his eyes, flickering through the semidarkness.

It was Vok. He walked slowly forward, his arms raised in a calming negating gesture. The light in his eyes blazed suddenly, and lines of concentration were etched into his face, as if he were fighting some titanic inner struggle.

"Ban," he called out. "I know you believe you are protecting your heritage, but you are wrong. You must let them go. We are on the verge . . ." Vok's voice choked up, and he staggered for a second, fighting for control. "On the verge of the *Awakening*. Here. Now. There must be no more discord, nothing but the harmony and the *One Voice*, or all that has gone before may be undone. Do you understand? You . . . might prevent . . . the *Awakening*."

He continued forward for about a half a step, sweeping his gaze in a wide arc over those facing him, then dropped to one knee. His eyes seemed to glaze as he fell toward the ground, and suddenly there were others at his side, those who'd only moments before been intent on overwhelming Janeway's small party, propping him up, holding him off the ground, and gesturing to their companions.

The attack was forgotten as quickly as it had begun, and Janeway found herself standing, facing a tall slender alien who seemed confused. He stared at her, then moved forward hesitantly. When he was closer, she saw that it was Ban, the one Vok had told her would be her contact among his people.

"The *Awakening*," he said reverently. "I'd never thought to actually live to see it—to experience it. Vok instructed us to leave you alone—that it was enough to bring your follower to enlightenment, and yet I would not listen. He didn't really want us to take her, I see now. I was so eager to be in charge, to lead the defense of my ancestors, that I forgot all of the lessons those ancestors passed down to me."

Janeway holstered her phaser and turned to the others. "We may not have much time to find our answers, now. I'm not certain that this tunnel is stable; let's get to work. If we can't find anything, then we'll have to count on The Doctor to come through on this one. I'd rather have something certain in my hand to take back."

Kim nodded, moving back toward the walls and the odd cryptic symbols, but Tuvok seemed entranced. He stood, staring back down the tunnel toward where Vok was being lifted gently to the shoulders of his followers.

"Tuvok," Janeway said softly, then again more urgently. "Tuvok!"

He turned slowly to face her, as though not really seeing what was before his eyes, then shook his head slowly and opened his mouth to speak.

"I . . ." He clamped his mouth shut and turned to where Kim was working.

"What is it, Tuvok," Janeway called after him. "What did you see—what did you feel?"

"I felt a very illogical urge, Captain, to lie down and sleep," he answered, not meeting her eyes. "It was a very *comfortable* sensation. I believe that I must keep myself busy, occupy my mind with the task at hand, or I may not be able to resist that urge a second time. The harmony is a very beautiful thing—I see now why they seek it so avidly."

Janeway stared at the back of her security officer's head. It was very unlike Tuvok to show a lack of control of any sort. She decided not to press the matter, and she followed her two officers to the wall. Time was running out, and the important thing was to find what they'd come this far to find and get out.

As she stepped toward the wall, however, time *did* run out. A long rippling crack, beginning somewhere in the depths of the tunnels and crackling along the stone floor, ripped between her and the others, and a chasm erupted beneath their feet, threatening to engulf everyone in the passage. Janeway jumped backward, reeling along the face of the wall, her arms pinwheeling wildly. Suddenly a side passage opened at her back, and she tumbled inside, losing sight of the main hall in the darkness and cracking her head painfully on the floor. Ignoring the pain, she scuttled farther in.

Across the way, Tuvok had done the same, reaching out to grab at Kim's arm—and missing. As the crevasse in the floor widened, Kim slipped over the edge, losing his footing in the loose stone and dust and scrabbling wildly at the wall for a grip, any sort of purchase on the crumbling face of the stone wall. Failing.

Janeway, who'd made her way to the opening in the wall once more, called out to him, and Tuvok dangled himself dangerously over the edge, but it was no use. Kim slipped down and away, and was quickly lost from sight in the rising cloud of dust and debris, a cry of shock and fear bursting forth from his lungs, then dying as he was engulfed in sound and vibration.

"Captain!"

Janeway struggled to hear Tuvok's words as he leaned out over the precipice again, calling out to her.

"Go farther in and try to make your way to the surface. I will attempt to do the same from here."

Across the brink, she nodded, tears stinging her eyes. Kim had been so young, so full of life and enthusiasm. As always upon losing one of her crew, she felt a quick stabbing pang of guilt, magnified by the closeness she'd felt for her young operations officer. She forced it aside. It was part of her job to be able to overcome such pain, to be able to set aside her emotions and carry on. Her responsibilities did not change with the loss of a single crew member, no matter how great the pain of his passing, and the rest of her people would need her—and Tuvok—to get through everything that was to come.

Turning quickly away to avoid the urge to clamber down after her lost officer, she ducked into the tunnels and began to run, banging off stone, hitting her head painfully more than once, trying to guess which trail slanted upward. When arms reached out, suddenly, circling her and bringing her to a halt, she cried out, reaching for her phaser.

"Please," came a voice from the darkness. "Let me help you. I will show you a way to the surface—I want to help."

She couldn't make out anything clearly in the darkness, but the voice was familiar somehow.

"Who are you?" she asked.

"It is Ban," he answered. "It is I who caused this; I am responsible for the attacks, for the destruction. Please, let me help."

She couldn't see him, and she had no way of knowing if he could see her, but she nodded. "If you can get me to the surface where I can reach my ship, I will be grateful," she told him.

He didn't speak again, but she felt his long slender fingers gripping her arm lightly, and a slight tug in the direction she'd been running. At least she'd been going the right direction.

What followed was a series of twists and turns that left her dizzy and disoriented. It occurred to her that it might be a deception, that he might just be leading her farther into the caverns to finish what he'd started, but there was something in the tone of his voice, something in the urgency of his movements and his grip on her arm, that told her differently. For whatever reason, he'd had a change of heart, decided that Vok was right.

Ahead, she saw a faint glow that quickly grew to a circle of light. An exit.

"This will bring you out near the place where your people landed," Ban told her, releasing her arm. "I must return. If the *Awakening* is truly to happen, then I do not wish to miss it, unworthy as I am of such a joy."

"My people," Janeway said. "Two of my officers are still down there, one probably dead—and you are still holding Ensign Kayla hostage."

"The one you call Kayla is being prepared for her *Long Sleep,*" Ban said wearily. "It may be, even now, too late to prevent that. The other two, those in the tunnels, I sent my own followers after them, but I do not know if they have made it out."

The sound of rending stone rose from beneath them, and a roaring filled the air. Janeway spun to stare out at the sunlight beyond the tunnel. She realized suddenly that it was the same sound as the vibration—the *One Voice,* rising to a crescendo of sound she wouldn't have believed possible. She turned back to where Ban had been standing, but the tall alien was gone.

With nothing left to gain from the tunnels, she turned and raced for the surface, praying that the others had somehow found a way off the planet, and that she could do so herself.

As she exited the tunnel, tumbling to the grass outside and lying, panting and gasping for breath on the violently unstable ground, she slapped futilely at her commbadge.

"Janeway to *Voyager.*"

At first she heard nothing, then through a crackle of static, she heard an answer, growing stronger. Was she hearing things?

"Captain!" It was Chakotay's voice. "We've launched probes, working within the harmonic resonance of the life-force. Remain stationary and we should be able to lock on to your coordinates in a few moments."

"Janeway, standing by," she answered, then slumped back to the ground and waited, trying not to think of Kim or Tuvok, trying not to lose the control she so badly needed. Moments later her form shimmered, then faded, and she was on board, rising from the transporter pad.

They were waiting for her with an injection of The Doctor's antidote. They made as if to escort her toward Medical, and she pulled free roughly, her jaw set in a grim line of determination.

Stone-faced, she said, "Get me to the bridge."

CHAPTER
13

As Paris and Kes made their way deeper down the darkened passage, the sounds of a battle floated up to them through the shadows up ahead. They hurried as much as possible, but the possibility of being discovered before they could be of any help was too great to allow for much speed. Their lack of familiarity with the tunnels hindered them as well, though the beam of Paris's light clearly marked where a great number of feet had passed before them (some Starfleet, some not). There were a great number of the Urrythans, and Paris noted two places, one to either side of the passage, where the natives' footprints diverged from the main path. A smaller group continued ahead as before.

"Looks like the Urrythans learn quickly," he commented. He pointed the beam of light to where the footprints headed off to one side. "It seems that some of our friends have moved around to set up an ambush."

Turning back to the main passage, he started forward again. "I hope the captain was ready for them."

Neither of them wanted to contemplate the other possibility. It was one thing to catch up and help the captain in a fight, quite another to have to follow her and free her from captivity or, worse yet, deal with the deaths of their friends.

They were encouraged by the sounds of battle that now reached them. The phaser fire was constant, so they weren't overwhelmed—yet. It seemed that their companions had not been caught completely off guard.

The stone floor and walls were beginning to vibrate, and the dust and debris falling all around them was starting to make Paris nervous. The vibration was sending an odd tingling sensation up his legs and into his spine. It seemed, almost, as if he could feel it all the way into his brain.

"It sounds like the whole place is falling apart," he said, spitting the words out like a curse. "We could've picked a better place to end up if there's going to be a quake."

"Not falling apart," Kes said, her voice far away and dreamy. "Awakening. The voice of the planet is growing stronger, more all-encompassing. There is such a joy in it—such release and celebration. What you feel is each cell—each separate note of the harmony reaching out and blending, weaving into a single note."

"Well," Paris commented dryly, "we won't be celebrating anything if we don't hurry up and get out of here. They can have all the harmony they want, but I wish they'd keep the volume to a safe level."

Ahead, the phaser fire stopped suddenly, leaving them with only the humming of the walls and their own rasping breath to break the silence of the passageway. Paris's heart lurched. Had they been overcome? Was he too late? He fairly flew down the passage, trying to eat up the distance between himself and whatever was happening ahead. He was so intent on his steps and his labored breathing, that he didn't notice the crack forming in the floor.

"Tom," Kes cried, "look out!"

He dove to one side at the last second, just as the stone beneath where he'd been standing disappeared in a steadily widening gap. Kes had caught up to him as he stumbled to the side, and he grabbed her by her arm, pulling her upright once more and dragging her into a darkened hole that opened to the right of him. They fell together, tumbling into darkness and chaos as the falling collapsing stone floor behind them raised huge clouds of dust to block what little visibility there had been before.

He could hear cries and screams from the tunnel beyond their own position, but he couldn't make any of it out. The sound was too distant, and the roar of the avalanche of stone and dust was still ringing in his ears, accentuated by the ever-strengthening humming sounds from the walls. He couldn't even tell if any of the voices he heard belonged to their own people or to the Urrythans; the noise surrounding them was just too overpowering.

He held Kes close, trying to protect her with his body as slightly larger bits of stone dropped free. There wasn't as much stone falling in the side passage, though, and a few moments later, though the steady thrumming vibration did not cease, the tunnels and the earth beneath them seemed to reach a state of equilibrium. There were still clouds of dust in the air, and occasional stones fell from the walls, but it did not seem as though the roof was going to fall in immediately.

"Let's go," Paris said, leaping to his feet and making his way back to the mouth of the tunnel he'd dragged them into. He stopped at the lip, playing his light down over the sides of the newly formed chasm that spanned most of what had been the tunnel's floor. It was deep, deeper than he'd have believed possible. He shuddered once, thinking of how they might have ended up had they been a couple of steps slower in diving to the side.

Along the length of the chasm's walls he could see the bases of the tall ancient pillars, lined up like giant silent sentinels. The crack in the earth seemed to have ended right at their base, as if it were clearing a space around them.

Beneath the floor of the tunnel, he could see more ruins, leading downward from where he stood. It was obvious that the network of tunnels they'd been traveling through had been built atop the ruins of previous civilizations. Crumbling doorways led off into deeper recesses, and there were stairs twisting and twining among the pillars, windows leading to great halls and chambers.

Paris was momentarily reminded of some old files he'd been scanning through on *Voyager,* art prints from Earth. . . . A man named Escher. The stairs seemed, at times, to lead to nowhere, ending where the next level would have been before the chasm opened up. Doors opened into thin air, and odd architectural mixes showed through where one generation's ruins bled into the next.

Then he leaned forward farther, squinting into the gloom. He'd seen movement below. Leaning dangerously far over the edge, he tried to pierce the shadows, tried to make out what it was that had caught his eye, but it was just beyond his sight.

"Kes," he said, "do you see something there?"

He pointed, and she followed—peering carefully over the edge. She didn't so much see the figure dangling from the ledge below as sense him. She reached out with her mind, probing, and the image became clearer. *Kim.* It was Kim, and he was in trouble.

"That's Harry," she said, backing away from the edge. "We have to get him out of there. He's on a small ledge, but I'm not certain how stable that ledge is. If he falls to the bottom of this pit, he'll never survive."

Paris had to think fast. He'd not come in prepared for a mountain rescue, but he did have a bit more equipment with him than he would normally have brought. Since they'd left the shuttle with no clear idea of when they'd return, he'd packed some survival gear. Among it was a length of synthetic line—he only hoped that it would be enough. He had some experience rock-climbing, as well, though he'd never expected it to pay off in quite so dramatic a fashion.

Leaning back over the edge of the chasm, he called out, "Harry, can you hear me? Are you all right?"

He could just make out a slight movement in the shadows below, and finally, a weak reply. "I . . . I think so. Can you get me out of here?"

"I'm going to try!" Paris shouted back. "Just hang on."

Turning to Kes, he said, "We're going to have to try and work our way down along this wall. If we can get directly above him, we might be able to reach him with the line. If not, I'm going to have to try climbing partway down and bring him up one step at a time. You'll have to stay up here on top to help us both out."

Kes nodded, the immediacy of their current task bringing back the alert shine to her eyes. She was sensitive to what was going on around her, but she was not under the planet's influence. Paris breathed a little easier. For a moment, as he'd watched her face and she'd described the sensation of the planet "awakening," he'd thought she might be about to check out on him. With Harry dangling over a cliff and the planet shaking down around his shoulders, it was good not to be alone.

They scrambled out of the mouth of their side tunnel, clinging to the shaking wall, and made their way carefully along the side. There was just enough of a lip left from the main passageway that they could shuffle along if they kept a good grip on the stone wall. Paris nearly slipped more than once, feeling the loose stone beneath his feet give way and tumble into the abyss below. His heart was hammering at double-time, and the sweat dripped down from his hair, which was soaked and matted to his forehead, to burn in the corners of his eyes.

Ahead, just at the mouth of a larger secondary tunnel, he could see that there was a ledge—wider than that across which they were climbing, and he made that his goal. He needed to get his feet firmly beneath him again, and he needed to do it soon. The sweat was making his fingers slippery, and the constant vibration of the walls was numbing him, tickling at his concentration.

Kes was following with surprising ease. Her smaller frame and lithe muscles lent her a grace on the tiny ledge that his frame and weight would not allow for. She nimbly scooted along in his wake, avoiding the spots where he broke loose fresh stone and finding handholds on seemingly smooth stone. After what seemed an eternity, they stood side by side on the ledge looking into the chasm. Paris took a deep breath, calming his nerves, and wiped the sweat from his brow with one sleeve.

From their present position, Kim was clearly visible beneath them. He was standing, looking up with his eyes shielded against falling debris. Paris saw that his friend was pressed tightly against the stone wall, as if he feared that the edges of his ledge might break free at any moment and plunge him to his death. He didn't appear to be too steady on his feet, either, and that made Tom nervous.

Working quickly, he opened the pack he'd been carrying and rummaged about until he found the length of line. It was thin and lightweight, taking up little room in the pack, but he knew that the small coil would be deceptively long. Due to the strength of the fiber, a greater length could be carried with less effort. It would hold the weight of two grown men easily—a fact he'd learned at the Academy, but that had now taken on important implications. The only question was the length; it was long, but would it be long enough?

He stuck his head over the edge and called out, "Harry, I'm going to lower a rope. When it reaches you, let me know."

Then he began to lower the line over the side of the precipice, hand over hand. The near end of it he secured to his belt to be certain he didn't drop it over the side. The shaking in the walls, while it didn't appear at that particular moment to be bringing the walls down, made him nervous. He didn't want any sudden lurch or shift in the earth to startle him into a mistake that could cost his friend's life . . . or his own.

He reached the end of what line he had available, and he'd heard nothing from Kim. Kes leaned over the edge and peered into the shadowy darkness, playing her light about the ledge below. She swept the beam over the stone wall beneath them, and she saw the line dangling, just out of Kim's reach.

"It's about two meters short," she said, pulling

herself back up. "We've got to find a way to get it lower."

"Harry," Paris called out. "That's all the line we have. Is there any way you can make it up higher—another ledge, anything? It's not far."

There was a moment's silence, then Kim called out hesitantly, "I don't think so, Tom. There's a ledge about ten meters up, but I don't think I can make it that far. I've twisted my right knee—that leg's pretty worthless."

Kim sounded cheerful enough, but there was a quaver to his voice that told Paris things were not as good as his friend was making out.

Cursing under his breath, Paris reeled in the rope and coiled it back up, then stuck his head over the side and scanned the sides of the crevasse directly beneath him. There was a ledge about five meters down, large enough to hold two bodies. He wasn't certain if it was stable, but then he wasn't certain that the ledge he was already on was stable, so it made little difference. Besides, the entire mountain was going to fall on them all if he didn't act and do so swiftly. That ledge would just have to do.

"I'm going down to that ledge," he said, turning back to Kes and pointing to the small space he'd spotted. "I want you to lower me with the line, in case I slip." Looking around quickly, he found a rounded outcropping of stone. He wrapped the line twice around this, gave the coiled length to Kes, and attached the free end about his waist. Then he dangled a length of the line over his shoulder and up through his legs, ready to play it out slowly, using his own weight and the force of gravity to keep him from sliding down too quickly.

"Pull it tight," he told her. When he was satisfied that the line would hold, he gave Kes a quick little salute and a nervous smile and leaped backward over the edge, beginning his descent.

"Tom," she called after him. He hesitated, looking up to meet her gaze. "Be careful," she said softly.

He nodded, then returned his attention to his descent. He'd done some rapelling in his Academy days, but it wasn't something he'd had a lot of chances to pursue in the interim. He found himself wishing he'd spent a bit more time on the holodecks honing those old skills. Something to keep in mind when, or if, he made it back to *Voyager*.

He moved carefully, but quickly, letting his weight support him against the pressure of his legs against the stone wall, dropping him bit by bit. Kes was doing admirably on her end of the line. It came free slowly as he descended, always providing the drag he needed to hold himself steady after each successive jump downward. In only a few moments he'd managed to cover the short distance to the ledge.

He experienced a brief moment of vertigo, looking down from where he now stood. The walls and pillars rose around him, shooting up to what seemed impossible heights and down to staggering shadowed depths. Below he could see Kim clearly now and the ledge his friend stood on, which was a bit smaller than his own. He didn't have a lot of room to work with, but it would have to be enough.

He groped about the wall behind him and found

what he needed, another protrusion of stone. Even with the pressure he could apply in lifting, Kim was going to have to help, or they'd never get him up.

"Okay, buddy," he said, "I'm going to lower this line to you now, and I want you to get it around your waist. You with me?"

Kim's features were white and strained, but he nodded. It was obvious that he was fighting the pain in his leg. He was leaning heavily against the stone wall, favoring the wounded leg. He was putting on a good show of strength, but it was obvious that there wasn't much left of his normally endless energy.

Paris began to lower the rope over the edge again, praying that his friend would be able to climb out once he had the loose end in his hands. If not, he was nearly certain that he would not be able to lift him, and with the line too short for Kes to secure it and lower him, he couldn't go down after him, either.

It seemed to take an eternity for the line to reach Kim, and a second for him to work it around his waist and secure it. When he was finally finished, he called up to Paris, who took a deep breath and got a tight hold on the line. He'd already located another stone outcropping, one that seemed sturdy enough, and he'd wrapped the line around this for support. Kes had dropped the entire line to him, so he had plenty to work with.

"All right," he said, trying to sound as cheerful and confident as possible. "I'm going to need your help, here, Harry. . . . Have you done any rock climbing?"

"A little," Kim answered shakily.

"Well, here's your chance to get in a little practice. Don't make any sudden moves. Test your handholds carefully—you're going to need to trust them with that leg bad as it is."

He kept talking. Though he knew Kim really didn't need his instructions to make the climb, he knew also that the younger man would be frightened and suffering from at least a minor case of shock. There was no way of knowing how many other injuries he might have sustained that he wasn't yet aware of. The constant flow of words was meant to help keep them both calm, to keep Kim's mind off the chasm falling away beneath him, and to bolster Paris's own sagging confidence.

The rope went tight in his hand, and Paris concentrated. He felt a bit of slack, and he knew that Kim must have begun his ascent. Pulling the line taut again, he held it tightly, waiting for more slack. He wanted desperately to look over the edge and monitor Kim's progress, but it wasn't possible. That might overbalance him and plunge them both to their deaths. All he could do was to lean against the stone, putting his weight on the line in case of an emergency, and pray.

It wasn't a situation that he was well prepared for; he was used to being on his own, depending on and worrying about himself alone. Now he had Kim to look out for, and Kes up above, waiting for him to lead the way back to the planet's surface and get them out of there.

Kim's progress was excruciatingly slow, but steady. After what seemed hours, but was obviously only a few minutes, Paris heard boots scraping against stone and heavy labored breathing.

"Just a little bit farther," he called out. "Slow and steady. We've got time."

He wondered, though, just how much time. The vibrations in the walls showed signs of growing in intensity again, and it might be only a matter of moments before the ledge he was standing on plummeted to the floor of the chasm below. He blanked this thought from his mind. As first one, then the other of Kim's hands reached over the edge of the ledge, he tightened the rope a final time, cinching it in place, and scrambled to the edge to pull his friend up beside him.

Kim collapsed in a heap, shivering as if with fever and trembling from the effort of his climb. Paris wasted no time.

"I'm sending the line back up to you, Kes," Paris called out. He released the line from around his waist and threw the free end of the rope up at an angle. It fell back to him, and he threw it again.

A moment later Kes called out, "I've got it."

"I'm sending Kim up first," Paris said. To Kim, he added, "It isn't very much farther, old buddy. You'll be up there before you know you started climbing. Are you ready?"

Kim looked anything but ready, but he grinned up at Paris gamely. "I'll do my best," he said. "I got this far."

Then he was on his feet, and all talk ceased. Paris grabbed under Kim's shoulders and helped to hold him erect as he groped for his first hand hold, beginning the painfully slow process again.

He could do nothing. It was up to Kim now, and Kes, who was slowly tightening the line from above, waiting, then tightening it again. She would not be able to pull Kim over the ledge above, as he himself had done, and Kim was tired. As far as they'd managed to come, the last five meters might prove more than they could manage, and he could tell by the growing strength of the tremors beneath his feet that time was a luxury they were not going to have.

"Come on, Harry," he said softly. "You can do this . . . I know you can."

And he was right. Somehow, Kim found the energy to scramble up the last few feet, and the rope was suddenly dangling back over the edge, directly in his face. He didn't hesitate. Wrapping the line about his waist, he fastened it securely and began his ascent. He was in a hurry, and he nearly slipped twice, but it was only a short climb, and moments later he was pulling himself over the ledge and dropping to the ground beside Kim's prone form.

"Let's go, buddy," he said. Standing, he wrapped Kim's arm around his shoulder and headed quickly into the tunnel ahead. He didn't know exactly where they were going, but he thought this was a bad time to bring that up. Either they would make it, or they would not—no need to bring up all the negative points that weren't painfully obvious.

They'd been moving for about ten minutes, and the passage ahead branched to the right and left, when they heard the voice. Paris spun quickly, his phaser at the ready, but he did not fire. There was no need.

"Please," the tall Urrythan said softly, standing before them with his hands upraised in a placating gesture. "There is so little time. I will take you to the surface, to your craft, if you will let me."

It was like something from a bad holovid, but Paris had no other options available. With a nod, he holstered his phaser and wrapped Kim's arm about his shoulder again.

"Lead on, friend," he said, hoping he wasn't making a big mistake. "We can use all the help we can get."

With a quick nod, the being turned and started off down the left fork of the trail. Paris followed, moving slowly as he supported much of Kim's weight. Kes moved close at his side, not speaking, but watching everything carefully. He noticed that the faraway expression was gone from her eyes. She seemed alert and ready, and he appreciated the support, though he wasn't certain how much good it could do them. One thing about her ability to sense what was up with the planet and its inhabitants was that she would have known if the alien were trying to trick them.

The sunlight ahead was like a dream, and Paris moved forward into it. He heard their guide speaking, but he paid little attention. All he caught were the important points. They would be free of the tunnels in a few moments, and they would be near the shuttle. They would have a chance.

Then the voice fell silent, and a moment later he

realized that they were alone. It didn't matter. They broke free into the lush greenery of Urrytha, and he gave a small cheer. Kim joined in half-heartedly, and Kes only stared at him, but he ignored them both. They had a chance.

Without a word, he started off down the trail toward the shuttle. The ground thrummed beneath them with energy and imminent—something. He wasn't certain that he wanted to know what that something was, but he *was* certain that when it happened he did not want to be a part of it. He wanted his console, free space, and a clear shot at *Voyager*.

Without really believing that it would do any good, he reached over with his free hand and slapped at his commbadge.

"Paris to *Voyager*," he croaked weakly.

When the answering voice returned over the circuit, he staggered, nearly dropping Kim to the ground.

"Mr. Paris, is that you?" Miraculously, it was Captain Janeway's voice.

"Yes, Captain," he replied. "I guess I have a few questions."

"They'll have to wait, Mr. Paris. Get aboard that shuttle and get up here. Now."

"Yes, Captain." Paris grinned. Then he remembered and added, "By the way . . . I'm happy to report that I have a certain young Ensign and a beautiful blond medical assistant here with me."

Kes smiled at him, and Kim managed a weak grin.

"Come on," Paris said. "Let's go home."

CHAPTER
14

THE PROBE THAT HAD MANAGED TO CONTACT BOTH
Janeway and Paris had not been the only one
launched. There were others, spread out across the
surface of Urrytha, placed so that the widest area
could be covered in the search for their crew members. There was a large gap in time from their last
contact, and considering the situation on the planet
below, there was no telling what might have happened, or where they might have gone or been taken.

While Chakotay was briefing the captain on everything that had transpired since she'd disappeared
into the jungle, Torres was feverishly continuing the
search for the others. She could have delegated a lot
of what she was doing—almost any member of her
engineering department could have conducted the
monitoring as accurately and professionally, but she
felt the responsibility to do it all personally. Harry

Kim and Tom Paris were down there, and against all the odds, the two had become her friends. She was determined not to let them down.

After a lot of playing with the frequencies, she managed to detect a ripple near the settlement in the desert, where they'd first spotted the aliens. Fine-tuning on that signal, she directed one of the probes in closer. What she was looking for was the signature of a commbadge, any of those that were missing. With the planet's own signal blending all life-signs to one, it was literally impossible that she would be able to beam anyone out by locking on to their own form. If she could get the commbadge, though, they could get them out. All she needed was coordinates, and she intended to get them.

The signal reception clarified somewhat, and she was able to make out that there were several distinct signals, but every time she tried to lock on to a particular one, the interference shifted. It was much worse in this area than it had been in the jungle with Janeway. She realized that she must not be as close to the source of the signals, because once the captain had called in, it had been only a matter of moments to lock on and get her out of there.

It was also possible that the nature of the harmonic signals in the jungle had been easier to navigate because the life-force signal in that area—the harmony, as Kes had called it—was more pure in nature. Once a harmonic had been achieved, there had been little or no variance, and B'Elanna had been able to work around that frequency without causing any more of a ripple in the overall signal than the Urrythans themselves did in their passing. Her signals were dampened, but not overpowered.

Just for an instant, a familiar signal flitted across her viewscreen, then vanished. With a small exclamation, she began searching for it, adjusting the sensitivity of her scanners and leaning closer over the controls, as if her proximity to the equipment could somehow cow it into submission. The signal was gone, but she knew what it had been. Kayla. That signal had been Kayla's commbadge.

"Captain," she called out. "I know the general area where they're holding Ensign Kayla."

"Well, get her out of there, then," Janeway said quickly.

"It isn't that simple, Captain," Torres said. Quickly she explained about the shifting frequencies and the interference levels. "Unless we can somehow get in there and administer that antidote, which should drag Kayla free of the *One Voice,* then I don't think we'll be able to get her out of there by transporter.

"Even if I could pinpoint her location, the chance of the signal breaking up is just too great. We could lose her before we ever got her off the planet. And the life-force is still increasing steadily. The stronger that signal grows, the less likely I'll be able to pick her out of it."

Janeway bit her lip. "I don't want to send anyone else down there," she said at last. "There's been too much loss already. Are we still in touch with Paris?"

"Yes, Captain," Fowler called out from the operations console. "They're just about to liftoff from the planet's surface."

"Hail him," she said, staring up at the viewscreen.

Moments later Paris's voice crackled over the line. "Paris here."

"Mr. Paris," Janeway said wearily, "are you up for one more rescue mission? We've managed to pinpoint the general area where Ensign Kayla is being held captive, and we need you to get in there and get her out. Without that antidote in her system, she's as invisible to our scanners and transporter as the Urrythans themselves."

"I suppose so, Captain," he replied slowly, "but Kim needs to be beamed directly to Sickbay. His knee is sprained, at the very least, and he's in a lot of pain."

"Have you administered the antidote?" Janeway asked quickly.

"As soon as we got to the shuttle, Kes took care of it," Paris replied. "You should be able to lock on to his signal in a few seconds."

Torres nodded.

"Janeway to Transporter Room," she barked, "Get him out of there. Doctor, we're beaming Ensign Kim directly to Sickbay." Then she returned her attention to Paris. "What about Kes?"

"If we're going in after Kayla, Captain," Kes answered for herself, "then I'd like to go along. Tom will need me to administer the antidote, and I seem to be the only one of us with any ability to sense the

Urrythans, particularly since the *One Voice* has grown so much more powerful. With the tricorders inoperative, I'd feel better doing what I can."

"Very well," Janeway said. Neelix was bobbing up and down at her shoulder, but she managed somehow to ignore him for the moment. "Mr. Paris, we've managed to locate the general area where they've taken Kayla by using these probes that B'Elanna has devised, but we can't get a strong enough locking signal to risk beaming her out. I need you to get in there and either get her or get that antidote into her so we can lock on to her signal. If you take one of the probes with you, you should be able to get it close enough for us to get a good lock."

"Right," Paris replied.

"We'll enter the coordinates into your computer. And Mr. Paris?"

"Yes, Captain?"

"Good luck."

Neelix would be ignored no longer.

"Captain, I *insist* that you send me to that shuttle. Kes may believe that she is ready for such a dangerous mission, but I assure you, I am a much better choice. I have more experience in this quadrant than anyone, and I . . ."

"Neelix, you're just going to have to trust me on this," Janeway said with a tired smile. "I assure you, Kes knows what she is doing. As for yourself, your courage is admirable, but I believe your services may well be needed here, and I can't risk sending anyone else down there. Besides, I don't know what happened down in that tunnel, but I don't believe these people mean us any further harm. They are too caught up in this *Awakening* to spare us much concentration."

"But, Captain . . ." Neelix began.

"I'm sorry, Mr. Neelix. With all the interference this planet generates, we can't be certain we could beam you to the shuttle in one piece. I know we got Kim out, but they are already moving, and locking on to them from those probes while they are stationary, and while they are in flight, are two different things altogether. You'll just have to wait with the rest of us."

Neelix bowed his head in barely controlled frustration, but then he nodded.

"One more thing, Mr. Neelix," Janeway added, her voice softening.

"Yes, Captain?"

Looking into his eyes so that he might read the sincerity in her own, she said, "I don't know the beliefs of your people, but if you have such a thing as prayer, now might be a good time to do it."

Paris dipped the nose of the shuttle back toward the planet and headed in. Kes was silent beside him, tuned in once more to the "voice" of the planet beneath them.

"Something is going to happen," she said softly. "Something wonderful. Can't you feel it?"

Paris didn't take his eyes off the viewscreen, but he answered, "No. I don't feel anything, but I believe that you do. I felt the vibration in that tunnel—and I saw the cracks in the stone—but I can't *feel* things the way you do."

"I'll try and describe it," she said. "It's as though the air itself was alive. I can sense your mind when you are near, but unless I concentrate on it, it's no more than a mild sensation at the periphery of my senses. This is different. This sensation is like one great mind, and it presses at me from all sides, intrudes into my senses without conscious effort on my part. It is so soothing, so calming and comfortable, that it is difficult to make myself force it away."

"Don't you be giving in to any alien mind-signals on me," Paris said, grinning. "I'm going to need all the help I can get in a few minutes here."

They were skimming along atop the tops of trees, sending flocks of birds fluttering off in all directions and dispersing the cloudy mist. The gardens still stretched out for some ways, and they needed to get beyond them and into the desert beyond. Paris sped up gradually, gliding along at an altitude that gave him quick glimpses, here and there, through the dense foliage below. They passed over several groups of the ruins they'd explored earlier, and he couldn't help but wonder if it was something similar to that which was happening below that had caused the destruction in the first place.

Kes had grown silent and meditative, and he decided not to interrupt whatever thoughts were occupying her. Instead he concentrated on the con-

trols and the terrain, zeroing in quickly on the area
the captain had indicated.

Kayla lay as still and silent as a sculpture in
alabaster. The color had drained from her already-
pale features as her metabolism slowed. The altar
upon which she rested was surrounded on all sides
by the blossoms of the *Ambiana,* fresh cut and
fragrant, replenished and replaced as they shriveled
and died. The air about her swam with the pollen—
was alive with it.

Around the altar, seated with legs crossed and
heads bent, were a dozen or so of the aliens. They
were singing softly, each a different note, a different
cadence and sequence of tones, and yet all of them
blended to a cohesive beautiful whole. It was as it
had ever been. Long years had passed since an elder
had reached the *Long Sleep,* and never had it been
reached by an outsider, or any so young as Kayla,
and yet the ceremony had suffered not at all from the
lapsed time.

The singers were there to usher her into the *One
Voice,* to wrap her deeply in the harmony and weave
her into its fabric. It would not have been possible
for any to accomplish this were it not for the ritual,
and the *Ambiana.* The proximity of the flowers, over
a long period of meditation, had brought these
twelve to a closeness with their ancestors that they
would never experience again until the hour of their
own *Long Sleep* arrived.

Each cadence of the ritual song, learned from

birth, one segment per child, was necessary to complete the whole. Each part was incomplete without the combination of all the others. Together, they reached perfect communion with the *One Voice,* and with Kayla prone between them, they were able to drag her into that sound—that "voice" created out of all their voices combined.

In her mind, what had been Ensign Kayla of the *Starship Voyager* was far, far away. She had retreated to a small warm place—an inner hideaway her mind had erected as a last bastion against the seductive pull of the aliens' song. On some deep primal level, she yearned to be a part of it, to give in and become one with that other, so insistent, so compelling. It was that fact—that there seemed to be only one other—that bothered her.

If she gave in to the insinuating comfort of the voice that intruded in her mind, she would be lost. There would not be her voice and the *One Voice,* but the *One Voice* alone, and Kayla would exist no more. She understood that it was an interval—a time between being and being transformed—but it did not matter. What arose after immersion in that single harmonic chord would never be what had entered in. Kayla would never rise again as Kayla, nor would she, in all probability, recall having ever *been* a being called Kayla.

It was that thin film of reason that was left to her, the desire to retain her individuality, to not be immersed in, then dissolved in, the whole. An alien whole. As comfortable as it felt, as beautiful as the harmony was, as certain—even—as it all made her that she could be a part of it, it was still not of her own people. It was not a way meant for her. She knew this, and she clung to it.

The aliens were unaware of her struggle. This was a moment of magic for them, a chance to taste that which was to come in their own lives—a bit of their version of Heaven on Earth. They would sit, and they would sing—continuing in an unbroken litany—until the ceremony reached its end and Kayla went to her *Long Sleep*. Completely.

That would not be for them to say—only Vok would know. Of them all, only Vok was close enough to the elders to know the truth in an initiate's heart. His own time was upon him, and he was away from them much of the time now—in his mind—communing with those who slept.

The singers did not even know that Vok had departed their midst, and those who were not part of the chant, who stood watch and waited for the return of Ban—and now for Vok, as well—grew nervous at the length of time their leaders had been absent. When Ban had left, he'd been very certain of quick and decisive removal of the alien problem. They had believed him—he spoke as one who knows.

Now with his return delayed more than three times what they estimated should have been adequate, what remained of his followers could not help but wonder what might have happened to detain him. Had he underestimated the star travelers? Had he met with them or fought with them? Could they have bested him? None of these was a question that they were equipped to consider on any practical level, though the questions—for all that—would leave them no peace.

And the ground had begun to tremble. They all sensed the source, the elders, but only those who sang—oblivious to their surroundings—knew the true import of the subtle vibrations, growing, shaking the foundations of home and mountain alike. The others feared trouble—feared the aliens. When Paris's shuttle appeared on the horizon, skimming rapidly above the desert like a great metal bird, the sentries ran gibbering into the midst of their fellows.

There was none left who might serve as leader. There were none who would face the invaders. Ban must have been defeated—possibly gone to the true death. This thought brought shudders and moans of fear.

As the Urrythans cowered and whispered among themselves, the singers continued their lonely vigil. As Paris touched down, just beyond the confines of the village, and clambered out of the shuttle, followed closely by Kes, the ground began to shake more violently, dropping loose stones from the buildings of the village and sending pots and implements crashing from shelves and tables.

The Urrythans didn't know if Paris was responsible for the quaking of the earth or not. Their senses told them he was not, but they were frightened, and disharmony was growing in their midst. They were cut off from the *One Voice,* helpless and alone. Paris and Kes began to advance slowly on their settlement, and they allowed it, scooting back toward the entrances to the caverns, abandoning posts and watching warily. What else could they do?

Paris didn't trust the silence. The probe *Voyager* had beamed to them before they reentered the atmosphere was now in place, halfway from the shuttle to the village, and throughout the entire operation of setting it up and testing it, they'd not seen a single one of the tall sorrowful Urrythans. Paris had worked with his concentration divided between the probe's controls and the small settlement, but it was a waste of time. Unless they were gathering their forces for some sort of attack, or waiting in ambush, the village's inhabitants were ignoring him.

"They are near," Kes told him, sweeping her gaze across what was visible of the settlement slowly. "I can sense their presence, their fear, but it is not like the larger combined voice of the planet. Each of them has a similar feel, like something that isn't quite complete, or not quite on the same wavelength—different enough from the *One Voice* for me to detect. Like imperfect stitches in a large tapestry."

"Why don't they show themselves, then," Paris wondered. "There are only two of us. Surely we don't make such an imposing image that they are afraid."

"They *are* frightened," Kes said suddenly, as if some vital piece of a puzzle had just snapped into place. "There are none of their leaders here. They must still be making their way back here from the caverns, if they weren't caught in the same quake that nearly got Kim and the others. They don't know what is causing the tremors—they may believe that *we* are responsible."

"What about Kayla?" Paris asked quickly. "Can you sense her as well?"

"No," Kes replied with a frown, "not exactly, but do you hear that sound?"

Paris stopped moving toward the village and craned his neck, listening. He did hear it, very low, a tune of some sort, like a chant or a very regular repetitive melody. Somehow the rumbling of the earth beneath his feet did not detract from it. It was as though the rhythm of the earthquake was somehow synchronized with the music. It was singing— and it was coming from somewhere deep in the settlement ahead.

"That must be the ceremony Vok mentioned," Kes said quickly. "He said that they were preparing Kayla for her *Long Sleep*. We have to stop them before there is nothing left of her individual mind. Come on."

She began moving ahead again, confidently, ignoring the fact that they were walking into an alien village full of potentially hostile enemies. Paris reached out, as if to restrain her, then, with a shrug, followed. She appeared so confident, so sure of her safety, that it was infectious. Besides, he didn't have any better plan in mind. It was difficult to get used to being around someone who had senses he did not, or, at the very least, senses he did not know how to use.

They slipped through the gate of the low-slung stone fence that surrounded the outermost buildings and into the dusty empty streets beyond. The oddness of the structures that lined the way on both sides struck Paris immediately. All of the buildings were tall and thin, as if someone had taken a group of perfectly normal homes, heated them up, and when they melted, dragged each up and stretched it. The windows were set in the walls just above the level of his eyes, and the doors stretched a good twelve feet in the air. It was familiar enough to be eerie, with all the perspectives skewed by the Urrythans' greater height. He also noticed that the walls were thick, the windows heavily shuttered and shaded. It appeared that even while above ground, they avoided the light as much as possible.

The music grew louder as they progressed. He thought, every once in a while, that he heard an individual voice among the layers of the chord, but each time it occurred, the sound slipped back away and blended itself into the whole. It was an amazing sound, captivating on deeper levels than any music he'd previously been exposed to. It was a revelation to understand the power that was *possible* from musical sound alone.

Then they smelled the flowers. Kes recognized the scent immediately and stopped Paris. "It is *Ambiana,*" she explained quickly. "It doesn't seem to have any effect on me, and it won't affect you, even in such a high concentration, with the antidote already in your system."

Paris nodded, taking a deep breath and rolling his

eyes heavenward for support. It was one thing to bring a cure to the planet for a group of *other* people who had been infected with an odd alien illness—quite another to walk right into the chemical that had produced that illness and trust your life to a drug that had only been developed that same day. They knew it had reversed the effects in the short term, but was it really a cure?

Only one way to find out, he thought grimly. *Here's to you, Doc . . . hope you knew what you were doing.*

As they moved farther in, Paris could see that the road opened up into a wider space ahead, like a square or ceremonial area of some sort. The sound of the chanting was growing in strength as they moved more deeply into the small settlement.

"There?" he asked.

Kes nodded. The sound surrounded them now, teasing at their minds. Even Paris could sense it. He could see that Kes was walking through it as if it were a physical thing. Her motions were slow and dreamy, as if she were walking through deep water. He moved closer to her, watching closely.

He was ready to get her out of there if she showed any sign of being controlled by the sound or by the pollen that surrounded them. He knew she was more sensitive to what was happening than he, and that could be a liability as well as an asset. On top of that, he could feel the sounds itching and tickling at his own control, and the urge to just stand still and become lost in the song was stronger than he'd have liked to admit.

Kes seemed to be fine, though, and a few moments

later, they entered the square. It appeared that, though more sensitive, she was also more able to control what she sensed, to not fall under its sway.

Paris stopped cold as Kayla's prone form, draped across the stone altar and literally buried in yellow blossoms, came into view. Surrounding her was a circle of Urrythans, caught up in the notes and harmonies of their song, oblivious to his presence.

The entire scene was like something out of a surreal nightmare. The circled Urrythans were swaying back and forth in a hypnotic rhythm and singing; the earth beneath them was shaking convulsively, joining itself to their voices. And like some lost princess, or sacrificial offering, Kayla lay before them all, silent and serene, draped in yellow. Paris had a sudden vision of the yellow blossoms as lilies, the ceremony as a funeral rite, and he began to move again.

As he approached the altar, his anger mounted, and he fed from it. Ignoring the hypnotic beauty of the singing, he stomped forward, purposefully mismatching the rhythm of his steps and the backbeat of the chant. It seemed to help—at least his mind cleared somewhat.

Kes moved at his side, keeping pace with him, though her features showed none of the intensity of emotion that the moment was bringing out in him. She seemed curious—fascinated—but not in any way angry.

As they reached the first of the Urrythans, Paris didn't hesitate. He pushed it aside, where it sprawled out awkwardly on the stone of the court. It was hard to tell if he had made any noticeable impression on the creature, or whether his action had even been noticed.

Like a toy that is tossed violently aside, the Urrythan continued singing, eyes glazed, canted over on his side. There was something wrong about it. Paris felt a chill transit his spine. What *was* this *One Voice* that it could influence these people to willingly give up control of their own minds?

He kicked the *Ambiana* blossoms aside as he went, reaching Kayla's side only a few moments later. Kes was there as well, moving up beside him so silently and gracefully that he didn't notice her at all until he saw her reach into a pouch on her belt and pull out the injection of antidote that had been beamed down to her. Paris said another quick prayer for the abilities of The Doctor.

As Kes reached out to administer the drug, a high shrill voice behind her cried out, "Stop."

The two of them turned as one, watching the odd group that poured from the mouth of some underground chamber a few hundred feet away. Kes hesitated, the antidote held hovering over Kayla, and Paris just stared, dumbfounded. It was then that the ground erupted, at last, and the sound engulfed them. Totally.

CHAPTER
15

Tuvok HAD COME TO ON THE COLD STONE FLOOR OF ONE of the tunnels shortly after the main tunnel had been split by the chasm. He'd leaped headlong into the opening behind him with no thought but escape, and when the dark path had turned suddenly to the right about three meters in, he'd not seen it in time. The solid stone of the wall had connected hard with his temple. He rose slowly, probing the knot on his head to assess the damage. The pain was disorienting at first, but his mental blocks quickly asserted themselves. Pain was the least of his troubles at that moment.

He would have no trouble in containing the pain until he got back to *Voyager* and had The Doctor look into it. His quick assessment showed no permanent damage, so he shifted his concentration to more important matters: escaping the tunnels and finding a way back to the ship.

He made his way back to where the passage opened into the main corridor, moving much more slowly and carefully than he had in his headlong dive, but he could make out very little with the small beam of his light. He called out twice, listening carefully, but there was no sound from the abyss that yawned in the center of the old passage, and he could make out no bodies or signs of life. No sign of Captain Janeway or of Kim. *Kim.*

He suddenly remembered how the younger officer had slipped away from them, falling into the crevasse. All other thought stopped for a moment, and he leaned heavily against the wall of the cavern. He had been fond of Kim. . . . The young man had had a bright future ahead of him.

This entire operation, from the first landing party to gather supplies, had been nothing but a long series of disasters. No matter that he'd been vigilant, and that all security measures had been strictly by the book. Illogical as it was, there were times when you just couldn't win.

He wished the captain had listened to his warnings, but he understood the logic behind her actions. They'd needed the food. Perhaps they could have gone about collecting it in a more professional manner, but there was no denying that the supplies had been necessary. If it had been only for the food and the water, they might have made it off Urrytha without a single loss.

The planet had sucked them in. It had mysteries in

abundance—plants, animals, sunshine. It was everything that the ship was not, and the crew, Captain Janeway included, had been too long without a real world beyond the confines of *Voyager*.

He made his way back into the darkened tunnel, mentally going over every detail, trying to ascertain if there had been any moment when he might have been more vigilant, when his security measures had been more lax than they should have been. He didn't blame himself, but he wanted to be certain in his own mind that he fully understood all that had gone wrong. The lessons to be learned from the type of losses he'd sustained in the last few hours would be deeply etched. . . . He did not intend to ignore them.

The vibration in the walls was distracting. He stopped and placed his hand against the surface, feeling the rhythmic pulse of it. Concentrating, he let his senses reach out, groping mentally for the source, for the reason. He could feel touches of it—the *One Voice* that Kes had spoken of—but he couldn't quite bring it into focus. As he released his mind into the life-force, the pain in his head snatched at his concentration, and he pulled away from the wall finally, continuing on his way. He could try again when the pain had subsided, or when he felt that he was nearer to the source. For now, the only thing that mattered was returning to the ship.

Logic told him that there would be other ways out of the darkened tunnels—probably many ways— and he needed to find one of them as quickly as he could. Vok, for instance, had come in a different way than he and the others had. The patterns of the tunnels did not seem to be laid out with the intent to obscure anything or to confuse. It was likely, he surmised, that he could continue moving down the passage he was in, and eventually a pathway to the surface would be available.

He was anxious to reach *Voyager*. Without the captain, and Kim, there would be a need for his leadership more than ever. Chakotay was a good officer, but he could only do so much on his own. That was another thing to be considered. Chakotay and Tuvok had not always seen eye to eye, and if they were to work together, compromises would have to be reached. Boundaries would no doubt move and be replaced.

He moved as quickly as he could, using his light sparingly. There weren't a lot of curves or branches in the passage, and he had little fear of losing his way, since he had no idea which way was right. He was counting on his senses to tell him when he was rising toward the surface, hoping to see some sort of light or feel a breeze from the open air above.

As he moved, he began to be aware of sounds that did not necessarily fit into the vibration in the wall. It took a moment for him to realize that what he heard was voices. Moving more cautiously, he followed the sound, pressing himself against the walls to use the shadows for cover. The hostility had seemed to end, just before the cave-in, but there was no reason to press his luck.

He wasn't certain how the Urrythans would react to his presence. When he'd last seen them, Vok had returned and stopped their attack, but that did not necessarily mean that they would welcome him with open arms. For all Tuvok knew, it could have had nothing to do with saving himself and the others. Vok could have been calling his followers to him because of whatever it was that was vibrating the walls. He *had* cried out something about the *Awakening,* about it being upon them.

If Vok's followers saw him, they might try to finish what they'd started, and his phaser was down below a twenty-five-percent charge. He couldn't hold out against any real number of them for long. He had no desire to fight them, but he hoped that if he followed them, they'd lead him to the surface and to freedom.

He peered cautiously around the next corner, and he saw them. They were about fifteen strong, walking slowly in a group. He saw that they were holding a long white object above their heads—Vok. It was the elder Urrythan's prone form that they carried. Had he been injured in the quake? It was difficult to make out in the darkness, but he seemed to be either sleeping, or dead. His body was still and silent, and though Tuvok couldn't quite make out their words, those carrying the alien leader seemed worried about something—nearly frantic.

The chant was meant, he sensed, to blend with the *One Voice* around them, and yet their agitation was fighting against them. The more they worried about their efforts, the less they seemed able to achieve their final goal. Whatever it was that was bothering them, it must be serious.

He kept back, following at a distance. His plan

was to follow them to the surface, then to slip away once there and make his way back to the jungle in the hope that *Voyager* would still be searching for him there. It might have worked, too, if it hadn't been for Ban.

The tall Urrythan, returning from taking Paris and his party to the surface, ended up behind Tuvok, and he managed through sheer luck to spot the Vulcan first. As he approached, Tuvok spun, leveling his phaser, but Ban held up his hands placatingly.

"Please," he said. "There has been enough fighting."

Tuvok did not lower his weapon, but he held his fire. If there was a peaceable way out of the predicament he was in, it would be the logical course to take. Besides, there was something in Ban's voice, the weariness behind his words, the new depth of sorrow in his already mournful countenance, that lent an air of sincerity to his words. Tuvok decided that, for the moment, the Urrythan truly meant no threat.

"It would appear that the journey into these caverns has proven to be too much for Vok," Tuvok observed, nodding his head in the direction of the procession that still moved down the passageway ahead, oblivious to their presence. He watched Ban's features, hoping that something in the depths of those long sorrowful eyes, or some twist of the Urrythan's features, would give him some indication of what was going on. He needn't have bothered. Ban was free with the information, and it was obvious that he was as upset as his followers.

"No," Ban replied softly, "it is merely his time. I was so selfish, so caught up in my bid to be a hero and prove that I was right, that I didn't pay enough attention to what was happening around me—to the thing that mattered most of all. I didn't notice.

"I spoke with him before I brought my people after you, and he didn't want us to go. He told us to leave well enough alone, to be happy that we were bringing the joy of the *Long Sleep* to the one you call Kayla, and to leave you to whatever you would do— that there was no harm you could cause. Even then I should have seen how weakened he had become on this plane, should have noticed how closely he'd become aligned with the *One Voice*.

"He has been withdrawn, spending more and more time in meditation and communion with those who have gone before, less with the day-to-day concerns of the people. Now my own foolish actions may have cost him the one thing that he wanted more than anything in the world—the chance to see the *Awakening* before he went to his *Long Sleep*. He used to sit with me and talk, telling me of the wonders he'd learned, in turn, as a boy, and he'd go on for hours about *Awakening*, the release of the spirits of the ancients to their great gift. It was his fondest dream."

"*Awakening?*" Tuvok asked quickly. "Would I be correct in surmising that it is this '*Awakening*' that is causing the quakes? It would appear that it is as destructive as it is wondrous."

Ban nodded. "Let us catch up with the others," he said quickly. "They are heading for the surface, as

I'm sure you are, and there is no way quicker and safer than that which we are now on."

Tuvok glanced back once, a flicker of guilt and remorse taking him momentarily back to that chasm, to the captain—and to Kim.

Ban saw the emotion flicker for a moment in the Vulcan's eyes, and he assured him, "I have already taken your companions to safety."

"My companions? The captain?" Tuvok was startled. He'd assumed the others were lost.

"The captain, yes," Ban replied, "and three others, two male, one female."

Between the throbbing ache in his head and the confused jumble of information that was being pressed upon him, Tuvok was having a hard time thinking clearly. Two males . . . another female . . . who could it have been? And was one of the males Kim? There was no way to figure it out now, but suddenly a great weight seemed to lift from his shoulders, and the pressure in his head lightened a bit.

"I will follow you," he said at last. "It is the only logical course of action. Without your aid, I might never make it to the surface at all."

Ban nodded, turning to hurry after his companions, who'd moved out of sight down the tunnel. The walls were shaking visibly now, and Tuvok followed, keeping a constant watch for more cave-ins or other pitfalls, hoping that they would make it out before any more floors or walls decided to cave in and bury them. Now that Ban had given him hope for the others, escape seemed more desirable—more critical—and the underground labyrinth through which they were traveling, in comparison, grew more ominous, more final in its embrace.

Ban did not seem concerned. He moved quickly but steadily ahead, and it was only a few moments before they reached the rest of his party. Perhaps he was more in tune with the planet around them, and could tell when things were about to get worse. The others acknowledged Ban's presence with a nod, but there were furtive glances and whispered words flying in all directions when they saw Tuvok come up at Ban's side—especially when they saw the phaser that he still carried, though his arm was loose at his side. Several of them remembered only too well the bite of the stunning ray that weapon could emit, and they were none to happy to have one of those who'd wielded that power trotting along at their side as if he belonged.

Realizing that it was a pointless caution, Tuvok holstered the weapon and kept close at Ban's side. He didn't want to do something that would alarm these others into violence. Not that he feared for his own safety, but they all needed to keep moving and get out of that tunnel. Within a few moments, they'd forgotten him, having more than enough to occupy their minds, and they began to bring Ban up to date on what had happened to Vok.

When Ban had left the others to do what he could for Janeway and the others, Vok had been on his feet and making his own way. He'd been shaky, but fully aware of his surroundings, calling out instructions weakly and helping to band the others together and get them moving as quickly and efficiently as possible. It had been that fact that had sent Ban on his rescue mission. As much guilt as he felt over the ill-concieved attack on the aliens, he would not have abandoned his own people to help strangers.

Now, though, Vok was beyond comprehensible thought. To see him carried as he was, helpless and unconscious while the wonder of a thousand lifetimes took place all around him, was heart-rending. Ban wished his own communion were deep enough to feel what his mentor now felt—to know that things would be fine.

"Is there no hope that he will regain consciousness in time?" Tuvok asked, trying to understand. "Doesn't he require a ceremony? When you kidnapped our crew member, Ensign Kayla, you mentioned preparations. Would he not be present, in some state, for those ceremonies?"

"The preparations should have already been completed," Ban said miserably. "It may be too late for proper ceremony—we will need to proceed very rapidly if we are to give Vok a true sending. It is my hope that I will be able to give him that, at least. The moment he felt himself being drawn into that final embrace with the harmony, we should have begun to prepare him for his journey. That extra bit of energy he spent getting to us in the caverns may well be what cost him his chance to last through the *Awakening.*"

"Are you taking me to where Kayla is?" Tuvok asked.

"Yes," Ban said quietly. "Do not think that you

can take her away from the ceremony, though. She has received a great gift, and there is no return from the *Long Sleep*. She is too far in, and there is no release for those who would send her—those who chant the ritual—even now."

"That is not true," Tuvok informed his alien guide. "Certain translations we had just managed to complete when you attacked us show that it was not only possible, in the history of your own people, but that at times it was forced upon those not deemed worthy. You may not know how it was done, but your ancestors *did* know. It is possible to prevent the *Ascension,* and to deny the *Long Sleep.*"

Ban looked at him in shock. "Forced upon those deemed not worthy. . . . I cannot fathom such a punishment. I cannot conceive of a transgression that would warrant such a thing. How would one live without the promise of another life?"

"I assure you," Tuvok said, "I have no reason to lie. If the tunnels had not collapsed, I could show you exactly what I am speaking of. The important thing is that there *is* a way to reverse the effects of the *Ambiana;* you could release Kayla to me. Our medical facilities are quite advanced—I'm certain that we could bring her back, given time."

"But you would be doing her a great disservice," Ban insisted. "The *Long Sleep* is a wonderful thing—to be one with the harmony of the elders, to contemplate the coming of the *Awakening,* and to prepare yourself eagerly for an entirely new existence? How could you take that way from her?"

"Your ways," Tuvok tried to explain, "are not *our*

ways. My own ways differ significantly from Kayla's, though we come from the same starship. It is possible that you are correct, and that what Ensign Kayla is experiencing would be wonderful for her. It is also possible that she is merely dying. You have no way of knowing this, because she is not of your race. What affects one person one way will not necessarily do the same for another. Would you risk killing her to bring her this enlightenment?"

"Killing?" Ban asked. "You mean the *Endless Sleep?*"

"If that is what you call it, it would be appropriate." Tuvok nodded. "I wish to take Kayla back to her own people. They have their own religion, their own beliefs; would it not be arrogant of you to believe your own to be the only possibility in the universe?"

Ban frowned, considering. He didn't answer. They continued down the tunnel, and after a few moments, Tuvok realized that the darkness was subsiding. He could feel fresh air against his face. They were approaching the surface, and it would soon be time to make a decision on what he should do. For the moment, it appeared that he could trust Ban and his followers, but things could change rapidly. He also needed to find out if Kayla was alive, and if so, figure a way to get her away and back to the ship. He was not about to leave anyone behind on the planet if there was a way he might prevent it.

Those carrying Vok's prone form began to chant, a monotonous, yet melodic chorus that seemed, at first, to repeat itself endlessly. After listening to it carefully for a few moments, however, Tuvok realized that it was varying subtly, changing from verse to verse, but in such small insignificant increments that the changes would not have been apparent to anyone not listening very carefully.

The chanting did not so much blend itself with the shaking of the walls as it seemed an extension of it. The air crackled with energy—palpable and very real. Tuvok felt it invading his senses, reaching out to him. The small flashes he'd gotten earlier from the wall had been nothing compared to the power of this bombardment of his mind. He was able to maintain control, his mental walls were strong and well-trained, but he was aware of the force surrounding him.

He could feel many voices within the chorus, and yet they were not so much separate voices as they were segments of one whole. He sensed, with shock, that Kayla was a part of it. Her contribution was not as strong as the others, not as refined, and it was not difficult, after a few moments of communion with the sound, to pick her out. In fact, Vok, who was not yet even prepared for *Ascension,* was more in tune with the harmony than she was.

She seemed to be finding a small niche in the whole, a part in the scheme of it, but barely—tolerated, not integrated, was the sensation he got. He wondered how long that tolerance would last, or if she would be able to compensate, over time, and merge more fully with the others. The alternative to this was not something that he was eager to contemplate.

The mouth of the tunnel was ahead, and from somewhere far inside himself, he found the strength to erect a more solid barrier against the voices—the sound. He closed himself off, concentrating on making his way forward and into the light. He could feel the power of the sound growing, expanding—could feel it like the pressure of water at great depths—but he held himself apart. The longer he maintained his control, the stronger it became, the further he was segregated from what was happening around him.

He'd heard something within the *One Voice* that might serve him well. Turning to Ban, he pulled him aside.

"I think I can help you," he said. "I have felt Vok's mind, his part in the *One Voice,* and I think that I can reach him. Perhaps I can bring him far enough back that he will be able to experience your *Awakening.* I cannot be certain, but I believe it is possible, still, to reach him. If he were not so far enmeshed with the life-force surrounding us, he might be able to regain the control he needs to make it through his ceremony."

"This is possible for you?" Ban gasped. "Vok himself claimed as much, for himself, but none of us—none of the younger ones—has developed far enough in the communion to read another. It is a great gift, one of the signs that the *Long Sleep* is near."

"He *is* slipping away," Tuvok said. "It would have to be done soon, and as I said, I can make no guarantees. I assure you, my own abilities come to me naturally, and I have always had them, in one form or strength. All of my people have them from birth. You see, I spoke the truth when I told you that my people and Kayla's were not the same."

Just then they came out of the tunnel into the street of the settlement in the desert, the first place that *Voyager* had noted the presence of the aliens, and the sight that met their eyes ended all thought of conversation.

Ban cried out, "Stop!" Then he was moving away from Tuvok's side, his gait a slow graceful lope that used the muscles of his long slender legs to their fullest. Tuvok took in the scene before him quickly, then set off after the long-legged alien at a dead sprint. Ban was headed for a raised stone platform, like an altar, and upon that altar Kayla lay prone on an overflowing bed of *Ambiana* blossoms. At her side, Paris and Kes stood, and they'd turned, startled, at Ban's outcry.

The altar itself was coated and layered in the yellow flowers; they were overflowing onto the base of the altar and down to the ground beneath. Around the altar, Paris, Kes, and Kayla was a closed circle of Urrythans. They were seated on the ground, their eyes closed and unseeing, singing a song—much like the chant that Ban's followers were still maintaining from somewhere at Tuvok's back, but more refined, more complete. The Urrythans did not even appear to be aware that their circle had been breached. They were too caught up in their song to resist.

Kes was holding something in one hand, poised

over Kayla's body, and as Ban approached, she turned back, pressing it against the young Bajoran officer's side.

Then the ground beneath Tuvok's feet convulsed like a living thing, rippling and tearing, sending him sprawling headlong in the street. He rolled with it, his reflexes preventing serious injury, and as he attempted to rise, he saw that Ban had fared no better than he. The tall alien had hit the ground hard, and was struggling weakly to regain his feet.

Ban was still struggling forward, though his attempts to regain his footing were failing. He was still trying to make his way to the altar and the circle of his people. He was still calling out to Paris and Kes, waving his arms in negation whenever his balance would allow for it, but it was no use. He couldn't make it to where they were clinging desperately to the supports of the altar, and they couldn't make it down from where they were.

Tuvok made his way to Ban's side. "There is nothing you can do," he said evenly. "I saw Kes administer the antidote. Kayla will regain consciousness soon."

"Then the others." Ban gestured at those arrayed about the altar. "There is nothing to bring them back. They will continue as they are, caught up in the song, until they feel the release—the joining of a new spirit to that of the ancients. They are trapped, and they will die."

Tuvok stared at the tall alien in disbelief. Then an idea occurred to him, and he began to move again.

"Come with me," he said abruptly. "We will bring

your leader, Vok, here, and we will awaken him. If anyone is close enough to your *One Voice* to reach your followers, it is he. Perhaps if he reaches his own 'release' the trance will be broken."

Ban didn't say anything, but he crawled after Tuvok. A few moments later, there was a lull in the quaking, and the two of them managed to regain their footing.

The others had been following much more slowly. They'd only just made it out of the mouth of the tunnel when the ground convulsed. Tuvok could see them up ahead, still chanting, scrambling back to their knees and moving forward. They weren't having the same trouble as he and Ban with the vibrations, but that was because they were in synch with them. They were caught up in their own chant—much as those singing before the altar were caught in their song. Tuvok realized suddenly that the two were one and the same, different levels of the same ceremony.

He reached them a few moments before Ban, turning to wait for the Urrythan to catch up.

"This will take a few moments." Ban gasped. "I will have to communicate with those in the front, guide them to the altar. It is not the proper ritual, but perhaps you are right. Perhaps it can work."

Then Ban turned away and began a chant of his own, a counterpoint rhythm that pierced the perfect symmetry of the voices of the others. It did not disrupt the flow of sound as much as it *altered* it, driving the tones higher, then lower—drawing certain phrases out a bit longer than they had been previously. It reminded Tuvok of a dam, changing the course of a stream or a river.

Whatever it was he was communicating, it worked. As they made their shaky progress forward, the column turned toward the altar. Somehow they managed to remain on their feet, moving with the shaking of the planet's surface in a way that Tuvok would have believed impossible, had he not seen it. He followed as quickly as he could, stumbling several times and scrambling back to his feet.

Paris and Kes still stood on the altar, and he knew he would have to reach them before Ban and his followers did, somehow. They had to get Kayla off of that platform to make room for Vok, and it would be a good idea to use the distraction of that moment to make their own escape. He wasn't certain if Ban had given up completely on Kayla, though it appeared that he had, and he wasn't about to take any chances on it.

The rest of the Urrythans, those not involved in either the singing or the chanting, were crying out and rushing about, ducking out of the cover they'd sought at Paris and Kes's arrival to rush toward Ban. They appeared to have no more true conception of what was happening than Tuvok himself, and it was obvious that their panic was eating away at Ban's control.

With a great effort, doing his best to synchronize his own steps with the rhythm of the chanting, Tuvok managed to break into a run and rushed at the altar. He teetered once, but managed to right himself, and moments later he was scrambling up the steps to stand at Paris's side.

"We have to get her off of here and out of the way," he shouted, trying to make himself heard and understood. "They are going to substitute their leader, Vok, in the ceremony, but we have to clear the way."

Paris nodded, and the two of them grasped Kayla's limp form and lifted her from the bed of yellow blossoms. Moving with extreme care, they began to descend the back of the platform. Kes walked at Kayla's side, helping to steady her as they moved steadily downward. Kayla had shown no signs of improvement, thus far, and Kes feared that if they didn't get her back to the sickbay soon, she might never fully recover.

They made it to the street, and they were moving toward the city's gates, fighting against the constant vibration and avoiding the small network of crevasses and cracks that were forming in the ground beneath them as best they could.

Suddenly Tuvok saw Ban break free from the crowd. The others continued upward, levering Vok's body toward the bed of flowers beyond as if the world had not gone crazy around them. Ban ignored his followers, concentrating on making his way to where Tuvok labored under Kayla's weight.

"Wait," Ban cried out, stumbling and almost falling headlong. "Wait. You said that you could help us . . ."

Tuvok hesitated. He had been on the verge of

promising his aid when they'd exited the tunnel and Ban was distracted by Paris and Kes. Now he had a decision to make. Kayla needed to get back to *Voyager,* and the way the planet was rolling and rending beneath them, there might not be much time to get her there. The ground beneath the shuttle could give way at any moment, and they could all be stranded. Kayla might die.

"We have to get to our ship," he grated, continuing forward. "Kayla is not fully recovered, and your planet is about to rip itself apart."

"It is the *Awakening,*" Ban pleaded. "All will be normal again, once it is complete. I need you to help me to reach Vok, to release my people."

"I cannot make that commitment," Tuvok answered. "My first duty is to the crew of my own ship."

"If you don't help them," Ban said with finality, his long sorrowful eyes deepening even further, "they will die. They will never ascend, they will sleep the *Endless Sleep.* Only myself and a very few others will remain."

Kes spoke up quickly. "We can get Kayla to the shuttle and get it off the ground," she said, reaching to take the young Bajoran woman's feet. "If there is anything you can do, Tuvok . . ."

For a moment he stood, torn, then he nodded. He spun and headed back toward the altar, Ban at his side, while Paris and Kes continued on toward the shuttle. It was only about a hundred more yards, but with the ground erupting all around them and the hum of the energy in the air, it seemed like miles. It was at that moment that Kayla moaned, shaking her head from side to side slowly, and began to struggle weakly in their arms.

Paris turned to look after Tuvok, but the Vulcan's form was all but lost in the chaos that had been the planet's surface.

CHAPTER
16

AFTER THE EXPERIENCE OF GETTING FROM THE TUNNEL entrance to the altar and halfway to the shuttle, Tuvok's steps were more certain as he made his way back through the gates and on toward the altar. The ground beneath him writhed and rippled oddly. If anything, it was less stable than ever beneath his feet. His mind, normally cool and controlled, was whirling. He had made a promise, and yet he felt that he should be on the shuttle with Paris and the others, on his way back to *Voyager*. He couldn't bring himself to push aside the new weight of responsibility his words had placed firmly upon his shoulders.

Part of it was his own desire to see what he could accomplish, to know—fully—what Vok and the others spent their lives seeking. He knew that there was a chance he could reach Vok, a chance that he could bring the tall Urrythan back, just for a moment, to this plane. He'd already been able to sense the other's mind, and that had been without effort. A true mind-meld would pull them together, and assuming Tuvok could pull himself free at all, he should be able to bring Vok with him. If it had been only for Vok, though, he would not have done it.

It was the others. He could not just walk away and leave an entire settlement of sentient beings trapped within a mental prison from which they could not escape. Not if there was a way he could help to set them free. Those who were not as attuned to their mental abilities would not understand in the way that he could—nothing could be worse than to be enslaved within your own mind without hope.

Of course, if he were to be perfectly honest with himself, he was curious. His own mental powers were considerable, and yet he had never felt anything as balanced as the communal life-force of these people. He had never experienced a mind, communal or otherwise, as powerful as what he felt here— as all-encompassing. There was something ancient, something enduring in the sensations it brought him. If he was not able to bring these people back from the communion that bound them, a communion that they were not physically ready to become a part of, then it might end. After tens of thousands of years—who knew how long—it would end, and he would be responsible.

It was difficult to envision a civilization that

ancient, that powerful in mental development, with so little technological advancement. They had gone blithely into this ceremony, depending on Vok to pull them back, not considering for a moment that there was a danger involved, or that everything might not turn out exactly as they'd been led to believe.

Ban helped him to keep his balance as they weeded their way through the circled singers and began the increasingly treacherous ascent of the altar. The *Ambiana* blossoms beneath their feet were slippery, adding yet another dimension to the challenge of remaining upright. Tuvok feared that the altar stone itself would crumble under the continual assault of the earthquake before he was able to reach the level where Vok lay. The pounding rhythmic vibration was still growing steadily in intensity.

"There is none living who has witnessed the *Awakening.*" Ban gasped, helping Tuvok up the last of the altar's steps. "We have only legends and stories, passed down from our ancestors, to describe what is happening. It is greater, even, than I'd imagined, more powerful than I'd dreamed. I can feel them, all of them, the ancients of generations past, joined as one. It is a glorious moment."

"I am not certain that your planet will survive this 'glorious moment,'" Tuvok commented. "It would appear to be ripping apart at the seams." He was hanging on tightly to the edge of the stone altar, his knees bent for balance and the knuckles of both hands whitened with the effort.

"It has happened before," Ban assured him, "and the planet is still sound. The legends tell us that this will be the fifth *Awakening* since our ancestors first inhabited this planet. That is what the *Awakening* is all about, Tuvok, our ancestors, bursting free of their constraints, awakening to new life and a new existence in the stars."

Tuvok did not comment on this. There was no time for a philosophical debate, and he was uncertain, in any case, whether he was ready to accept that the quakes were anything other than a planet destroying itself. He turned to Vok, steadying himself against the altar, and placed his hands carefully on the thin pale forehead of the Urrythan leader. Closing his eyes in concentration, he pushed outward with his mind, reaching for the familiar barriers that would delineate the other's mental walls, searching for the way through, for the key to unlock what was beyond those walls.

He felt a momentary pang of guilt. To meld with another's mind was not something one normally undertook without the permission of the second party. It was dangerous—not to mention the most serious breach of privacy he could imagine. There was also the matter of Captain Janeway's orders— he could still hear her light reprimand. "No more mind-melds without my permission—is that clear?"

But he had heard the old Urrythan voice his desire, above anything else in life, to witness what Ban claimed was about to happen. He'd heard that from Vok's own lips, and that request would have to serve as the permission he needed. There was no way to ascertain, now that he had gone on to the next state of his existence, how he might feel about being dragged back, but at least they were acting on wishes Vok himself had voiced.

Then there was the matter of the others, those circling Tuvok even now—the followers, the ones who would carry on this tradition, this communion, through the next ten thousand years. Vok had, foremost, seemed to value those he led. He had carried the yoke of responsibility well. Tuvok knew that he would not begrudge his followers a few moments of his *Long Sleep* in return for their safety and continued existence.

Then it was too late for further worry—too late for anything but concentration. He felt his own thoughts slipping through the membranous walls of Vok's mind, and he was in. The sound—the song of the *One Voice*—was overpowering within. It overrode everything, nearly dragging Tuvok into its spell. He fought it, keeping his thoughts focused on his task. He was searching for a bit of what had been Vok, some part that had not yet been consumed by the *One Voice*. He needed something to link the Urrythan's mind back to the physical shell that housed it—something that would push aside the call of the harmony and create an *individuality* within Vok's mind.

At first there was nothing. Vok seemed not to exist as a separate entity, but to have become another facet in the song—another harmonic of the central melody of the voices of his ancestors. Tuvok probed more deeply, pushing aside the veneer that was forming over the entity that he'd met in the garden what seemed an eternity in the past, inserting small discordant jolts of mental energy with surgical precision. Just as he was about to give it up for lost and make his way out, he found what he needed.

It was little more than a thread of thought— something that didn't fit exactly, something that, while it was molding itself to fit the whole, had not yet finished the process. Perhaps it was what the ritual they'd been performing on Kayla was meant to weed out—the last vestiges of anything that might link the elder to the physical world he'd left behind. Tuvok grasped at it, wrapping his mind about it and trying to pull it free from the energy that was trying to claim it, to mold it to fit the pattern.

He worried at it, pressing around it with his own thoughts. He insinuated images from the world he stood in, the ruins, the gardens, the tall looming *Ambiana* plants with their brilliant saffron blossoms, images of the Urrythans arrayed in a circle around him singing, tinged with the near certainty of their impending death, and images of the coming *Ascension*. He thought of the tunnels, the walls that had surrounded him, the vibration of the earth and the ripping chasms that continued to split the surface of the planet.

He had no way of knowing what might work, so he tried everything at his disposal. He could see that the thread was unraveling from the tapestry of sound and energy surrounding it, was aware that he'd interrupted the careful weaving of the song, but his own strength was failing.

With a final effort that drained what was left of his reserves, he grabbed the thread with mental fingers and withdrew. He did not release the thought, but dragged it with him, feeling it coming up against the alien's mental walls, then through. He felt himself falling backward, felt arms reach up to grab him and support him. He didn't know if he'd succeeded in bringing Vok back to the world, or if he'd yanked that last vestige of what had been Vok free forever, consigning him to his *Long Sleep*. In any case, he'd done all that he could.

His head was throbbing where he'd smashed it on the tunnel wall, and his eyes were blurring as the world came back into focus. He was laying back against the shaking earth, strong hands beneath his shoulders supporting him. The *Ambiana* blossoms were all around him, their scent filling his nostrils, and the chanting and singing filled the air. He thought he heard words, but he couldn't be certain, and he fought for clarity, fought to regain his feet.

As if swimming up from a great depth, he returned to full consciousness. The voice he heard cleared— it was Ban. The Urrythan was shaking him, calling out to him, and he turned, trying to answer, but managing only a croaking gasp. He saw the relief that flooded Ban's features, transforming the long sad features, just for a moment, into an odd carica-ture of a smile.

"I thought you had gone one with him," Ban said.

"Vok?" Tuvok asked, sitting up slowly, "Is he?"

"No," Ban said softly. "He has not come back to us. I fear that they are lost—all of them."

"But . . . I felt him come free. Are you certain?"

At that moment a low moan floated down through the continual chanting and singing, and both of them looked up quickly. Vok's arm, which had been lain carefully across his chest, crossing his other, had raised and flopped over the side of the altar.

With a great effort, Tuvok levered himself to his feet. His head felt like there were tiny hammers pounding against it from the inside, but he forced himself to move. Ban was already at his leader's side, shaking him gently.

"Wha . . . what has happened?" Vok asked, his eyes flopping open lazily. "Where am I? How have I come here? Ban?"

"It will be all right," Ban said soothingly. "We have brought you back from the *Long Sleep*. You are still needed . . . just for a short time."

"Back?" Vok tried once to sit up, fell back against the *Ambiana* blossoms, then tried again and succeeded.

"This ceremony—it is for me?" At that moment he saw Tuvok for the first time, and he sat up the rest of the way. "What is happening here, Ban?"

"You collapsed in the tunnels," Ban explained. "When you came in after us, preventing the disaster I was too blind with pride to see, it stole the last of your energy."

The ground gave another powerful lurch, nearly tossing the three of them clear of the altar platform, and Vok's eyes took on a sudden and intense light.

"The *Awakening* . . ." he said with awe. "You've brought me back in time to witness it . . . I . . ."

"There may not be much time left before whatever is going to happen, happens," Tuvok cut in. "If there is something we must do to free these others from the grip of your *One Voice,* I suggest that we do it now."

"He is right," Ban said, gesturing to Vok's followers. The original circle still sat as before, singing in time with the undulations of the ground beneath them, oblivious to what was happening around them. Those who'd been in the tunnels had ceased their chanting in confusion, but the rippling cracks in the planet's surface had driven them randomly about the settlement, where they hid and watched the altar from the shadows.

Vok took it all in quickly. He did not appear concerned, but instead smiled.

"They are one with the *Awakening,*" he said softly. "There has been no more complete, no happier moment in all of their existence. Even the ritual of the *Long Sleep* could not have brought them to this state—to this union. If Kayla had completed her journey, they would still be in this union. How could they let it go?"

"But they cannot free themselves," Ban nearly shouted. "How can they make their way to the *Long Sleep* if they sit here and sing until they die?"

"They will not," Vok said, laying his hand on Ban's shoulder softly. "They will be released at the moment of the *Awakening*. Do you not remember the legends? When the elders rise to their new beginning, the *One Voice* here on the planet will be weakened. It is up to those of us who come after to rebuild, to restore its strength. When the elders release us, these will be released as well."

"That may be true," Tuvok said, "but if the earth crumbles beneath them and they fall to their deaths, they will not be arising to any level at all. There must be something we can do?"

Vok looked down at his followers, suddenly becoming aware of the physical danger of what was taking place.

"I . . . Ban, we must get them to the main cavern."

"Is it wise to make your way underground during an earthquake?"

"The main cavern is possibly the only truly stable spot on the planet," Vok explained quickly. "The stone that supports it stretches deep into the bowels of our planet—it is solid and immovable. Mountains have grown and crumbled on the surface, and yet that one place has remained untouched. If there is any place that will not crumble beneath us, it is there."

Ban nodded. He leaped to the ground in a surprisingly graceful motion, considering the length of his limbs, and began calling out to those who hid among the shadows of the settlement. They responded quickly, once he'd made the move to take charge, as if they'd only been awaiting his words—knowing already where they needed to go.

Then, grabbing one of the singers beneath his bony arms, Ban set off at a trot, half-carrying, half-dragging the chanting Urrythan toward the entrance to the main tunnel. It was a couple of hundred yards distant, and with the earth shaking and rippling beneath him, avoiding the cracks and crevasses that had formed in his path, it was a long arduous journey.

Tuvok followed more slowly, grabbing a second singer, and suddenly the Urrythans were all around him, taking their companions in their arms and moving as quickly as they could toward the tunnel entrance. He struggled to keep up, the tall being's larger clumsy form slowing him down, along with his own fatigue and the pounding in his head, but he pushed it all aside, focusing on the goal ahead. With the help of the others, it took only a few minutes to get them all to safety, but it seemed like hours. After making the journey, fighting every step of the way, Tuvok turned and looked back.

Vok was the only one who had not joined them. He'd risen to a kneeling position on the stone altar, and his eyes stared skyward expectantly. Tuvok saw that Ban was already making his way back to where his leader waited, and, not really knowing why, the Vulcan leaped back out of the cave entrance and followed. He didn't know if Ban planned on dragging Vok physically back to the caverns, or if he just wanted to be close to the elder at the last moment.

Either way, it seemed appropriate, after all that had happened between the three of them, that he be there as well, to finish what he'd begun.

Whatever it was that was causing the planet to buck and rock crazily was becoming even more violent. It was obvious that something significant was imminent, and Tuvok wanted to know what it was. He sensed that his life was in danger, and if that was true, he wanted to understand why. He wanted to be a part of whatever was to come, or to witness it, at the very least. The *One Voice* called to him, and he responded. The time for fear was past.

There was also the logic that if *Voyager* was to find him—if they managed, somehow, to pierce the odd interference and get a lock on him—it would only happen if he was in the open. The altar was located in the largest open space of what remained of the settlement.

The place was a wreck—a ruin. He saw now what must have happened in the past, what must have been the end of the past civilizations, and the immensity of it nearly made him stagger. If the elders slept their *Long Sleep* for more than ten thousand years, and the civilization that had built those huge gardens and elaborate temples had been destroyed in a similar cataclysm to the one that was taking place before him, then how old must this race—this planet—be? And those elders ascending—they would be the very ones, or some of them would be, who had *built* that city, who had tended those gardens.

He stumbled along in Ban's wake, fighting for

balance with each step. A sudden ripping sound filled the air, and he saw the ground before him open suddenly. He had no time to think. With a grunt of exertion, he leaped, stretching the muscles of his legs to their limits and reaching toward the opposite side of the chasm, which seemed to recede, even as he flew through the air toward it.

Ban heard him cry out, and he turned. With a cry of his own, the tall Urrythan leaped to the side of the new rend in the ground, reaching downward and grasping Tuvok by his extended arm. Even as he slammed into the side of the crevasse, nearly losing consciousness as the breath was knocked from his body, Tuvok felt himself being levered upward. Ban was surprisingly strong, and it was only seconds later that they stood side by side, Ban's arm supporting him as they made their way forward once again.

As they neared the altar, Vok noticed their approach, and he called out to them in a loud ecstatic voice, "It is happening. The moment is upon us!"

Turning to look in the direction that the elder's eyes were focused, Ban and Tuvok stood, shoulder to shoulder, bracing one another, and watched. There was no further safety to be found closer to the altar. Whatever was to come, whatever miracle or disaster was about to befall them, they would meet it where they stood, and they would meet it together.

After leaving Tuvok behind, Paris and Kes had helped the now-awake and staggering Kayla to the shuttle. She would have had trouble making the transit in her condition under normal circumstances; with the earth heaving and leaping beneath them, it was next to impossible. Paris found himself nearly carrying her at times, and the three of them were cast to the ground repeatedly. He pushed onward doggedly. He didn't know what to expect, but he knew he wanted to face it behind the controls of the shuttle, not staggering across the uncertain surface of the planet.

Kayla was barely coherent. She had no concept of who she was, or where they were, and her lost faraway expression made it clear that, while she was awake and walking and had actually uttered a few words, she was anything but back to normal. Her condition was another time limit on their actions. Paris didn't want to think about how he'd feel if they didn't get her to Medical in time for a full recovery.

Miraculously, the patch of ground where they'd set the shuttle down was still intact. It was canted a bit to one side, but otherwise unharmed. When they reached it, Paris wasted no time, hefting Kayla to his shoulder and carrying her quickly up to the hatch. Kes scrambled up after him, and as he set about powering up the small craft's systems, running through the lift-off procedures as quickly as possible, she got Kayla strapped in and settled, then slipped into the seat at Paris's side.

"Let's get out of here," he said, firing the thrusters. The shuttle lifted smoothly from the ground, and he took it up quickly.

"We need to get out of this atmosphere so we can get her beamed to Sickbay," he said, "but once that's done I'm going back for Tuvok."

Kes nodded. "I'll go with you."

"There's no sense in that," Paris said with a frown. "If I make it, there's nothing that you could do to help me, and if I don't, that would just put you at risk for no reason."

"Tuvok is injured," Kes snapped. "If you get him out of there, he's going to need medical attention. I'm going back with you. And if something was to happen during his mind-meld, there is no one else who could reach him. You know that's true, Tom."

Paris stared at her, thinking hard, trying to find a flaw in what she'd said so he could justify having her beamed out, but he failed. The fiery glint in her eyes told him that any attempt he made to dissuade her would be met and matched, and he decided not to bother. They were in it together, then.

The shuttle climbed rapidly through the planet's atmosphere, leaving the heaving chaotic quakes behind. In moments they broke free, and Paris immediately activated his comm panel.

"Paris to *Voyager,* one to beam up."

"Who is it, Mr. Paris?" Janeway's voice snapped back. "And why aren't you all coming in?"

"It's Ensign Kayla, Captain, and I think you should beam her straight to Sickbay. Kes and I are going back down there after Tuvok."

"Tuvok?"

"He showed up shortly after we did, Captain," Paris explained. "He was with a large procession of the aliens, and they were carrying their leader, Vok, on their shoulders. When we left they'd replaced

Kayla with Vok on their altar and had continued the ceremony."

"Then why is Tuvok still down there?" Janeway asked.

"He stayed of his own free will, Captain," Kes cut in. "There was some problem with the ritual—some danger to the Urrythans. He'd promised to try and reach Vok's mind and bring him back before it was too late."

"I hope that it isn't too late now," Janeway commented. "Get in and get him out of there, Mr. Paris. I don't care what else happens, I want him off that planet and all of you back on this ship as soon as possible."

Turning to Chakotay, she barked, "Get Kayla out of there now. We don't have any time to waste."

Chakotay nodded, and she dismissed him from her mind, returning her attention to the shuttle. Before she could say anything further, though, Paris's voice crackled over the speaker.

"Aye, Captain," Paris said, smiling. "We'll get him. Shuttle out."

Without further words or hesitation, he dipped the nose of the small craft and plunged it back toward the surface of the planet below, hoping that, somehow, a stretch of ground large enough for him to land on would still be intact when he got there.

"Captain," Ensign Fowler called out from his console across the bridge, "I think you might want to get a look at this."

Janeway turned from where she'd been watching Paris's shuttle disappear from the screen as he returned to the planet. "What is it, Ensign?"

She was already moving toward him when he answered. "The life-force interference has doubled in the last few minutes, alone," he said quickly. "And it's rising. Something is about to happen, and it's going to be big."

"Janeway to Paris," she snapped, slapping her commbadge hastily, "pull up. Do you read me, Mr. Paris? Something is about to happen down there . . . pull up."

The only answer was the silence that had consumed the bridge, and she returned to her seat to wait. Whatever was going to happen, the show was about to begin.

The first of many pillars dropped away suddenly, and there was a flurry of motion, a fountain of incredible color, a burst of sound. Like dominos they followed, one after the other, the song expanding and crackling with energy, assisting the next in line from the outside with its own release. As the shells of stone fell away, the voices burst free, released, and leaped forth to the clouded sky.

The motion was as relentless as the tide, as inevitable as the wind. Centuries came and went and came again, and the cycle was repeated. What had been would be again, what had lain to rest would rise and take flight. The *Awakening* had begun.

Tuvok and Ban stood, each bracing the other, leaning into one another heavily, and they watched. There was nothing visibly apparent, but they knew that it was only a matter of time. The cadence and volume of the sound had increased so drastically that it poured across the surface of the planet toward them like a flood. Nothing could be that loud, that powerful, and cause nothing visible—nothing that they could watch. Even if it meant that it would flood across them and obliterate them from the face of the planet, they watched.

The tremors had increased to such a level that stone buildings were actually crumbling to dust around them. The huge quakes themselves seemed to have ended, and yet the buzzing hum of energy that rippled across the planet was growing in power and strength. What had been jagged irregular motion had stabilized to a hum, a steady state of animation that tickled up through Tuvok's bones.

He could feel it surrounding him, washing over and through him. He was not one with the *One Voice,* and yet he could feel it resonating through his being, sending thrills of electric harmony through his mind. It was entrancing. Even had the ground beneath him buckled at last, threatening to plunge him to his death, he could not have ignored it. There was a perfection to the life-force, an effervescent sensation of elation that would not be denied.

The sound grew to the roar of an avalanche, rising in volume steadily as it approached, and far in the distance, in the direction of the gardens, the first visible signs of what was to come became visible. Straining, he could see great gouts of dust blasting into the air. Like the aftermath of a series of explosions, clouds formed, lining themselves symmetrically against the horizon. That line of clouds was approaching, along with the avalanche of sound, and they stood, awaiting it, mesmerized. It was strange—illogical. Clouds were an act of nature, and they did not line up in ranks. Planets did not just explode.

Vok had risen from his knees and was standing, even as Ban and Tuvok were, standing and balancing somehow atop the stone altar. He teetered madly atop the remnants of the bed of flowers that had so recently held Kayla's prone form, dancing back and forth, balancing in eerie grace. His arms were raised toward the approaching madness, and his eyes were alight with energy, his sorrowful elongated features twisted into the most all-encompassing expression of ecstasy Tuvok had ever encountered. It seemed, over and over, that the tall old Urrythan would fall to the ground and be swallowed, or that his strength would fail, but it did not happen.

Tuvok turned away from Vok and back to the clouds on the horizon, fascinated. The dust was beginning to clear in some areas, in others it was just beginning to rise, giving the overall impression of a giant kaleidoscope. He wasn't certain when it had begun, but he became suddenly aware that the clouds were interspersed with flashes of color, flashes that grew more and more persistent, spreading across the sky.

He stood and watched, scarcely able to breathe, so rapt was his concentration, and an odd sensation of liberation, of freedom beyond his comprehension swept over and through him. He felt sensations that could not have been his own, but that were shared in such earnest delight and wondrous power that they could not be denied. Somehow something was communicating with him, gifting him with a magical communication of hope and gladness, of sheer love of life.

His control was crumbling. Long years of learning to subjugate all emotion, of depending on logic alone as a goal and a way of life, seemed to pale to insignificance against a seemingly limitless backdrop of pure emotion. He felt tears streaming down his cheeks, but he did not move to wipe them away. He watched and he listened and he experienced. He did not understand it, nor did he try. For once it was enough just to be—to have a part in something grand, something amazing. There would be time enough, should he manage to live through whatever was happening, to think back on it and try to make sense of it all.

Almost the instant they dipped back into the planet's atmosphere, Paris knew they'd made a mistake. The shuttle lurched, nearly ripping free from his controls, and he fought to bring it back level. Something powerful and violent was imminent, the energy of it crackled in the air, and he could sense it as well, hovering about him, like a great cloud of anticipation. His sensors were scrambled, their readings either wildly inaccurate or dead. . . . The instruments were worthless. He couldn't trust any of them, and they were still flying blind, heading toward the planet, or in the general direction of it, through dense cloud cover. It hadn't been so thick when they'd pulled away from the planet, and he realized nervously that he had no way of knowing how close they might already be, or how much farther they would have to travel, before they would break through the cloud cover and see the planet's surface.

Kes was sitting, rigid eyes staring straight ahead, and at first Paris mistook her posture for one of fear. He wouldn't have blamed her, under the circumstances. Even best of pilots likes to know where he's at when flying. On the other hand, Kes wasn't prone to bouts of debilitating fear. He had no time, at that moment, to try and comfort her—time enough if, and when, they landed.

The hull of the shuttle was beginning to shudder, buffeted by some force he could not identify. There was a roaring sound surrounding them, engulfing them, and no matter what he tried, he could not get a fix on their position. It was more like flying through water than air, as the forces knocked them first one way, then the other. He held on grimly.

"Kes," he cried out, trying to make himself heard over the vibration of the shuttle's hull.

There was no response. Releasing the controls with one hand, risking having them torn from his grip completely, he reached over to shake her shoulder roughly. "Kes!" he called out again, much louder this time.

She turned to him with a dazed quizzical expression on her face. She saw him, but it was obvious that she was not quite registering what she saw, not really all there. Something was distracting her. She started to mouth a response, but whatever words she'd planned failed to reach her lips. She just stayed as she was, mouth parted slightly, staring.

Paris got the feeling that, though she seemed to have acknowledged his presence, and she'd turned toward him, her eyes trained directly on his face, she did not see him at all. Something was going on, something that she could sense, or that could sense her, something she couldn't rip herself free from.

Whatever was to happen in the next few minutes would determine their fates, and it looked as if, once again, he was on his own.

He whipped back around to grasp the controls, and he was just in time to see the viewscreen come clear for one long moment. In that instant he caught a glimpse of the surface of the planet beneath them, then it was obscured again, then visible. He got the images in a sort of flashing series, like a strobed light, but he was able, at least, to get some idea of their position, and he breathed a bit easier. They were flying through a series of clouds.

Suddenly something burst upward beneath them with jarring force, knocking the shuttle sideways and nearly ripping the controls from his hands once again. He fought wildly for control, righted the shuttle just in time to be buffeted again from the far side. There were a series of explosions, or air pockets, rising from beneath them, and he was caught up in their grasp, being tossed from one to the next like a rubber ball.

Throwing caution to the wind, he increased his speed, rushing along, keeping the shuttle just above the level of the trees, skimming over the junglelike gardens as if the craft were nothing more than another large insect. Small shocks were still reaching them, and his control of the craft was anything but certain, but they seemed to have outrun whatever it was that had nearly blasted them from the sky. At least he could see.

Paris glanced over at Kes again. He hadn't been

able to check on her for the last few minutes, but now that he had control again, his concern for her returned. He saw her shake her head, as if clearing her mind, then she blinked and turned to stare at him, eyes wide.

"We have to see," she said, putting her hand on his arm. "What's happening back there, we have to watch it. I have to know—to understand. Tom?"

He stared back at her, wondering if the aliens had somehow managed to derange her mind. She seemed lucid enough.

"We have to find Tuvok," he replied. "We have to get him, and get out of here, Kes. . . . You heard the captain."

"We will," she said softly, "but there is nothing we can do until this is over. Believe me. I've sensed their power, their joy . . . such joy, Tom. I have to see them."

"Who?" he asked. When she didn't answer, he heaved a sigh and turned back to his controls once more. "Well, we aren't seeing anything from up here," he said. "I've got to set this thing down before one of those blasts puts us there the hard way, or this crazy interference knocks out every system on the shuttle."

He began to scan the surface below them, looking for anything stable enough for them to land on. Most of the surface had been exposed, one way or another. Trees that had been growing for hundreds of years had been uprooted, rock formations had crumbled to dust, and what had been a long flat expanse of desertlike land stretching beyond the gardens was now a map of tortured ruins with cracks and crevasses crisscrossing its surface in all directions.

He saw what appeared to be a plateau, resting on the strong base of a mountain, and he headed for it. The ground there seemed relatively undisturbed, and there was nothing that could fall on them, nothing that could topple and crush them. As long as they managed not to fall into a crevasse or be swallowed whole by the ground beneath them, they should be able to survive whatever was to come.

They were still many kilometers from the settlement where they'd left Tuvok, and he decided that, bending his orders as it was, the decision to set down would be the safest. Even with the explosions that had buffeted them about so roughly seemingly left behind them, he wasn't certain if he could navigate the growing turbulence to bring them safely as far as the settlement. With a deep breath and a short prayer, he picked out a spot and took it in.

He felt the shuttle settle to the earth, and he suddenly became aware of the trembling in his hands. He'd been so intent on fighting the shuttle's controls that he hadn't realized how tense he'd become—how taut his nerves had grown. The ground was still shaking, but not with the quakelike tremors they'd experienced before taking off. The frequency of the vibration had increased to the point that the surface seemed to tremble, as though the entire planet were being brought to some point of resonance that was more defined, and yet somehow less destructive.

The shuttle settled, and he released the breath he'd been holding with a gasp. Kes was moving before he could even get the engines shut down, lifting the hatch and scrambling out and down to the ground. She stumbled a bit at first, but righted herself quickly, as if coming into alignment with the vibration. By the time Paris had unstrapped himself and followed her, she was standing, one hand holding on to the side of the shuttle for support, staring back the way they'd come. Her eyes, once more, were far away.

Paris stepped up beside her, put one hand on her shoulder, and grabbed the shuttle with his other, swinging his head until his own gaze followed Kes's into the distance. He had none of Kes's, or even Tuvok's, psychic ability, and yet he could feel something. He could feel some sort of emotion draining from the planet—from the air—draining into him and filling him. It was a strange sensation, a bit frightening, used as he was to the confines of his own psyche, and yet somehow exhilarating—a feeling of liberation.

He found that he was smiling widely, and he couldn't tear his eyes from the clouds in the distance. There were voices as well, very faint but distinctive, whispering through his mind. They were so similar that it was difficult to tell where one stopped and another began—cries of delight, bits and flashes of memory brought to life and transmitted, sensations he couldn't begin to fathom or to explain.

The sensation was very similar to what he'd experienced when he first learned to pilot an aircraft. It was a feeling of release from restrictions—of freedom. He remembered how space had stretched before him, limitless, ready for him to explore. No one else could have been a part of that moment for him, and yet here on this planet, so far from Earth that it was difficult to put it into any type of perspective that made sense, he was sharing that moment . . . living it again. He knew, somehow, that the beings behind those voices, the beings so full of joy and release that their minds and emotions were overwhelming his own, were sharing that memory with him. They delighted in it, communing with him and transmitting their own memories in return.

He would never, willingly, have allowed another so close to his thoughts, his dreams, and yet he felt no ill will. Their joy was contagious, infectious in ways he couldn't begin to fathom. There was nothing that could have happened in that moment other than the communion that *did* happen.

The depth of it was overpowering. There was a wealth of imagery, a vast ocean of thoughts and dreams, cities and ruins, jungles, deserts, and oceans. There were starships, races he'd never dreamed of, caverns so deep and dark that no light penetrated their darkness, and yet he perceived what was there—knew it as they had known it. He recognized in passing some of the places he'd seen on the world, and yet they were as they had been, not as they now were . . . alive, where they were now nothing but ruins and shadows.

It was nearly too much for him to accept at one time, and his mind was nearing complete overload, when suddenly the cloud cover broke. His eyes widened, and without noticing, he tightened his grip on Kes's shoulder. As wonderful as the experience he'd just shared had been, it had not prepared him for what now met his eyes.

They were immense. Diaphanous wings, flashing like woven crystals, tossing captured rays of light in rainbow-hued glimmers of beauty and wonder.

Paris could make out the features of the aliens—Vok and the others—in their forms, though the creatures flowing up like a fountain from the gardens were much taller, longer and more slender, translucent. The span of their wings was incredible, and they just kept coming, moving up and away, heading into the clouds above to be replaced by a myriad of others.

The ground was stabilizing, the trembling dying to a murmur of its former strength, though the flood of images and memories did not diminish. It had moved into the realm of the mind, released from the planet's physical restrictions. The buzz of energy was dissipating as well, fading like a pleasant dream, unwinding itself from Paris's mind one tendril at a time, until he was able to move, to shake his head and clear the rest of the cobwebs.

He craned his neck, watching as the last of the creatures disappeared above them, parting the clouds and disappearing within them, trailing the length of its gauzy fragile wings behind it. In the wake of their passing, the planet was swallowed by silence.

Kes was still not moving. Her eyes had filled with tears, then overflowed, sending salty rivulets running freely down her cheeks. Her hand gripped the ship so tightly that the skin of her knuckles was white from the effort, and she was trembling.

Paris realized how tightly his own hand was gripping her shoulder, and he released her, moving closer and pulling her against him. She collapsed into his chest, her eyes still trained on the clouds above. She was shivering, and he saw that her hair was matted to her neck with sweat.

How much more powerful must that experience have been for her? With her ability to share the thoughts of these creatures, her sharing of what must have been their group mind—the life-force reading that had caused them such difficulty since their arrival on the planet—how much more deeply must she have shared that moment?

"Kes," he said softly.

She didn't answer, at first, but then she pulled back, raising her eyes to meet his own concerned gaze. She was smiling, and with one hand she reached up to brush the tears from her cheeks.

"I'm all right, Tom," she said finally. "But . . . they were so—wonderful. And old. They have seen so much, experienced so many things, yet it is just a beginning."

"I sensed that, as well," Paris replied. "It felt as if

they were on the verge of something great and wonderful, something new and thrilling to them."

"They were answering a call," Kes said distractedly. "I couldn't make it out—not really—but I could feel it teasing at the edges of their thoughts. They are drawn to it—destined for it. They are gone."

"But . . ." Paris frowned. "They must just have flown to some other part of the planet?"

"No," Kes said, "they are gone. Their time here is done."

"How can they fly in space?" Paris asked, half curious, half wondering. "Those wings would be of no use."

"They have power," Kes replied. "They have more power than anything I've ever felt—more knowledge. They don't need the wings to fly."

He took a last lingering look at the clouds, imprinting the image in his memory, then he turned back toward the shuttle.

"Let's get Tuvok and get back to the ship," he said. "It's time for us to be gone, too."

Tuvok watched in wonder as they took to the sky, hundreds—maybe thousands—of slender shapes, their wings flashing about them in sparkles of color, their minds wide open and shouting mental adulations, bursts of pure joy.

He felt their lives, their dreams, their memories, all open, shared with whoever or whatever might wish it. Shared, even, with those who might *not* wish it. He felt Ban, who still leaned heavily on his shoulder, trembling. The voices called to him; Tuvok could sense this. He felt the overwhelming emotion that the winged creatures evoked, wonder born of Ban's lifetime of preparation brushing against the proof of his faith, the truth beyond legend. Tuvok could share in that emotion, and yet there was something deep down in Ban's own spirit that called back to the aliens, that yearned toward them in a way that Tuvok could never match.

He could feel Vok, as well, could feel the yearning that rolled from the elder in waves as he watched his own ancestors rise to another level—another world. He sensed, as well, the loss—the silencing of the voice that had linked them, one to another. It was not gone, but it was much reduced. Vok's was one of the stronger minds left, the foundation—Tuvok realized—of the future, the beginning of another cycle.

When the last of them had disappeared into the clouds, Tuvok pulled his gaze free and swept it over the ruined settlement. He didn't pull away from Ban, not immediately. The tall Urrythan was still trembling, still caught up in the moment, and Tuvok was afraid to remove his support. Then Ban moved, like a man coming awake from a deep pleasant sleep.

The yearning was still there—it was nearly palpable in the air surrounding them—but it was not an unpleasant sensation. Though their ancestors had departed, leaving them on their own to follow as they might, it did not bring the Urrythans to despair. Instead, it had brought hope and strength.

They now had visual proof of the faith they'd kept for ten thousand years. Now, more than ever before, they knew the truth of their convictions.

"You will have to rebuild your homes," Tuvok commented, finally breaking the silence.

"We will build in a different place," Ban answered. "It is only right that we leave our ruins here to commemorate their *Awakening*—that we share in their new beginning by creating one of our own."

"Ban . . ."

Vok, who'd fallen back to his knees as the vision released them all, was canting to one side weakly, and Ban had to move quickly to keep him from falling from the altar.

"It is time," Vok said calmly. "You must gather the others, and you must begin my ceremony. I have put off the *Long Sleep* longer than I should, and it is calling me back."

"We will do as you say," Ban assured his leader. "I will have the others bring fresh blossoms, and we will clean this area that we may begin anew. You will be first. We will follow. One day, we will see them in the stars."

"I have lived a long life, thus far," Vok said softly, a smile washing serenely across his face, "and I have a new beginning to look forward to. I have seen that which my parents and my parents' parents only dreamed of and talked about over their fires at night. I have been a part of the wonder of the *Awakening*."

He turned to Tuvok slowly, and he reached out to take his hand weakly between his own. "You have given this to me, and I will not forget it. I will sleep now, and when I rise, you will be long gone to whatever awaits your spirit. When I rise, I will seek you out, if it is in my power, and I will find a way to thank you. When the next *Awakening* finds my people, your memory will be shared with them, your spirit will linger with ours."

"There is no debt owed," Tuvok assured him. "I have shared in your experience as well. It was difficult to resist. Illogical as it seems, I feel as though I am in your debt."

"We will meet again, Tuvok of the *Starship Voyager*."

With those final words, Vok lay back on the stone altar and closed his eyes to the world. Ban and Tuvok watched him for a long moment, then Tuvok released the Urrythan's hand, laying it gently in place across his thin chest.

In the distance, they could hear the shuttle's engines and Tuvok knew that the moment was at an end. *Voyager* awaited, with all its various problems and difficulties, and he had a responsibility to her. He turned away, walking toward the gates of the settlement and beyond as Paris banked in and brought the shuttlecraft down.

"Wait," Ban called after him, and he turned, raising his eyebrow slowly.

"Yes?"

"Please," Ban said, "if there are still supplies that your people need, if there is anything that I can do for you—anything that will make up for all I have done . . ."

"I will inform the captain of your offer," Tuvok assured him.

"It is well, then," Ban said, the odd smile flitting across his face again.

As Tuvok turned away once more, the alien added, "I hope you find your way home."

CHAPTER

18

ON *Voyager,* the air was charged with anticipation and with worry. There had been no word from the shuttle, no sign of life at all on the planet before, and frustrating as it was, all there was for the crew to do was to wait, and to see what might transpire. Everyone on the bridge was gathered around and beside the captain's chair, silent and brooding, letting the closeness calm their nerves as it might, watching what they could see of the events taking place on the planet below.

They had long since given up trying to pierce the life-force reading. Though the harmony and purity of the signal had grown to unbelievable stability and power, they could no longer reach the probes. Nothing they had could override the interference from the planet itself. The life-force readings had continued to grow, moving to levels beyond any scale they could record, and with their instruments worthless, all that remained was the waiting.

They had seen flashes, traced sudden anomalies in the readings from the planet, that seemed to indicate a series of small explosions on the surface, all in the area of the gardens and the ruined buildings where they'd first made landfall. They couldn't make out anything through the dense foliage, but bursts of dust were being catapulted into the sky by whatever was happening below, sending up clouds of debris that hung in the air, floating across their viewscreen and obscuring their view of the planet even further. The explosions were of enormous power, and this factor added to their growing apprehension over their missing companions.

There was a void on the bridge in the absence of Paris and Tuvok, a gloomy cloud hovering about them as Neelix wrung his hands and paced back and forth, worrying over Kes. The feeling of helplessness was overpowering, and the sensation of anticipation, the aura of inevitability that hung in the air, was staggering. There was something building, something beyond their comprehension, and yet calling out to them on levels each could understand. It was a frustrating moment, a case of events far beyond their control, and Janeway didn't like it at all.

The door slid open, and Neelix entered the room once more. His smile had returned, though it was obviously forced, and he held a large tray in one hand. On the tray was a steaming pot, beside which rode a group of mugs. The scent of whatever was in that pot was anything but encouraging, and they all looked at him in amazement, unable to fathom how he'd had the audacity to interrupt the moment.

"I thought you could all use this," he said. "It is a particularly tasty tea—I stole the recipe from the Kazon. Besides the flavor, this blend has the particular effect of bringing one's nature into balance—it is used in Kazon religious practices to calm one before combat. I know we face no combat, or I certainly hope not, but I thought it might help, all the same."

"Thank you, Neelix," Janeway said absently, accepting a mug of the tea and sniffing at the steam that arose from it without looking. Suddenly, she snorted, leaning forward and nearly spilling the hot brew on her lap.

"Neelix." She gasped, setting the cup down. Around her, others were having similar reactions, and glaring at the squat little alien with a mixture of anger and disbelief.

Looking hurt, but not surprised, Neelix turned to her.

"Yes, Captain?" he asked.

"What *is* this?"

"It is made from boiling the stomachs of a particular species of lizard which has first been fed on a healthy portion of several roots and herbs that render the toxins in their digestive systems neutral. It is a very interesting process."

"I'm sure it is." Janeway sighed. She pushed the cup as far away from her as she could get it, then returned her gaze to the viewscreen.

Suddenly what had been a cloud-covered, green, blue, and tan world was transformed. It was only a small area, she realized, but growing fast, a splash of vivid color against the backdrop of mist and cloud. It was expanding, crossing the clouds and moving closer at high speed.

"Chakotay, what is that?" she asked. Deep inside, she knew he would have no answer, but she needed to ask. Somehow breaking the silence and setting the burden of explanation on another allowed her to galvanize into action.

"No idea, Captain, but whatever it is, it's moving toward us pretty fast. Not as fast as a starship, or an incoming weapon, but fast."

"Shields up," Janeway barked. "Computer, magnify sector forty-seven, factor one hundred."

The screen blinked and they were watching an exodus. One after another they came, a montage of color and sparkling light. Like tall lithe angels, the elders of Urrytha took to the sky, gauzy wings spread and eyes wide, expressions of pure joy masking their previously sorrowful features. What Janeway had originally found to be tragic in their countenance had molded itself to a truer form—an absolute. She could, if she thought about it, transform Vok's image in her mind to such an expression, and she wondered—even as she was caught up and lost in the spectacle below them—how she might have missed such a possibility in the alien's face. She had done the old Urrythan an injustice within her mind, and she hoped that the opportunity to right that would present itself—when her crew came home to *Voyager*.

It was becoming obvious that, despite their caution, they'd overlooked a great many things. The *Awakening*. She'd heard the Urrythans speaking of it, she'd seen the inscriptions, seen the pillars—had they been some sort of cocoon? They'd looked upon all of it as superstition, religious mumbo jumbo. The Urrythans had their faith, as Janeway herself and the others of her crew had *their* own faiths, and yet she had been too blind to see beyond the differences, too blind to notice how much of what had been said and written was born out by the events and circumstances that had surrounded her.

Kayla had been bound for such an end, and would it have been wrong? Had they been incorrect to deny her a place in something as wondrous as this one day? Or would her body have rotted, not making the transformation, dying within the embrace of Urrytha's voice?

There was no way to know. As the Urrythan elders continued to flow upward, a fountain of flitting soaring bodies, the ship began to hum. At first it was just a slight vibration, tickling at her senses, then Janeway realized it was something more—something different. Something was invading her mind, her senses, and yet she did not feel defiled or violated.

She wondered why she'd bothered to have the shields raised. Nothing else that they'd tried had in any way changed the course of this life-force. Why would the shields be any more effective? There was something in the feathery tingling touch of the vibration that calmed her fears, held her to her silence, despite the possible risk. The closer the aliens came to *Voyager,* the more certain she was that the shields had never been necessary. In any case, she was certain that they would make no difference at all in what was to come, whatever that might be.

Tearing her eyes from the screen for just a second, she swept the room with her gaze, checking to see how the others were reacting. Chakotay and Fowler sat enraptured, clinging to the armrests of their seats. Their consoles went ignored—everything went ignored—except for the vision that filled the viewscreen. Her training urged her to reprimand them, to call them back to their senses and their duties, but her instincts vetoed the thought. There was nothing they could do.

The images on the screen were all-encompassing, filling their vision, even as the life-force within the aliens reached out to their minds. It was not so much the colors or the sound that grabbed her and held her spellbound, but the combination of sensory input. There was a subtle vibration, but even as her mind named it as such, she realized that it was much more than that. It was a sound—a song. Somehow it was powerful enough to penetrate the ship's hull, yet subtle enough to play like a wonderful symphony on their emotions—on their nerves.

Suddenly the perfect harmony that was building in Janeway's mind was shattered, and she realized that what had brought her to her senses was a sound—a crash. She whipped around in her seat, scanning the bridge for the source of the sound, trying to get her mind alert and ready for trouble.

She released the tension in her shoulders almost as soon as she'd made the turn. Neelix, transfixed by the screen, had dropped his tray, falling back heavily into the nearest seat and ignoring the mess he'd made. He seemed unable to pull his gaze away from the screen, and his hands, which sat loosely in his lap, were trembling. She had a fleeting moment to her own thoughts, a moment where she felt closer to the Talaxian, wondering what images his mind was building for him, what emotions the sound and vibration would bring him.

The Kazon tea was pooling on the floor, setting off at odd angles in slow-moving rivulets. She watched it for just a moment, fascinated, realizing that the vibration of the hull was causing the patterns of the liquid. Then she turned slowly back to the screen.

They were close now. She wanted to tell the computer to turn off the magnification, to prolong the moment as they came nearer and grew to full size again, but she couldn't form the words. There were words, but they were not her own. There were voices—hundreds, maybe thousands of voices—all speaking at once, and all making sense.

They didn't seem to interrupt one another, those voices, but to blend. It was like hearing a chord—a multipart harmony—of spoken words. There was melody to it, as well, but she felt that it was communication, not just song. There was an intent behind the words, and the intent seemed to be release. They were releasing their past, both figuratively and literally, sharing it with whoever or whatever came into their path.

There were images—histories, tragedies—and throughout it all, there was an undercurrent of faith, of rest and calm, of building and rebuilding. She knew the cities below as they had been, and as they had fallen—as earlier generations of these creatures had risen to their new existence somewhere out there in the stars. She experienced the gardens from rows of seedlings to mature cultivated beauty to wild overgrowth and jungle—to now.

The yellow blossoms were ever-present. At first, they were kept apart in small secure gardens— guarded by priests—administered in small doses. As civilizations fell and grew and fell away again, as generations passed the secrets along in their own ways—changing the words, molding the faith—the flowers were moved to the gardens, where Urrythans could walk freely through them, gathering the sacred pollen into their systems.

She knew the sorrow of those who had not been chosen, as well. Vok was wrong. Not all of his ancestors had gone on to the *Long Sleep*—not all had been found worthy. Over the years, the centuries, as the culture of Urrytha had degenerated to living beneath the ground in caves and the grand cities and civilizations of the past crumbled slowly around them, the rituals had been warped— changed.

The more of them who went to their *Long Sleep,* the greater their combined voice, the stronger their influence on those still living, and the less of the *Ambiana* was necessary to produce the *Long Sleep* in those who remained on the surface of the planet. The influence of the elders was calming, as well, and those who would have been deemed unworthy in the larger flourishing civilizations were weeded out or changed—reformed. They did not exist in the later groups, but were replaced by calm intelligent communes—single-leader systems that sought only the release that Janeway now witnessed and were willing to wait literally thousands of years for that release. Indeed, they eagerly sought the opportunity to sing their single-chord song for what would have been an eternity to a human.

Besides this, those in the later years had begun to go to their *Long Sleep* more rapidly—they had less time to become enamored of the world, of building and expanding, of progress. They spent their days, more and more, in preparation for their *Ascension,* without thought to living the lives allotted to them.

Then they had left the gardens behind, moving to the desert so that the pollen would not overtake them too rapidly—before they could prepare. They avoided the ruins of their ancestors cities and stayed clear of the gardens, shunning the knowledge recorded in the ancient writings. All that mattered was the preparation for communion with the *One Voice.* They lived and breathed for *Ascension.* They were the last of the cycle.

Now the elders were departing. Janeway felt them sweeping around and past *Voyager,* felt the center of their combined consciousness pass through her like the eye of a storm—calm, perfectly balanced—and then they were gone. As they receded, their message—their voice—preceding them into infinite space, on to whatever awaited them, whatever drew them away from their homeworld of ten thousand plus years into the limitless reaches of galaxies and worlds without end.

The sudden absence of them left a void that drew the breath from each and every member of the crew. It was an incredible feeling of emptiness—of loss—but thankfully it didn't last. As their minds slowly regained their normal thought patterns, they began to analyze and compare, using the experience they'd gained to filter through their own experiences. No one spoke for a long time—moments, hours?

Finally Janeway pushed firmly against the arms of her chair and rose to her feet. The planet below was just that again, a planet that resembled Earth. She had responsibilities, things that required her full attention, and her own ruminations over what had just happened would have to wait.

"Ensign Fowler, see if you can get that scanner on line now. Something tells me that the life-force interference will not be a factor."

Her words, breaking the long silence, galvanized them all into action. Neelix, apologizing profusely, went to get something to clean up the mess he'd made. Chakotay moved over next to Fowler and assisted with the scanners. They moved sluggishly at first, but it seemed that the normalcy that the aliens' departure had thrust upon them gained in strength with each passing moment. They had shared in another's world, if only for a moment, but now they were back in their own.

"Lieutenant Paris, this is *Voyager,*" Janeway said, "do you read me?"

There was a moment's pause, then Paris's voice came back, loud and clear.

"I read you, Captain," he replied. "We had to put down when that . . . whatever it was . . . happened. We're proceeding to where we left Tuvok."

"Very well," Janeway replied. "Tuvok, this is Janeway, do *you* read me?"

"Yes, Captain," Tuvok replied. "I am awaiting the arrival of the shuttle."

"Get back here," Janeway said softly. "Get back here as soon as possible. Janeway out."

"Captain?" The Doctor's image popped onto the viewscreen.

"Yes, Doctor, what is it?"

"Ensign Kayla, Captain. I am not certain exactly what happened, but a few moments ago my instruments became useless. Immediately prior to that fluctuation, I noticed that she had dropped into a deeper level of sleep. More relaxed. She has awakened now, and all traces of the toxin seem to have disappeared."

"Your antidote would appear to be working admirably," Janeway noted.

"You don't understand, Captain," The Doctor continued. "My antidote neutralizes the toxins, returning the nervous system to its normal functional mode. Ensign Kayla's system shows no indication that there was ever an antidote or a toxin. It is as though she'd never been infected in the first place."

Janeway didn't answer. There was no way to explain to The Doctor what they'd experienced, no logical way to lay out for him her experience. She knew that what he had witnessed was a direct result of that song—that harmony—that had brushed against their existence as it heralded an Exodus. She had no idea how that interaction had caused Kayla's miraculous recovery, nor did she know how she knew that the Urrythans had been responsible. She just knew.

A snippet of verse from her past returned to her, something her father had read to her from old Earth's Christian Bible came to her mind suddenly, and with a clarity she'd not experienced since much earlier in her life. "And death shall have no dominion," she said softly. Somehow, it seemed very fitting at that moment.

"Captain?"

"Never mind, Doctor. I don't think you'll need to worry about her now," Janeway said at last. "Don't ask me to explain, because, I assure you, I cannot."

The Doctor looked perplexed, and more than a little annoyed, but he did not question her further, and a second later the screen went blank. Smiling, Janeway returned to her seat to wait for Paris to bring the shuttle home.

* * *

Though operations had returned to normal, nothing on *Voyager* was moving very quickly. The crew moved about their assigned tasks placidly, calmly. There was little speech—almost no interaction of any sort. They were lost in meditative silence, the first real peace they'd shared since being dragged from their home space.

Chakotay noticed the silence, and he appreciated it. Not being needed, at that moment, he slipped quietly off to his stateroom and sank into the chair at the head of his table. He closed his eyes and fell into the trance more quickly and easily than he ever had in the past. He moved inward serenely, seeking his guide—seeking his silent special place.

There was a lot to absorb. He'd never felt anything so deeply spiritual, not in the jungles with his father, not in his own spirit journeys. It had been a pure moment of cleansing, a moment in which centuries of knowledge and evolution had passed into and through his own belief system. It had changed nothing, really, but it had altered his perspective.

He had always known that his spirit must move on beyond his present form, but to truly believe that? Belief in the unknown is not an easy thing, especially for one grounded in a life of harsh physical reality.

When they'd come to Urrytha, he knew he'd been guilty of swift, and incorrect judgment. He'd seen the Urrythans as primitive, seen their beliefs and their legends as naive and destructive. He'd not had the vision to look beyond the obvious, and this both saddened him and soothed him. He knew he'd grown in the last few days—grown in ways he'd not even realized were necessary.

As his spirit world closed in around him, and the world faded, he smiled.

In the sickbay, Harry Kim slipped from the examining table, wondering at his leg, which felt better than it had any right to, and made his way across the room to stand beside Kayla, who was just rising.

"I'm glad to see you safely back," he said, smiling and holding out his hand.

She met his gaze frankly, returning the smile. "I hope I didn't make you nervous down there, Ensign," she replied.

"Maybe a little." Kim was blushing now, but he knew he had to see the moment through.

"There is someone waiting," he said softly. "Someone that I love very much. I hope you can understand that."

Kayla nodded, but she didn't release his hand. Slowly Kim pulled away and headed for the door. He felt as if an enormous block of granite had been lifted from his shoulders. Kayla's smile grew wistful as she watched him depart, then followed more slowly.

The Doctor, standing to one side, merely watched them both in consternation, remaining silent. Nothing that had just occurred should have been possible. For the first time in a long time, he felt the definite urge to terminate his program.

CHAPTER
19

IT TOOK VERY LITTLE TIME FOR PARIS TO NAVIGATE THE short distance to the Urrythan settlement, and yet the flight seemed to take a pleasant eternity. The Urrythan elders were gone, the *Awakening* complete, and yet the emotions they had triggered, the images they'd shared, lived on. They passed low over the gardens and the ruins, most of which were buried now, taking in the changes to the planet silently.

Where the huge pillars had cracked and crumbled, releasing those who'd slumbered in their embrace, the earth had erupted and moved, covering what had been visible and unearthing things that had not. There were still ruins, but they were different, older, and in many places they were running deeper beneath the surface of the planet. There was a whole new face to the landscape, and this seemed somehow appropriate. Nothing would be the same, and yet

Paris knew from what he'd experienced that one day it would be the way it now was once more, and the cycle would continue.

Much of the foliage had been buried under new soil. He knew that it would grow again, making its way slowly back to the surface and re-creating a semblance of what had been, but it would take time. The section of the garden that had held the *Ambiana* was nearly gone, and that would, he thought, be the greatest change wrought on the planet's inhabitants.

"The flowers are buried," he commented, breaking the silence he and Kes shared. "I wonder what will become of Ban and the others."

"They will return," Kes said with certainty. "They have blossoms at their settlement, and they will find a way to bring them back."

Kes had been distant, lost in a world of her own, since they'd returned to the planet. Now that the silence had been shattered, it seemed that she had a lot to tell—a lot to unload and sift through her mind.

"They will change, you know," she said softly. "It is a cycle, and we have witnessed the beginning of it . . . of the new cycle."

"What do you mean?" Paris asked, knowing the gist of what she said was true, but knowing also that her understanding of it would be more complete. "It appears to be more of an ending than a beginning." Even as he said this, he recalled the sensation the huge winged Urrythans had caused in him as they erupted from the ground, ascending to new life, and he knew that what he'd said was wrong.

"They will not have the great number of *Ambiana* blossoms that they have had," Kes explained slowly. "It will take them longer to reach their *Long Sleep*—many of them will never live to see it. They will grow away from their roots a bit, and those who remain true will grow fewer, will tuck themselves away.

"Then the cities will begin to grow again. Other things will take precedence. Art, technology, the *Ambiana* and the priests who tend it, the *Ascension* and the tales of this day will fade, inscribed in stone, or on paper—recorded, then tucked away and forgotten until they are only tales for children, and ritual for the faithful.

"They will grow, though. As more of them reach the sleep—as more of them join in the chorus—in the chord that forms their voice, their influence will grow. Vok will be the first—it is the pattern of his voice, that which he has learned from those who have gone, and that which he will learn over the course of their lifetimes. He will build the new voice, the new song, and one day—one glorious day—he will ascend."

"Maybe he should change his name to Adam," Paris said with a grin.

"What do you mean?" Kes asked.

Paris just shook his head. "It would take *way* too long for me to explain," he told her. "I'm just remembering my own family's beliefs. I never took them very seriously as a child, and I didn't take these people seriously, either. Now I guess I've got some thinking to do."

"We all do," she replied.

They continued on in silence, and soon they were setting down near the settlement. They found Tuvok alone, seated on a patch of clear earth large enough for the shuttle to land, waiting. His eyes were closed, and he was seated in a position of deep relaxation— legs and arms crossed.

He did not acknowledge their approach, but once the shuttle had gently touched down a few meters away from him, he opened his eyes and looked up. Just for a moment, before the inscrutable mask of logic slammed shut on his features, Paris was certain he saw a flash of very deep, very raw emotion. It passed so quickly that he couldn't be certain, and he turned to Kes. She was already looking at him, an odd little smile curling her lip, and he knew she'd seen it, too. An amazing day, all around.

They opened the hatch and Tuvok joined them in the shuttle, strapping himself in in silence.

"You don't seem as glad to see me as I thought you might be," Paris prodded, unable to hide the wide grin that had spread across his features.

"I am relieved to be returning to the ship," Tuvok said dryly.

"You're not sorry to be leaving your new friends?" Paris continued, unable to resist. "You seemed to be getting pretty close, last time I saw you."

"My actions," Tuvok retorted with a hint of indignation, "were the only logical course at the time. I had given my word to help them, and I did everything that I could. Now, if you will get us off this planet, I'd like to get to the sickbay and have The Doctor look at my head."

Paris's smile widened. Innocently, he added, "Then why did you wait for us? With the interference gone, there's no reason you couldn't have just beamed to the ship."

Tuvok didn't answer. He just stared out toward the settlement they'd left behind. Too much had happened in the past few hours for him to join in Paris's joking, and he was too worn out, mentally and physically, to truly be bothered. His distraction led to another period of silence, a comfortable silence, and in that silence, they lifted off and headed for *Voyager*.

As they neared the cloud cover, Paris kicked it in, leaving the planet behind rapidly. It was time to get home.

Despite all that had happened, *Voyager* did not depart her orbit of Urrytha for several days. In the aftermath of their troubles, they still needed supplies, and with The Doctor's antidote, the sudden burial of most of the *Ambiana* blossoms, and the cooperation of Ban and his remaining followers, the collection of those supplies was a quick, pleasant experience.

They did not linger with the Urrythans, nor did the natives seem disposed toward spending much time with them, though Tuvok and Kes were invited to, and attended, the final segments of the rituals that sealed Vok away for his *Long Sleep*.

When the ceremony was over, the two of them lingered near the newly erected pillar. It was still moist, softer than its elder predecessors. At the base the story of Vok's *Ascension,* and that of the sixth *Awakening* were inscribed in Urrythan characters. Above this, Ban had asked Captain Janeway to inscribe the same story in universal characters, so that if any of her people—or any other travelers from Federation space—were to find the place in the next ten thousand years, they might have more of a chance to understand more of his descendants than she and her crew had been given. He also insisted that *Voyager* and her crew be honored by the inscription of the parts they'd played in the final moments.

Kes and Tuvok stood side by side at the pillar's base, their hands pressed softly against its surface. There was no overwhelming vibration, nor a grand harmonic chord to draw them in, but they both sensed the tranquillity and slowly maturing strength that was Vok. They knew that Ban and some of the others felt it, as well. There would be more—a new forest of monoliths to greet the coming centuries, a new voice and a new dream.

Turning away, they saw Ban watching them from the shadows of a nearby tree, respecting their silence, but waiting. Tuvok moved forward first, extending a hand.

Ban took it, meeting the Vulcan's gaze. "You have done us a great service," the Urrythan said. "We will not forget."

"I did what had to be done," Tuvok replied. "There are no thanks necessary. I do not know why, but I believe that you would have done the same for me."

"I'm not certain of that," Ban said reflectively,

"but I would like to believe that, if it was not true before, it is true now."

"We must leave now," Tuvok said abruptly. "Thank you for your hospitality—"

"Thank you for everything," Kes cut in, her eyes bright and shining with an inner light that was somehow brighter than Tuvok had ever seen it. "You will not be forgotten, either."

Ban nodded, then stepped back.

The three of them stared at one another for a long moment of silence, then Ban turned away, returning to his followers and his future.

"*Voyager,*" Tuvok said slowly, "two to beam up."

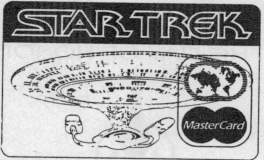

Look for STAR TREK Fiction from Pocket Books

Star Trek: The Next Generation®

Star Trek: Deep Space Nine®

Star Trek: Voyager®

Flashback • Diane Carey

Coming Next Month from Pocket Books

INTELLIVORE

by

Diane Duane

Picard leaned back in his seat, looking up at the screen, now divided between the away team's view and a view of *Oraidhe's* bridge. "The question, now," he said to Clif, with whom he had been talking while watching the teams finish their work, "is what to do with this vessel."

"Well," Clif said, looking slightly quizzical, "its crew has abandoned it. By the laws of salvage, it belongs to anyone who now comes along to claim it. *We* could do so . . . but frankly, Captain, I don't relish the idea of dragging this thing along after us while we're on patrol."

"Jean-Luc," said Ileen from the bridge of *Marignano,* "if you feel you might want to have another look at it later, why not just leave a sensor buoy with it, set to notice if anyone comes along and shows interest. If anyone does, the buoy can notify us . . . and also broadcast a message that this vessel is under investigation. She sat down in her center seat and smiled a big, bright, sunny smile. "You might even slap a Q on it."

"Quarantine?" Clif said, acquiring a rather artificial look of shock.

Picard smiled a little bit himself. "Weren't you telling us, Ileen, that some of the settled worlds in this area had been troubled by sporular angue fever?"

Captain Maisel nodded innocently. "Virulent stuff, that. And opportunistic. Four systems down with it, at least."

The three Captains nodded gravely at one another: Riker, who had come in partway through the discussion, smiled a very sideways smile, touched his commbadge, and started having a quiet discussion with someone in Engineering about a marker buoy.

"Protective measures aside," Maisel said, "if I came across a ship like this, in this part of space, when all kinds of people have heard the kinds of stories about this area that I have . . . I wouldn't want anything to do with the thing: I'd leave it right where it was."

"We might as well do the same, for the moment," Clif said. "We have other concerns."

"Agreed," Picard said. "More than ever, now, I'm eager to touch base with the people on that colony ship; I want to make sure they get where they're going safely."

"Yes," Clif and Maisel said almost in unison.

"Let's make it so, then. Mr. Data—"

"Laying in a course, Captain, and datastreaming it to *Marignano* and *Oraidhe.*"

"Very good. Let's go. If anyone wants me, I'll be down in Sickbay."

The Alpheccan lay on one of the diagnostic beds, the screen above it showing a most unusual internal arrangement of which Picard could make out absolutely nothing. Crusher was standing with her arms folded, a whole range of diagnostic tools lying to one side on a table while she gazed thoughtfully at the screen. Standing next to her was a tall balding man with an open, friendly face.

"Captain," said Crusher. "Oh, Captain, this is Doctor Spencer, Jim Spencer, from *Marignano.*"

Picard nodded to him. "Pleased," he said.

"He's worked with Alpheccans before; I haven't, really," Crusher said.

"Clinic work mostly, on Alphecca Four," said Spencer. "But they're not that common a people outside their own system: normally they don't care for star travel much—religious and cultural reasons. However, as you see, there are always exceptions to the rule . . ."

Picard nodded, looking at the screen again. "Correct me if I'm wrong, but he—he?—appears to have two of everything."

"Nearly," Spencer said. "With the possible exception of the brain, which would seem to be bad luck for this gentleman."

"Why? What's the matter?"

"Well—" Crusher gestured them all away from the bed, and they walked into her office and waited for the doors to shut. "He's dying, Captain; I'm afraid there's no question about that. I could prolong the process, but ethically I'd be on shaky ground."

"The problem," said Spencer, "is not so much that he's dying, but that, as he is at the moment, he shouldn't be alive at all."

"He seems to have incurred some kind of brain damage," said Crusher. "And it's a very peculiar kind, because in terms of actual trauma to his analogue of the cerebrum and cerebellum, there *is* none. His autonomic nervous system is perfectly intact . . . except that it seems not to be working properly: it's slowly losing function, giving up the business of running his breathing and heartbeat, and the process would seem to be irreversible. When I have to sign his death certificate . . . something which I'm pretty sure I'm going to have to handle in the next few hours—the proximate cause of death will be heart failure secondary to cerebellar dysfunction. But that will *not* be what killed him. I don't know what did."

Picard sat down, concerned. "Some kind of weapon, perhaps?" he said. "Or exposure to radiation, perhaps—?"

Crusher and Spencer shook their heads in unison. "No chance, Captain," said Spencer, "or very little. The only weapon this man had any contact with would have been someone's blaster or disruptor. That damage we repaired. But no known radiation, or infectious agent, can cause these effects.

"The problem is that this Alpheccan's brain is *intact,* Captain," Crusher said, sitting down on her desk and staring at her screen as if simply staring could make it give up some answers. "It has no reason to be failing. Its electrical action is somewhat reduced, but that clinical sign could be commensurate with the effects of shock. While the patient suffered considerable blood loss, that's been replaced, and the loss alone wasn't enough to cause the profound unconsciousness we see here, or, for that matter, to cause any kind of significant 'brain damage'—that kind of trauma leaves detectable signs in the cerebral vascularization."

There was a soft *cheep* from the screen. Crusher looked out of her office toward one of her staff who was standing by the bed with an instrument in his hands and a "yes or no?" expression on his face. "Half a second," she said, and went out.

When she came back, her face told the story. "That's it," Crusher said. "His dorsal heart just stopped for the third time, and his ventral one hasn't been working for the last hour. I told Mike not to bother with another restart; it serves no purpose."

Picard nodded sadly.

Crusher sighed and sat down in her chair. "Captain, if you're looking for a fast diagnosis from me, I don't have one for you. We'll get started on the autopsy right away. Jim, have you got time to spare?"

"Plenty. I'll gown up."

"Analysis is going to take a while, Jean-Luc," Crusher said; "when I run into a clinical picture this barren, I don't like to rush. If you'll check with me tomorrow about this time, I may have some initial indications for you. But I have to say, I can't guarantee much of anything."

"All right, Doctor," Picard said, getting up. "Let me know if anything of interest comes up before then."

He went out past the Alpheccan, glancing only briefly at him as he passed. It might have been a trick of the somewhat subdued lighting in Sickbay, or the dark complexion, or something about the way the Alpheccan's face was shaped: but Picard could not get rid of the impression that that face wore the faintest shadow of a smile. Coupled with the dark, empty eyes, it was an uncanny effect. He went out, turning the situation over in his mind. *One more mystery . . . one more among too many, for so early in the mission.*